THE NEWMARKET MURDERS

THE NEWMARKET MURDERS

THE SECOND KIT & MARY ASTON MYSTERY

JACK MURRAY

Books by Jack Murray

Kit Aston Series
The Affair of the Christmas Card Killer
The Chess Board Murders
The Phantom
The Frisco Falcon
The Medium Murders
The Bluebeard Club
The Tangier Tajine
The Empire Theatre Murders
The Newmarket Murders
The French Diplomat Affair (novella)
Haymaker's Last Fight (novelette)

DI Jellicoe Series
A Time to Kill
The Bus Stop
Trio
Dolce Vita Murders

Agatha Aston Series
Black-Eyed Nick
The Witchfinder General Murders
The Christmas Murder Mystery
The Siegfried Slayer (Oct 2023)

Danny Shaw / Manfred Brehme WWII Series
The Shadow of War
Crusader
El Alamein

ISBN: 9798397425537
Imprint: Independently published

Cover by Jack Murray after J.C. Leyendecker

For Monica, Lavinia, Anne, and Baby Edward

The Runners and Riders

Kit Aston...................... *Dashing, highly intuitive amateur detective and former spy*

Mary Aston.................... *Beautiful, brave and brilliantly smart*

Chief Inspector Hook... *An old friend of Kit's from school & university*

Gerry Tudor.................. *Owner of Tudor Stables, husband of Tamsin, brother to Chris and Carol*

Tamsin Tudor.............. *Wife of Gerry Tudor*

Carol Harrison.............. *Sister of Gerry and Chris, the widow*

Chris Tudor.................. *Brother of Gerry and Chris, horribly injured during the War*

Roger Sexton................ *Friend of Carol's, owns business in Newmarket*

Vincent......................... *The venerable butler of Gerry and Tamsin*

Jason Trent...................*Friend of Carol's, banker*

Bryn Cain......................*Lawyer for the Tudor family*

Teddy Harrison.............*Husband of Carol Harrison*

Damien Blythe...............*Employee at nearby stables*

Two of these people will die.
Two of them were involved in these deaths

Part I: Under Starter's Order

Newmarket, Cambridgeshire, England: November 1921

'I've killed him.'

'What?' exclaimed the voice on the other end of the phone line.

'I've killed him. I didn't mean to. I think he's dead. The blood,' cried the woman. It was a howl of fear.

'Carol, calm down,' urged the man. Such advice is always guaranteed to be well received by members of the opposite sex. The words were barely out of his mouth before he had to hold the receiver away from his ear as the young woman lashed out at him with an impressive array of profanities that would have made a stable manager blush.

The storm abated when the young woman realised that the help and counsel she required would not be forthcoming if she continued in a similar vein.

'I'm sorry, I don't know what to do.'

'What happened, Carol?' asked the man who had been moments away from hanging up and leaving her to her fate and the dead body.

'He hit me. Again.'

'The beast.'

1

'He was a beast. We argued. He accused me of having an affair with you. He slapped me. There's a bruise,' sobbed the woman. 'He was going to hit me again. I swear he was. I was afraid. I...I...'

The tears resumed, forcing the man to bite his tongue. He was thinking furiously. What he said now could affect the rest of his life never mind hers. While the sobs throbbed down the phone line he considered his options. He could drive there. It would only take a few minutes. What if someone saw his car? True, it was late. This was the country. Most people would be in bed by now. Still, it was a risk. What was his plan?

Carol's tears remained a distraction to him, and he almost asked her to keep quiet so that he could think. Why did they get so emotional? This was a time when emotion was a luxury. Stone cold rationality was needed, and he was the man she'd called. A smile crossed his face.

'Carol, listen to me,' snapped the man.

The crying ceased immediately. This was gratifying. He stood a little bit more erect. They like decisiveness.

'We have to play this smart. Let me handle it. You have to be brave old girl. You did nothing wrong; do you understand? It was self-defence. Now, you know that, and I know that, but a jury may not see it that way.'

The sobbing resumed. The man cursed himself. He'd tried to keep his voice neutral and unemotional. He'd tried to make her see sense, but he was dealing with someone who was beyond rationality at that moment. Time to change tack.

'Carol, what's done is done,' said the man. He was within a whisker of adding "there's no use in crying over spilt milk" but wisely swerved away from that land mine. Spilt blood more like. Yes, his credibility would have been shot had he added that banality.

Think.

'Look Carol, I'm going to come over. Do nothing except what I tell you.'

'Yes,' said a weak voice.

'Now, I want you to pack a bag now,' said the man and then he outlined what he intended doing.

'You'll go to Gerry and Tamsin's. Don't, whatever you do, say anything about what's happened. As far as Gerry is concerned, you've had an argument. It's over. Yes, say it's over. Don't tell him that he's been hitting you. Knowing Gerry, he'll be over in a minute with a shotgun and a spade.'

'Yes.'

'You understand? We have to change the story of what's happened. Stay at Gerry's. Say nothing. Avoid people. Try not to seem jumpy. We have to avoid any hint of suspicion in your actions. The police will come. In fact, it's essential that they do. When they tell you that he is dead, then you can break down. You cannot do so until you hear the news. In the meantime, you are angry, Carol. Very angry. You just want to leave him. Tell Gerry that you have had enough of Teddy's accusations and lies. Tell him that life with him has become unbearable. You want out. You want to divorce him. In fact, say that you told him you wanted a divorce. Believe me, Gerry will understand. Between you and me, he never liked Teddy. No one did, Carol.'

He grimaced as he said the last line. It was probably true, yet it felt like a veiled criticism of her taste. Well, why not? She'd married the wrong man. Everyone knew that. Everyone except Carol. She was the most beautiful woman in

3

the county. She could have had her pick of any man. Him, for instance. But no. Not her. She had to pick the biggest bounder that the good Lord had ever created to set fatuous female hearts a-flutter. Well she made her bed. The thought of Carol in bed with Teddy felt like his heart had been stabbed with a pitchfork. He shook his head hoping to rid himself of that image of her lying seductively in marriage bed.

Stop!

'Carol, are you still there?' A sniff suggested that she was. 'Look, hang up now. Remember what I say. Say nothing to anyone. As far as you are concerned, Teddy is at home, drinking as usual.'

'Yes. Yes, I'll do that. What will you do?' asked Carol.

'Don't worry. Trust me. This needs thinking about. We must make sure that you are nowhere near the scene. I'm coming over now. You need an alibi, darling.'

Darling.

There. He'd said it. Well, why not? Teddy was out of the way at long last. It was time to correct the error she'd made. She'd called him. Not one of the other admirers that still swooned around her like love struck stable boys.

The line went dead.

1 Thursday

Hyde Park, London: November 1921

'What do you see?'

Mary Aston felt her heart stop momentarily. This was not through fear or shock, only sadness. She was sitting by the Serpentine, a large lake in the middle of London's Hyde Park. It was late morning. A low mist draped the surface of the water hiding the ducks, although the heads of a few swans peeked out over the top like periscopes.

'It's so beautiful, Rose, I can barely do justice to what I see,' said Mary honestly.

She and Rose Hunter were with a group of half a dozen women or more. They were all sitting by the lake, buried under layers of clothing, a very English picnic. A couple of the women had young children with them. An older woman, an American lady, spoke up.

'Anyone ready for a picnic?'

This was met with a chorus of assent from the ladies. Two of the ladies climbed unsteadily to their feet and went to help the American lady.

'Well?' asked Rose. There was a smile on her face. Her sightless eyes gazed at the water. Mary felt tears sting her eyes

5

as she gazed at the young woman. Rose was in her late twenties with dark hair and large brown eyes. She was blind but had not been born this way.

'Well,' began Mary. 'There is a low mist over the lake. I can see some swans and even a few ducks.'

'Yes, I hear them.'

'Noisy aren't they?' laughed Mary. 'The trees still have a few leaves. They're all around us, brown, gold, copper and red. It's so beautiful, Rose. The sky is a bit grey. The grass, too. Or perhaps it's silvery, I suppose. With beads of mist. Or frost.'

'Yes, rather chilly, I noticed.'

'So, I have some news,' said Mary. 'Kit spoke to Major Cyril Entwistle. He's the Member of Parliament, we mentioned. He's agreed to represent your petition for divorce. Once he heard the circumstances of your case, and what Ron had done to you, he needed very little persuasion.'

'Thanks Mary. Do you think we can win?'

Mary paused for a moment to control the emotion in her voice.

'Things are changing, Rose. Since the War we've begun to win rights that should be ours. The law has been an ass for far too long. He nearly killed you, yet you cannot be granted a divorce without a private members' bill. That's plainly wrong and more ministers are recognising this.'

'None of them voted for by you or me,' said Rose. There was colour in her cheeks now. Anger.

'This will change,' said Mary. There was a hard edge to her voice, too.

Mary took Rose's hand. Neither wore gloves, so it was cold to touch. They sat in silence for a few moments. It was a

6

comfortable silence. Rose was naturally quiet, yet her presence had a reassuring quality.

'What you two gabbing about,' asked a young woman approaching Mary and Rose. She was a little older than the two young women, but not much.

'An MP has agreed to sponsor a private bill for Rose's divorce, Dulcie,' said Mary.

'That's great news, my darling,' said Dulcie, leaning over and giving Rose a hug. 'Best thing that ever happened to me. Thanks Mary. You and Kit were proper good to me.'

Mary smiled at Dulcie Palmer, but her eyes were full of sadness. She, like Rose, had been badly mistreated during her marriage. She knew Kit suffered a little from survivor's guilt following the War. Sometimes she wondered if she did not feel a little guilt too. Her marriage to Kit seemed the very embodiment of bliss. Her work with women who needed shelter and protection from abusive marriages was probably a form of atonement, not for sin, but for the good fortune that had mostly marked her life.

The three women sat in companiable silence gazing out towards the lake. On the other side they saw two women pushing perambulators. Both were a similar age to the three young women. The tranquillity was broken when one of the babies began to cry. The three women immediately smiled sympathetically.

'I don't suppose I'll have one of those,' said Rose. There was a wistfulness in her voice, but no self-pity.

'Why not?' asked Dulcie.

Rose shrugged then replied matter-of-factly, 'Even if I wanted to be with someone again, and I'm not sure that I do,

7

I suppose there are so few men after the War and, well, who'd want to take me on now?'

Dulcie laughed dismissively at this.

'Rose, aside from maybe Mary 'ere, there's probably not a prettier girl in the park than you. Lots of men would give their right arm to be with you when you're back up and walking. Them bones will heal, then they'll be all over you. Just you watch. It'll be harder work for someone with a clock like mine.'

Mary and Rose laughed whilst reassuring Dulcie that nothing could be further from the truth.

'Trust me, 'aving a good heart is all very well, but it's the body surrounding it that they want,' said Dulcie. This provoked more giggles from the three women which brought another one of the party over.

'You folk look like you're having far too much fun. What's going on?' This was Isabella Rosling. She sat down alongside the two women. The accent was American, the tone demanding. This was a woman used to leading or, at least, being obeyed.

She had come to London before the War with her husband who was a banker. Mary had come to know her the previous year when she had worked, undercover, as a maid in the house. At that time, she and Kit where on the trail of a jewel thief known as 'The Phantom'. Mary had grown to admire Mrs Rosling. She certainly impressed her as a more capable and intelligent woman than her husband who was a board member of a bank. To the credit of her husband, Mary sensed that he recognised her ability too and treated her as an unofficial partner in the business.

'Have you told the ladies the news, Mary?' asked Mrs Rosling.

Rose piped up at this, 'Mary told me that an MP will sponsor the private bill for my divorce.'

Mrs Rosling turned in surprise to Mary, 'Entwistle has agreed? Well I never. Well done to Kit. I didn't have Entwistle marked down as a supporter.'

'When Kit took him through the particulars of Rose's case, the beatings as well as pointing out the obvious double standards at play, he came around. I think it helped he's ex-army like Kit.'

'Well, it's certainly brightened up this rather grim day,' said Mrs Rosling. 'Where is Kit, by the way?'

Mary grinned towards the American lady. 'You'll be glad to hear there's a little more good news to brighten your day.'

'Go on,' said Mrs Rosling, leaning forward.

'The house we purchased in Lambeth for these women will have an added layer of security that will cost us nothing and won't burden the police.'

Mrs Rosling clapped her hands together in delight. 'That's wonderful. Has he called in the army?'

'In a matter of speaking,' said Mary enigmatically.

The Windmill is a pub that for almost five hundred years has allowed thirsty freeborn Englishmen of Lambeth the opportunity to congregate and converse on the great matters of the day while lubricating their vocal cords with the local ale. Since the 1850's, it had even permitted entry for members of the smarter sex to provide a degree of

9

moderation to the level of conviviality and boisterousness that was always guaranteed in such a palace.

Just as Mary was sharing her news about the proposed safekeeping arrangements for the women's refuge in Lambeth, Kit was toasting the pact with his new partners. It is doubtful whether or not the Elephant Gang would have considered themselves an equal opportunities employer had such terms existed then. However, in practice, this is what they were.

Women played a variety of roles within the gang. They were, unofficially of course, affiliated members who comprised what had become popularly known as "the Forty Elephants". This was a loose collective of women who had dedicated themselves with an enthusiasm that bordered on zealotry to the principle of free enterprise and earning a living through the work of their hands. That these hands were often to be found in other people's pockets was only a minor moral consideration. Their biggest motivation was to earn a crust while avoiding the 'pokey'.

Sitting at the table with Kit were Charles and Bert McDonald, the leaders of the Elephant Gang. Also in attendance were Alice Diamond and Maggie Hill, who were *de facto* leaders of the Forty Elephants. Last, and certainly not least, given his heroics in an earlier report from your humble chronicler, was Dan 'Haymaker' Harris. 'Haymaker' was a former middleweight boxer whose ranking had never reached the dizzy heights of the top ten and probably not in the top twenty either. What he lacked in terms of any basic defence he more than compensated for in the size of his heart.

'I owe you one,' said Kit, lifting his glass of ale and then taking a generous slug.

10

Charles 'Wag' McDonald laughed derisively at this. He said, 'I think we're long past the point where you owe me just one your lordship. The list has grown a little too long now.'

'How do you treat people, might I ask, who do not settle their debt?' asked Kit.

'Don't ask,' said Bert and Kit did not.

'It's a good cause,' pointed out Alice Diamond.

Wag looked in the direction of the impressively menacing young woman. She was as tall as he was, and probably weighed in at light heavy. In short, she was not to be messed with and few did. Still, Wag was not a gang leader without having a fair share of chutzpah.

'You're all heart, Alice. Always said that.'

Alice let that one pass. Her on-off boyfriend Bert would be the one to suffer if Wag took the mick.

'I don't think that it requires much on your part,' pointed out Kit. 'Once people in the area know that this is under your, dare I say protection, then I imagine the young women there will be safe. And this is where our friend Haymaker can help.'

'Anything, your lordship. You know that.'

'Just show a face,' said Kit.

'Bloody hell, Haymaker's boat will scare them girls away, not just their husbands,' said Maggie Hill.

Haymaker had the good grace to smile at this, but the McDonald brothers looked unamused at the red-headed Miss Hill. They said nothing because, despite her diminutive stature and their position as two leaders of one of the most feared gangs in London, she was as likely to attack them as talk to them about the weather. Definitely a young lady to

11

treat even more like a ticking time bomb than the rest of her gender.

The conversation turned to another subject close to all of their hearts: horse racing. The Elephant Gang had interests in the world of gambling and, as Kit knew they would be, very interested to hear about the weekend he had ahead of him at the house of a friend who was a race horse owner and trainer.

'Is he the one that owns Northern Glory?' asked Wag McDonald.

'Yes, Gerry struck gold there. You heard the story? It all came about by accident. Glory's daddy, Boner's Delight, was a bit of a lothario. One night he burst out of his stable because he was in the mood. He found his way into the stable of a filly...'

'Juliet's Gift,' interjected Bert. 'I made quite a bit of money on her back in the day.'

'Well Juliet's Gift to Gerry was a potential Derby winner after Boner's Delight covered her.'

'Unbeaten in four races, I know. I saw him earlier this year in a novice race, he walked away from the rest like they were on crutches.'

Kit eyed Wag before saying, 'And were they?'

Wag looked affronted at such a calumny. 'Leave it out your lordship. Not our style. Anyways, you lot are much worse. Half those races are fixed and we're the ones that get rinsed while your lot are quaffing champagne and stuffing cucumber sandwiches down your gobs.'

This was a combination that Kit had never considered before. It was one or other in his book. 'I'll pass your menu suggestions on to cook.'

'Have you a stopwatch, your lordship?' asked Wag.

Kit thought for a moment before replying, with a knowing smile, 'No. Am I going to come into possession of one by this evening?'

'Consider it a *quid pro quo* for the service we're providing you,' said Wag.

'Promise me that this will have been honestly acquired,' said Kit. His eyes were on Alice Diamond as he said this and his tone a little more serious.

She grinned back at Kit.

'You know me.'

'My point exactly,' said Kit, rising from his seat. 'Next round is on me.'

2 Friday

Tudor Stables near Newmarket, Cambridgeshire, England: November 1921

The sky was darkening over the Tudor Stables, yet it was barely four in the afternoon. The shortest day of the year was a week away. A chill breeze rustled the branches of the wood-environed field bending the tops of the trees backwards. Kit and Mary Aston strolled towards the fence surrounding the paddock.

Tudor Stables was a thriving yard used by many thoroughbred horse owners to train promising two-year-old and three-year-old colts and fillies. It was one of many such stables in the flat countryside surrounding the world-famous Newmarket racecourse.

Kit and Mary were in the company of Gerry Tudor, who owned the estate and the stables. Overlooking the estate, on a slight rise, was their impressive Georgian mansion. Kit and Mary joined a man in his late thirties. Gerry was an atonal symphony in tweed. He put on the wax jacket he had been carrying on his arm and fixed his tweed cap.

'Chilly,' said Gerry. He was not a man known to use one word when a nod would suffice. He leaned over the fence with eyes squinting beneath the cap as he fixed his attention

14

on half a dozen colts being led up a slight incline towards the stables.

'That's Northern Glory over there,' said Gerry, pointing to a big, rangy colt at the back of the line. 'He's with Leonardo's Pride. They're great friends. Glory won't go anywhere without him. We've used Leonardo as pacemaker for the last two races.'

'It certainly worked,' commented Mary, putting a small pair of binoculars to her eyes. 'How many lengths did Glory win by?'

'Seven and nine respectively,' said Gerry proudly. 'He won't find it so easy when we step up in class but, well, perchance to dream.'

'Derby?' asked Kit. He was gazing at the colt through a rather battered pair of binoculars.

'Let's start with the Guineas and see how he goes,' replied Gerry. 'Look, they're coming over now.' He glanced at Kit's old binoculars. 'Ever thought of a new pair?'

'Don't,' said Mary. 'I've tried. He won't be separated from them.'

Kit put the binoculars down and said to Gerry, 'I went through the War with this pair.'

'Here they come,' said Mary.

The horses were indeed heading in the direction of Kit and Mary. Steam was rising from the horses as they trooped towards the stables after their workout. Mary smiled and glanced at Gerry. The estate owner was smiling. There was something about Northern Glory that made him feel like a child in a sweet shop. His face was permanently ruddy; dark hair, flecked with grey stuck out from beneath his cap. He put on a pair of spectacles with thick lens which made him

15

seem more like a university don at the nearby universities rather than a racehorse trainer with a potential Derby winner at the stables. He nodded to Mary who reached inside a pocket crammed with carrots.

'A horse races on its stomach, trust me. You'll be his friend for life, Mary,' said Gerry with a grin. Northern Glory made a beeline for Mary when the carrots came out. 'I told you.'

The horse began to nibble at the carrots. He was joined by his friend, Leonardo, who did likewise with a carrot held out by Kit.

'How was it?' asked Kit to the stable lad holding Northern Glory's lead.

'Wonderful. It feels like you're flying, even when he's cruising along.'

'Do you want to go for a ride on Glory tomorrow?' asked Gerry.

Kit and Mary chorused 'No thanks.' Gerry laughed at their collective cowardice. Kit was unabashed. He shrugged and said, 'He's worth too much. I wouldn't want to be the cause of any misfortune to a potential Derby winner. You and Tamsin would have my guts for garters. Are Carol and Teddy joining us this weekend?'

The mention of his sister and her husband caused a shadow to fall over the features of their friend. This was noted by Mary, but missed by Kit who was busy rooting around his pocket for some more carrots.

'I was going to let Carol mention this but, well, you may as well hear it from me,' said Gerry in a very serious tone. 'Carol came to us a couple of nights ago in tears. She says she's left Teddy and has no intention of going back.'

16

'Good Lord,' exclaimed Mary. 'But why?'

'Carol didn't say, but I think he hit her. I was going to go round and sort him out, but she begged me not to.'

'Has Teddy been up to the house?'

'Yes once, but he keeps calling on the telephone. Crying according to Vincent. You know what Vincent is like, inveterate snob. He didn't think much of Teddy to begin with and frankly his emotional outburst was the final straw. He was happy to hang up on him. Carol's instruction, by the way. She's going to London next week with Bryn to meet a barrister to understand what action she can take. Devilishly difficult if you're a woman.'

Kit and Mary exchanged glances at this.

'We may be able to help you there, Gerry. You say that this beast may have been hurting her?' asked Mary.

Gerry nodded grimly. Then he said, 'You'll hear tonight. Bryn Cain is joining us for dinner; not sure you've met him, Kit.'

Kit thought for a moment before saying, 'Yes, I remember him from your wedding. Did he take over from his father?'

'Yes, that's the chap. Carol confirmed to Bryn that Teddy had hit her,' said Gerry. His face had tightened now and looked as if he was ready to explode. His large, calloused hands gripped the fence. They were the hands of someone from the country. Kit glanced at his own. Soft and slender, like a pianist.

'You don't need me to tell you,' warned Kit, 'it's imperative that you do not go and knock seven bells out of him, tempting though it may be.'

17

'I never liked him, Kit. Always knew he was a wrong 'un, but Carol wouldn't listen. Fell for his smooth charm. He's not like us. A city boy. Never fitted in.'

Kit patted Gerry on the back. They had been friends since school. Gerry and his family had spent their life with horses just as their father and grandfather had, before them. Gerry spoke in staccato sentences as if he were an army major, which he had been for a couple of years. The tragedy of the War's brutal annihilation of human life was matched only in savage cruelty by the manner in which animals were treated over this period.

At the start of the War, Gerry and his younger brother, Chris, had facilitated the mobilisation of tens of thousands of horses from Britain to join calvary regiments and help with the work that needed to be done in transporting arms and men around. They did so little realising the hell into which these animals would be sent. It didn't take long for the horrifying reality to hit home. For a man who adored horses, the sight of seeing these animals treated with almost inhuman ruthlessness made the War a particularly brutalising experience. Over eight million horses, donkeys and mules had been killed during the course of the War.

The scars of war lay deep within his friend, Kit knew. Unlike his brother who had gone on to the Royal Flying Corps, the scars inflicted on Gerry were invisible. Every now and then, however, the memory of what he'd been through came back and overwhelmed him. This was the same for Kit too but, since meeting Mary, he rarely if ever, experienced any episode.

They followed the horses towards the gate and then Mary happily took up the offer of Northern Glory's bridle. She patted his neck to show that she meant him no harm. The colt nodded at that moment which pleased Mary greatly. She led him towards the stables, following the other horses. Leonardo's Pride had to make do with Kit. He did not seem much enamoured of this which amused Gerry and Mary.

'I think young Glory got the better deal there,' laughed Gerry.

The stables were a combination of corrugated metal and timber from the nearby forest. The smell of hot horse inside was almost tangible in the air. Mary led Glory into his enclosure and handed the bridle over to the stable lad. She watched as he undid the girth buckle and gently slipped the saddle from the horse. Northern Glory's nostrils were still inflamed from his gallop. His heaving flanks rippled with prominent veins. Mary stroked him behind the ear as he nibbled a few more carrots.

'We should go up to the house now,' said Gerry. 'Leave the lads to it.'

'Yes, good idea,' said Kit.

'It will give you some time to freshen up before pre-dinner drinks,' said Gerry.

They walked up the hill towards the large Georgian mansion. Mary drew her coat around her. There was a definite bite to the chill in the air. Up above the clouds were blackening ominously.

''I don't like the look of that,' said Gerry gazing upwards. The hurried towards the house as a spray of rain began to fall lightly.

When they reached the door, Mary asked Gerry, 'What time should we come down?'

'I think seven,' replied Gerry.

19

'Will Carol be joining us?' asked Kit.

'Yes, I think so. She's putting a brave face on things, poor girl, but I'm sure, in fact I know, she's dying to meet you, Mary. She'll want to see what sort of girl managed to bag Kit.'

'I think you'll find it was the other way around,' said Mary, but there was a mischievous glint in her eye.

'I stand corrected,' laughed Gerry good-naturedly.

'I usually am,' agreed Kit.

Gerry nodded his head and said, 'Quite right, too. '

Standing at the door to greet them was Vincent, the Tudor's venerable butler. Vincent was around sixty years of age, but his manner and values belonged to a bygone age that had probably never existed outside of the pages of Victorian romances and comic novels. For all his snobbery, a characteristic sadly lacking in his master, Vincent was adored by everyone.

Vincent had not only seen the Tudor family grow up, but he had also seen friends such as Kit Aston over many years, which meant he had a healthily respectful disrespect for each and every one of them and their modern attitudes. He clung to the old ways like a mother to a young child: a combination of carer, coach and custodian.

'Mr Harrison phoned an hour ago. I said Miss Carol wasn't in,' announced Vincent as Gerry entered into the large hallway. A couple of footmen were busy erecting a Christmas tree.

'Rather early, isn't it,' said Kit nodding towards the tree.

Vincent nodded slowly which amused Kit.

'Never too early, old chap,' said Gerry gaily. 'What did you say to that blighter?'

'I told him she was at doctor's. She had a rather nasty bruise on her cheek.'

Gerry laughed and clapped Vincent on the shoulder, 'Well that was a bit of cheek all right. Well done Vincent.'

Vincent was caught between disapproval at the familiarity and a confusing mixture of mortification and gratification at receiving praise. He chose a middle course which, in England, is to remain impassive and seek to move the conversation on to neutral territory.

'Will there be anything else sir?'

'No, thank you Vincent.'

Just as the butler departed, the phone in the hallway rang again. Vincent picked it up. He turned immediately upon hearing the voice to Gerry and raised a disapproving eyebrow. Gerry was over to the phone in a flash. He did not listen to anything that was said he merely launched into a tirade.

'Now look here Teddy, I've good mind to drive over there and give you a damn good thrashing. And I will of I catch you over here. Do you hear me? Hello? Hello?' The caller had obviously hung up.

Gerry slammed the phone down and marched angrily away to the library leaving Kit and Mary staring in wonder at the violent outburst they had just witnessed.

3

'What's Teddy like?' asked Mary. She was standing by the window looking at the rain falling in sheets onto the ground and bouncing back up. Lights from the house reflected off the growing puddles on the grass. It was a little after six in the evening and the sky was a black canopy. As she stood there fixing her earring, she saw a car come up the driveway. It was coming at quite a clip. It went into the garage. She heard a car door being slammed shut but could not see who had been driving.

'I never liked him,' said Kit. 'Thought a little too much of himself. He came the odd time to Sheldon's. I remember Olly used to lampoon his voice something rotten.'

'Oh, why was that?'

'He just had the most awful drawl, and he would say things like,' at this point Kit put on a rather irritating voice dripping in smug superiority, 'doncha know.'

Mary laughed at the voice and Kit's rather elegantly dissolute pose.

'He was rather awful really, but the blighter always seemed to be popular with the girls. Good looking, I suppose,' said Kit albeit reluctantly. Mary smiled towards her husband and strolled slowly over to him to help with his tie.

Kit gazed at her and asked rather reluctantly, 'Are you planning on getting dressed?'

Mary shook her head. She reached up and undid Kit's fairly poor effort at making a tie. Then she spent a minute or two longer than was strictly necessary in fixing it. Her efforts were not in the least helped by her husband.

'What's Carol like?' asked Mary a few minutes later.

'I think at one point every man in Cambridgeshire was chasing her,' replied Kit, admiring the dress Mary was holding up.

'Were you?' asked Mary with a smile. This was dangerous territory even for a man as obviously smitten as Kit. Luckily, truth was a shield that would protect him, and the truth was pretty good.

'Actually, she and Olly were an item briefly. The War clouds put an end to matters and Carol was not the sort to wait at home for her man to return. She ended up with Teddy.'

About ten minutes later, they heard another car drive up to the house. It parked out at the front. Neither went to see who it was as Kit was otherwise engaged in delaying Mary getting dressed and she was letting him.

'Teddy did not go to France?' asked Mary after another several minutes had passed. A rumble outside seemed like an echo from the guns of Flanders. Mary got up from the bed and looked outside to see if there was any lightning.

'No, he had a gammy leg which exempted him from fighting. I may not have liked him, but he was certainly very smart in an arrogant and officious way. He joined up in 1916 because he had experience of retail. To be fair to him I'm sure he did a good job in supply. He was also a good deal older than her. She's my age, but I would put Teddy at forty.'

'Well, in this sense, you're a good deal older than me,' pointed out Mary, eyes twinkling.

'True,' acknowledged Kit. 'And to answer your question, no, I was never interested in Carol despite her wealth and good looks.'

Kit put his arms around Mary's slim waist, 'I think I made the right decision.'

There was only one way to respond to this and Mary did so with an enthusiasm shared by her husband. It took a gong from Vincent, twenty minutes later, to interrupt the couple. Pre-dinner drinks were to be served.

The hall of Tudor Mansion was wood-panelled and full of equestrian paintings. Aside from Munnings and Stubbs, it was not a genre that appealed to Kit. They descended the stairs and joined Gerry in the drawing room. With him was his wife Tamsin. Kit's raised eyebrow was greeted with a roll of the eyes from Gerry.

'Even in the midst of crisis, we can't deny Carol her big entrance,' said Tamsin.

Tamsin Tudor was always delightfully wicked. She was a country woman who disliked superficiality, snobbery and pomposity in any form. She had hated Teddy from the day and hour they had met. Mary smiled at this barbed comment and decided immediately that she liked Tamsin.

'Tamsin never made any effort to disguise her dislike of Teddy. I have to admit, old girl, you were bang on,' said her husband, Gerry.

'Of course I was bang on, as you say and less of the old,' said Tamsin, fixing Kit and Mary their gin and tonics. Then

24

she took Mary by the arm, cast a meaningful glance in Kit's direction and said, 'Now, I want to know what kind of a woman would make you give up any hope of having me.'

'Tamsin,' exclaimed Gerry, but he was laughing as he said this.

'She never changes,' said Kit, raising a glass to the two ladies who were now standing side by side by the window. Gerry clinked his glass with Kit's.

'Long may it continue,' agreed Gerry. He glanced sharply towards the window as the thunder seemed to make the sky buckle under its anger, 'Gosh. Awful night.'

Mary gazed up at Tamsin. While Mary was five feet three, on tip toe, Tamsin was closer in height to Kit and Gerry, who were both over six feet tall. She gave Mary an appraising look and said, 'I hope you don't mind me.'

Mary laughed. Her eyes were shining as she said, 'I heartily approve of anyone who throws my imperturbable husband off balance.'

'I think we're going to get on rather well, Mary and, for the record, my dear, it is all too evident why he would have set his cap in your direction. Methinks Carol won't appreciate the competition, but perhaps I'm just hoping.'

The door opened and Mary spun around, expecting to see Carol. In fact, it was the family lawyer, Bryn Cain. Kit and Cain shook hands while he bowed to Mary. His dinner suit fitted snuggly over a well-made frame.

'As ever, we await our Queen, Carol,' said Tamsin.

Mary grinned at her new friend. Tamsin was a brunette with a smile that exuded good humour and no little mischief. She appeared to have avoided make up entirely which Mary heartily approved of. Her dress was plain without any trivial

25

detailing. Mary was glad that Kit had guided her in selecting her weekend wardrobe. She sensed that the down-to-earth woman facing her was not overly appreciative of frivolous females.

And then Carol entered the room.

All eyes turned to her as she made her entrance. She did not walk so much as float with her arms held up either side as if she were running her fingers through long grass. The dress was by Lanvin, the diamond necklace by Tiffany and the eyes were from the icy Arctic tundra. She turned her beautifully sculpted face and Mary gasped. A purplish and yellow discolouration on her cheekbone seemed to pulse through the light covering of make-up that she had applied. Kit immediately went over to Carol and kissed her on her other cheek. He gazed sympathetically at her.

'Gerry's told you,' said Carol. It wasn't a question. Kit nodded, and then turned to indicate Mary.

'Let me introduce you to Mary,' said Kit.

Carol broke into a smile when she saw Mary. There was genuine warmth in the smile and Mary felt a moment of remorse for having felt a little cynical towards Carol. She had been hurt and the scar was clearly not just physical. Mary immediately went towards and gave her a hug. This spontaneous gesture prompted Carol's eyes to glisten with tears.

'Thank you. You are everything Kit said you were.'

Mary smiled at this and replied, 'I have him well trained.'

This brought a roar of laughter from Tamsin while Carol managed a smile.

'You must show me how, my dear,' said Tamsin. 'I still have trouble with my pet.'

26

Gerry rolled his eyes at this to Kit and said sotto voce, 'Here we go.'

'I find a combination of biscuits and denial of treats works wonderfully well,' said Mary, ignoring the three men and addressing her comments to the two women.

Carol smiled, but it was clear to Mary that her eyes belied any suggestion that she was enjoying herself. Still, she managed to respond in a kind which Mary had to admire, 'I like your stick and carrot approach. He's a very lucky man, I can see.'

Just then the phone began to ring in the hallway. Silence fell on the group for a few moments as the phone rang and rang. Then Gerry spoke up, 'Tamsin and I instructed Vincent not to answer it.' His voice shook as he spoke. Kit assumed it was the anger within him that had no escape valve.

After the phone had stopped ringing, Vincent entered the room and informed Gerry that dinner would be served. They left the drawing room and went into a large dining room. This room, rather like the hallway, was full of equestrian art showing racehorses, hunting scenes and a couple by an artist who had tried to depict racing without, apparently, having seen either a horse or, indeed, a race before. Kit stopped by it and stared aghast at the elongated shapes that were meant to depict horses.

'Good Lord,' said Kit, at last.

'Hideous isn't it?' agreed Tamsin before adding wickedly, 'It's rather grown on me over the years. I have a soft spot for absurdity.'

It was clearly going to be impossible to avoid talking about Carol's situation, so she broached the subject once they were all seated.

'I find talking about adultery, abuse and annulment goes so well with Oxtail soup, don't you think?' said Carol.

This brought some smiles around the table. Tamsin and Bryn Cain both raised their glasses, in approval. Gerry looked uncomfortable, noted Kit. Outside the thunder rolled a little more loudly.

'The truth is, Kit, Mary, I've left him. I should have done this years ago, but the night before last was the final straw,' said Carol. She pointed to the bruise. 'With Bryn's help I will divorce him.'

'I had no idea Teddy was like that,' said Kit.

'Oh, indeed he was. I never said anything because I knew Gerry would pay him a visit with a shotgun and put it to a use that the manufacturer's never intended.'

This brought a smile from Mary and a chuckle from Tamsin.

'I think I like you better without him, my dear,' said Tamsin and she appeared to mean it. Kit glanced towards the hostess and marvelled at her. Tamsin disliked society events and hobnobbing with her peers. This was their loss because she had an unusual, yet winning, combination of down-to-earthedness mixed with no little sharpness of tongue. Gerry adored her as much as he feared her. They made a great team. Gerry was a brilliant racehorse trainer while Tamsin ran the business with an eagle eye on the bottom line. And she loved horses as much as her husband.

'When are the boys back from school?' asked Kit, noticing a framed photograph on the wall.

'I'm afraid you'll miss them. They're not back until next Friday,' said Tamsin, wistfully.

'What ages are they now?'

'Steven is thirteen, quite the young man now, while Hector is eleven.'

'My goodness, the time goes quickly, doesn't it.'

Tamsin said nothing while smiling sadly. Images of two baby boys flashed across her eyes. Little made her sentimental, but this was the one exception. Just to have had them as babies a little longer. Just a little longer.

The brief silence that followed Kit's comment was shattered by the sound of the phone ringing again. No sooner was it trilling in the hallway when, outside the window, they saw one then two sets of car headlights blaze across the curtained windows. The black canopy of cloud had well and truly broken now, and the rain was pelting off the ground.

'Good Lord,' said Gerry. He looked pale.

'What on earth is going on,' exclaimed Tamsin. She rose from her seat. As she reached the window to look out Vincent entered the room. He seemed distinctly peeved by the turn of events. As any student of national characteristics will tell you, an Englishman peeved is a man bringing a lifetime of repression to bear on containing his escalating anger. It seemed he would choke on the information he had to convey.

Suddenly the air seemed to leave the room as a crash of thunder coincided with the lights dimming and an explosion of light outside.

Carol screamed.

Everyone had turned to the window and saw what she had. A figure had been silhouetted against the curtain of the French windows.

29

The lights were back on just as Vincent burst into the room. His usual disdainful composure appeared momentarily to have parted company from him. In its place was a distinctly ruffled manner which reminded one of a vicar dealing with a child crying mid-sermon. Through lips that appeared to have been glued together, he managed to splutter the message he'd been sent to convey.

'Sir, the police have arrived.'

4

Kit was the first to respond to this rather dramatic announcement. He strode to the door of the dining room. Standing there was a uniformed officer. A sergeant. The sergeant looked at Kit in his black dinner suit, the very epitome of English upper class breeding and found any words he'd intended to say abandon him.

'Uhhhh,' said the police sergeant. To add clarity to this rather enigmatic utterance, he pointed in the direction of the French windows.

'Darling,' came Mary's voice from inside the room.

'Coming,' said Kit.

Inside the room, Gerry had thrown open the curtains to reveal that there was a man in a raincoat and a felt hat standing outside. He opened the French windows and the man stepped inside with a slow nod of thanks to Gerry.

The man removed his felt hat and surveyed the room impassively. The new arrival was somewhere in his fifties or perhaps early sixties. Tufts of grey hair stuck out unapologetically from over his ears and few strands of grey hair remained on his otherwise bald pate. From underneath bushy salt and pepper eyebrows, a pair of intelligent, humorous yet unsentimental eyes fixed on Carol just as Mary said, 'Darling'. Those eyes thought Mary. They were compelling and knowing in equal measure.

Kit entered the room and stopped in his tracks as he saw the man. If Kit was shocked to see the man, the reaction was no less intense from the new arrival. His face fell and a scowl appeared on his face.

'Hookie,' said Kit and his face lit up in a warm smile.

Hookie seemed a little less enamoured by the reunion. The scowl grew rather than diminished. He looked as if he might roll his eyes, but iron discipline stopped any display of petulance.

'Please tell me you're not staying here,' said the man known as Hookie.

'I am, old chap. Sorry, we are. This is my wife, Mary,' said Kit turning to Mary, who was looking unusually confused by what was happening. A slight frown creased her forehead. Her eyes narrowed as she gazed at Hookie. 'Mary, please may I introduce Inspector Douglas Hook. He and I go way back.'

Mary peered sideways at her husband. Kit knew this look and he groaned inwardly.

'There's probably a few things I hadn't mentioned about my past, darling.'

The detective stepped forward and held his hand out to Mary. They shook hands. He said very gravely, 'It is a pleasure to meet you Mary. Quite what made you marry this young man escapes me. You have my sympathy.'

'I think Kit will need your sympathy when I've finished with him, Inspector Hook,' said Mary, but there was a hint of amusement in her voice.

'It's Chief Inspector now,' corrected Hook, glancing scornfully at Kit. Then he turned to Gerry Tudor and nodded to the stables owner.

'I'm sorry to disturb you on such a horrible night,' said Hook. He then turned to Tamsin who was standing beside Carol. 'Tamsin, Gerry; is it possible that I may have a few moments alone with Mrs Harrison?'

Tamsin glanced at Carol who had grown even paler since the arrival of the policeman. She said, 'Of course, Hookie.'

'No,' said Carol suddenly. 'No, I want you all here. What has that beast done, Chief Inspector? He's a liar and a brute. If you must know, with Bryn's help, I'm going to divorce him.' Carol had turned towards Bryn Cain and then back to Hook. His eyes widened slightly as he saw the bruise on her face.

'Did your husband do this?' asked Hook. Unable to trust her voice, Carol nodded confirmation. Gerry stepped forward at this point.

'Hookie, Carol has left Teddy. He's treated her abominably as you can see.'

Hookie said nothing to this. The thunder rumbled once more, but he did not blink as he studied Carol.

'When did you leave him?' asked Hook, his eyes narrowing.

'Why do you ask?' said Bryn Cain almost as a warning to Carol not to speak. She ignored him.

'Two nights ago. I'm not going back whatever he says,' said Carol. She was framed by flickering light in the sky.

'I don't think he's going to say much now,' said Hook. 'We found a man in the kitchen of your house. Dead.'

33

A crack of thunder seemed to shake the house never mind its occupants.

The detective glanced towards the window and back before saying as much to himself, 'I feel like I'm in a badly written play.'

Carol collapsed weeping into Tamsin. There had been an undefinable edge to her manner all evening and it was as if the levee had come apart. She sobbed uncontrollably on Tamsin's shoulder. Mary went immediately to her while the three men did what men usually do in these situations and stared mutely at one another.

'I say Hookie,' said Gerry, finally. This is as far as a wealthy English landowner will push admonishment. For students in the use of English English as opposed to American English, the key in making your repressed feelings felt is to add more emphasise in the word 'Say' while proceeding not to say anything about what has upset you in the first place. It is upon such indirect communication that an empire was built. Perhaps if Victorians had used American English, rather than English English, Britain might have been holidaying in Magaluf earlier rather than invading hot, foreign climes.

Hook shrugged unapologetically. 'Perhaps the ladies could take Carol away for the moment.'

Tamsin nodded to Gerry and both she and Mary led Carol away. When the door closed Kit went over to the drinks cabinet.

'What would you like Hookie?'

'To be somewhere else,' admitted Hook truthfully.

'Sure?' said Kit holding up a bottle of gin.

'I'm on duty,' pointed out Hook. Then he added, 'Best make it a small one.' He watched as Kit poured some gin into a glass before adding a touch of tonic to it. He brought the drink over and Hook took a seat without being asked. Kit sat down and then Gerry.

'So, Hookie, what's all this about?'

The detective took an appreciative sip of the gin and then fished in his pocket and extracted a pipe. He spent a few moments lighting it then took a puff or three.

'About half an hour ago, we received reports of a gunshot. This was confirmed a few minutes later by a phone call from a man named Roger Sexton. Do you know him Gerry?'

'Yes, of course. He owns a horse box business. We get our horse boxes from him.'

Hook glanced towards Bryn Cain who had said little so far. 'I suppose you know him.'

'Yes,' said Cain who, as a lawyer, appeared to invoice by the word. He popped a cigarette out of his case and put it in his mouth. He offered one to Hook who accepted it but put it behind his ear.

'Well, Mr Sexton and another gentleman named Jason Trent, were invited to the house of Edward Harrison this evening. They knocked on the door of the house but there was no answer. This was strange as Mr Harrison had specifically said to them to come at six o'clock. They went back to the back door and opened it. Just at that moment there was a gun shot. A shot gun blast, I should say. They found a dead body inside the kitchen. The shot left a bit of a mess, I can tell you. I wouldn't be surprised if they are both in shock.'

'So Teddy topped himself,' said Gerry in wonder.

'It would appear to be so,' said Hook. The serious tone of his voice was in contrast to his evident enjoyment of the gin.

'Was there a suicide note?' asked Kit. This brought a grimace from Hook. He glanced sideways at Kit and wagged his finger.

'No,' said the policeman.

'No, there wasn't a suicide note or no to my involvement?' asked Kit innocently.

'I think you know very well what I mean Kit,' said Hook. 'You haven't changed I see.'

'Nor you, Hookie,' said Kit appreciatively. 'I knew Teddy. Not well, of course. He never struck me as the kind of man who would kill himself.'

'Did he strike you as the kind of man who would act so cruelly towards his wife?' asked Hook, sardonically.

Kit thought for a moment before replying, 'This was less of a surprise.'

Hook kept his eyes fixed on Kit as he asked, 'You were not keen on the man.'

'No. No, not really,' admitted Kit. 'Would you like to know where I was between four and six this afternoon?'

Hook waved his hand dismissively. 'Let me enjoy my pipe,' said the detective before adding ominously, 'We have a long night ahead of us.'

At this point an unlikely albeit welcome interjection came from Vincent who had been standing quietly observing events with his usual combination of gentle condescension.

'Sir, what about dinner? Cook was most insistent that it be eaten now.'

All eyes turned to Vincent. He stood there looking decidedly decided that it must be eaten. In the face of such

36

stubborn observance to cook's imperatives there was only one response and Chief Inspector Douglas Hook was just the man to deliver it.

'Capital idea.' said Hook before supplying a very English solution to a tricky problem. He said, 'May I join you?'

'Of course, Hookie,' said Gerry a little nervously. 'Vincent, why don't you tell the ladies that we are having dinner.'

Vincent disappeared while everyone turned to Hook. He offered a smile that reminded Kit of a cat gazing at a mouse going about its everyday business without a care in the world, utterly unaware of what lay ahead.

'Why don't you sit at the end of the table, Hookie?' said Gerry. 'Guest of honour.'

'I hope you still think that when all of this is over,' said Hook ominously. He walked slowly to the end of the table. Kit shot him a look and for a moment their eyes fixed on one another.

In that moment, the ten years since Kit had last seen the detective melted away. Kit had attended school near Newmarket and gone to university in Cambridge. During this period he had come to know Douglas Hook very well. They had worked together, usually unwillingly on Hook's part, on several police investigations.

As if reading his mind, something that Hook did with an alarming proficiency, he asked, 'How are your friends, Olly, Spunky and Chubby, Kit? As he asked this, Vincent placed a plate of veal with vegetables on in front of him. 'I hope they survived it all.'

'They all survived. Olly fell by the wayside a little,' replied Kit enigmatically.

'He was always a rather wild character,' observed Hook. 'I'm glad you all made it through.'

'And Abbie?' asked Kit. Abigail Hook was the detective's daughter. She was around five years older than Kit. Then a thought struck Kit and he added, 'And Philip?'

'Philip survived,' said Hook. 'Some scars. Abbie's fine, thank you. She's relieved he made it through, naturally.' Kit nodded and nothing more needed to be said. Those that survived all carried scars of some sort. Hook turned his attention to Gerry. There was a distinct sadness in his voice now. 'And Chris?'

Gerry smiled but there was desolation in his eyes.

'You know,' he said. He shrugged and could think of nothing more to say about his brother.

Hook nodded while Kit remained silent. Of course he knew what had happened to Chris. The horror had left its mark permanently on Gerry's brother. It seemed extraordinary to think it, but changing the subject of the conversation to the death of Teddy Harrison was a blessed relief for all.

'What happened?' asked Kit, looking at the detective.

'I would like to find out more myself,' said Hook. 'We were called out to Mr Harrison's house following the reports of a gunshot. The two young men I mentioned were already there. They were the first to find the dead body.

'Teddy?' said Kit.

Hook peered sideways at Kit. Then he ate a mouthful of the veal and raised his bushy eyebrows in approval. It seemed only right to have a sip of the wine. This also met with his appreciation.

'You do have a rather good table Gerry, I must say. Now what was I saying? Oh yes, the young men, Roger Sexton and Jason Trent were there standing by the dead body. We've brought them to the police station to answer questions.'

Gerry was a countryman. He liked horses. They liked him. Despite his privileged upbringing, he had been missing on the day they taught false airs and graces. His reactions to anything surprising were just like him, honest, direct and without any attempt at concealment. His mouth fell open.

'You seem surprised,' said Hook. This was a classic piece of understatement from the detective and just at that moment Kit felt a stab of nostalgia for the man and the cases they had worked together on.

'I, well, yes,' said Gerry which hardly clarified why he was surprised only that he was flabbergasted.

'Why?' asked Hook just before taking another sip. His tone, as ever, was dangerously conversational. He took another sip of the wine and nodded at Kit's untouched glass. Kit almost smiled at the performance, but he was trapped. He could not warn Gerry that the detective was already setting traps. Yet another part of him wondered why he would do so? There was always something else in the background. Hook never revealed his cards too early, and he was usually the last to set down his hand. The hand was invariably stuffed with aces.

'They're friends,' spluttered Gerry.

'Of yours?' asked the detective.

Kit could not breathe. He could see where this was heading.

'No, not mine, I suppose. More Carol's.'

'So, the two young men that found the dead body at her husband's house were friends of Carol's?'

By now the penny had dropped even for the honest, but less-than-bright Gerry.

'I say Hookie, what are you suggesting?'

Hook did not answer because, just then, Mary entered the room to a clap of thunder outside. It was as dramatic an entrance as the detective's earlier and Kit almost gave his own clap of approval. Mary stopped at the door; her slender figure was framed against the bright light in the hallway as she surveyed the three men sat at the table. It was immediately clear to her that there was an atmosphere in the room. Mary turned to Gerry.

'We've settled Carol in her bed. She's dreadfully upset as you may imagine. Tamsin wants to give her a sleeping draught.'

'Won't she be needed to identify the body?' asked Gerry.

'Oh, don't worry about that,' replied Hook. 'There's not much left of his head to help her.'

5

'Let her sleep,' said Hook gently. 'Perhaps, Gerry, you could go to her. I think families should be together at times like these, don't you?'

Gerry was out of the chair like a sprinter at the starter's pistol. He was clearly upset at the events of the evening, but his dash for the door suggested that there was more on his mind than just concern for his sister. Kit wondered what his old friend's game was and he was in no doubt there was a game being played. In this regard, he was very much cut from the same cloth as his beloved uncle, Eustace "Useless" Frost, the late husband of his aunt Agatha. They both had minds that contained wheels within wheels all of which had their own set of wheels, too.

'Cain stood up also. He fixed his eyes on Hook and said, 'Perhaps I should head down to the station. Mr Sexton was once a client of mine.'

'Was?'

'We fell out,' was the drawled response from Cain.

'It's good that you have an opportunity to build some bridges once more,' said Hook. Cain smirked at this but didn't rise to the bait. He sauntered out of the room watched by the detective.

Once Gerry and Cain had left, Hook turned to Mary with a beatific smile. Mary smiled sweetly back at him. They were like two fencers sizing one another up, liking what they saw and savouring the match ahead.

'So, how do you know Kit?' asked Mary. As an opening thrust, it was innocuous enough on the face of it, but Kit had already felt the scratch. Hook's smile widened. He understood all too well what Mary was asking and he was not a man to pass up the opportunity to add a nick to the one Mary had already left.

'You mean Kit has never mentioned me?' he asked in mock surprise.

'Never,' confirmed Mary. She was not looking at Kit even though she was speaking to him. At this point it might have been difficult to see him as he was busy trying to bury himself into his seat.

'Shame on you, Kit,' said Hook with mock severity.

'Oh for goodness sakes, Mary,' exclaimed Kit laughingly. 'Don't fall into his trap. He makes Machiavelli look like a teddy bear. If you must know, I saved his life.'

Mary's eyes widened and she swung her head in the direction of the detective.

'I saved yours, too,' pointed out Hook defensively.

'More by accident than design.'

Hook flicked his hand in a manner that suggested such fine details were for minions to deal with. Then he said, 'I deal with outcomes. You lived therefore I succeeded in saving your life. Of course, if you had not interfered then the issue would not have arisen.'

Kit's grin broadened, but he shook his head sceptically before adding, 'And you may not have caught the murderer.'

'I think we both know I would have. You youngsters are always in such a rush. No attention span. Anyway, I fear we may be boring your charming and, I can see, very bright wife. Tell me, Mrs Aston, no, assure me, that you, at least, are above the childish antics of amateur detection.'

All eyes turned to Mary. She smiled and shook her head slowly.

'Sorry, Chief Inspector, I'm afraid I'm with my husband on this.'

Hook rolled his eyes and his mouth fixed into something midway between a grimace and a scowl. Kit was having none of this though.

'Go on, admit it, Hookie. You've missed me.'

'Like I miss appendicitis.'

Kit looked fondly at the detective. It was easy to misunderstand Hook. His face was often set to grouchiness. A frown was never far away from his mouth, his eyes often conveyed quiet desperation, and he had the patience of a three-year-old boy. Kit understood that most people hid behind a mask. Not Douglas Hook. This was him. He was irascible, impatient and impossible in equal measure and highly intelligent. An alumni of Kit's own school, a graduate of Cambridge in law, he had shocked both his college and parents alike when he chose to join the police.

This was typical of the man that Kit had come to know in his younger years at school and then college. While his manner was all too transparent he used it as a shield when the occasion demanded: he always kept something back.

Always.

'It sounds as if you had quite a few adventures. I look forward to the book series,' said Mary mischievously.

43

'Oh yes,' said Hook, a mirthless smile on his face. 'Inspector Hook Investigates, open bracket, assisted by irritating public schoolboy, close bracket.'

'I doubt Conan Doyle will be losing sleep over the competition,' noted Kit.

The detective paused for a moment and said carefully, 'Agatha knew Doyle didn't she? How…?'

'Going strong,' replied Kit anticipating the question. 'She misses Eustace dreadfully, though.'

Hook nodded before responding, 'Yes, I can imagine she would. He was quite a man. I imagine you miss him, too.'

The memory of his uncle, the lop-sided smile, the Byzantine mind, made Kit pause and collect himself. Tears stung his eyes. He nodded but said nothing.

Hook immediately punctured the emotional air by adding forlornly, 'Would that you were more like him, Kit.'

'Rather than?' smiled Kit.

'A dashing, too-good-to-be-true amateur detective?' suggested Mary, eyes twinkling in the low light. 'He is smart.'

'And devilishly good-looking,' suggested Kit.

'As I was saying, he is smart.'

Hook raised a glass to this comment thereby confirming the early good impression that he and Mary had of one another. The mutual appreciation society was interrupted as Kit brought matters back to the case in hand.

'What's really going on, Hookie?' asked Kit. This was greeted with an innocent shrug of the shoulders and his hands splaying out in a "search-me-guv" manner. 'No Hookie. I know you. You're here for a reason beyond being the bearer of bad news. There's something not quite right about what happened. I can tell. My money's on the fact that

44

two men arrived just as he blew his own head off. We both knew Teddy Harrison. This wasn't his style. If he were going to top himself and that's a jolly big if, he would have drunk himself senseless and added a bit of something to the cocktail and bingo, he never wakes up. The Teddy Harrison I know would never have blown his head off. Then we have the two young men arriving on the scene as he did all this. How well did they know Carol? I think we both know this was not a marriage made in heaven. He was an out and out bounder. I'm now wondering about Carol.'

While Kit was saying this, Hook was looking ever more depressed. He set the knife and fork down and rested his head on his two hands.

'You're not to become involved,' said Hook, but his heart wasn't in it.

'You're a betting man, I seem to remember. What odds would you give on that?'

A couple of hours later, Kit and Mary were back in their bedroom while Chief Inspector Hook was his way home to the cottage he shared with his wife, midway between Cambridge and Newmarket. Carol had taken a sleeping draught and was sleeping peacefully in her childhood bedroom. Gerry and Tamsin retired to bed, unspoken questions in the air.

Vincent, meanwhile, helped to clear away the plates from the table with a leaden heart. He adored Carol, hated Teddy. Yet even through the mist of his own prejudices and snobbery, he sensed that the wonderful news of Carol leaving that hateful man was likely to turn into an inquiry of the most sordid kind. What the newspapers would make of this the Lord only knew, but it was an ill wind that had brought that vile excrescence, Edward Harrison, into the lives of this family and it had returned to take him away. But what else would be ripped away?

Vincent paused for a moment as he stared at the uneaten food on his master's plate. What had happened that evening in Newmarket town that should see a man take his own life? And who had driven away that afternoon from the house? Vincent stopped himself thinking any more about such matters. It was a suicide. This was a matter for the police and an inquest. He had made a life from upholding standards, not asking questions that were not his business.

Hook was a dangerous man. His presence boded ill for the family. Of this, Vincent was sure. And what of poor Master Chris? How would this affect his fragile state. His thoughts were interrupted by the maid who came into the dining room to carry away the remaining plates. He watched her go but said nothing.

Upstairs in their bedroom, Kit waited for the interrogation to begin. Mary's technique was nothing if not novel. She began with a few kisses to soften up the suspect. Then she stared up at him through narrowed eyes that dared him to dissemble.

'So,' began Mary. Never has this word been invested with such a sense of threat as Mary managed just then. 'Saved lives, slayings and schoolboy shenanigans. I want to hear all,' said Mary. So far, so good, thought Kit. I might just have gotten away with this one. Such illusions rarely last long in the merciless memory of any woman. No minor infraction is ever waved away and dismissed. They all count. Equally.

'And then you can explain to me why you had never thought it worth mentioning before.'

'Errr…' began Kit who was usually more fluent than this.

The next hour was an entertaining walk through his memories as Kit outlined several cases that had heralded his career in amateur detection. They sounded worthy of a series of books, to Mary and she said as much.

'I learned everything I know from Hookie,' concluded Kit, 'but probably not everything he knows. He is deceptively smart.'

'There's no deception. I had that feeling right from the beginning,' admitted Mary. Then her face became more concerned. A frown appeared and Kit guessed what was on her mind because it was on his also.

'There's something about this case that has him concerned,' said Kit.

'Will he tell you?' asked Mary.

'Oh yes. He grumbles a lot. He enjoys that. To be honest, so do I when he does it. He'll tell me. For once, though, I'm not sure I want to know.'

'Yes, I see what you mean. Do you think that Mr Hook thinks that Carol or Gerry are involved?'

Kit shrugged and held his hands out. He walked over to the window and stared out at the front lawn. 'I don't know, darling, but I am worried about that. Gerry wouldn't hurt a fly. He's the gentlest man I know. He was destroyed by the War; and what it did to Chris; what it did to his horses. I couldn't imagine him doing anything after that to hurt anyone, but Carol is his sister. If anyone was mistreating her

47

then who knows? Tell me, did you see him return in the car before drinks?'

'I couldn't see who it was. I only saw the car pull into the garage.'

Kit stared out into the night. The driveway leading from the edge of the estate to the front of the house was lit by lamps. The garage was situated to the right of the house. If someone left from the side door then it would not be possible to see who it was. Mary stood beside Kit by the window. Her arm circled around his waist. She noticed a light on in a room at the end of the house which blocked their view of the garage.

'Let's go to bed,' said Mary. Those were Kit's favourite words, and no second invitation was needed.

A few hours later, in the middle of the night, Mary awoke with a gnawing hunger. She had not had the opportunity or, perhaps, the appetite to eat earlier. She was ravenous. Rather than wake Kit, she decided to sneak down to the kitchen and find something to eat. She was sure no one would mind.

Mary padded over to the chair where her dressing gown lay. She settled into her slippers and crept quietly out of the room. A little earlier she had been down in the kitchen with Tamsin and Carol following the shocking news, so she knew her way around. Making her way down two flights of stairs she walked along the corridor to the kitchen. There was a light on.

Mary was surprised by this as it was not yet three in the morning. It seemed too early for cook to be up preparing food. She approached the kitchen stealthily, not wanting to disturb who was inside, curious to see who it might be. There was definitely someone there. She could hear cupboard doors opening and shutting.

Then she remembered an important fact that had not been a consideration when she embarked on this voyage. Hadn't Kit mentioned the fact that the mansion was haunted?

When Kit had mentioned it, in passing as usual, she had immediately dismissed it as a joke. However, it is an inalienable truth and may one day be proved empirically by scientists who view life through a more Gothic prism, that we are more susceptible to believing the worst of the most innocent of sounds when we are alone, at night, having been told our location may be a metropolis for paranormal manifestations. Or some such rot.

Mary's heart was beginning to beat a tad faster now. It was not exactly fear. There was an element of her that had never lost a yen for schoolgirl adventures. Sneaking down to the kitchen in the middle of the night in a house that might be haunted fell right into this category. She inhaled deeply to regain control of her breathing and slowly peeked her head around the corner.

Standing directly in front of her was a man in a dressing gown. It was Gerry making himself a midnight snack.

Mary knocked the door and moved inside the kitchen. She said, 'Hello.'

The man that spun around was definitely not Gerry. He was wearing a mask over his face with holes for his eyes, nose and mouth. A large knife gleamed in his hand in a hand that was shaking.

A scream split the night.

The next morning around ten, Kit and Mary were in the dining room helping themselves to an extravagant country breakfast. Fresh eggs scrambled or poached along with enough sausages and bacon to fuel an army battalion.

'I think I would have screamed also,' said Kit to Mary as she told him about her midnight adventure. Then he added, 'Poor man. You must have frightened him awfully.'

'I hadn't realised I presented such a fearsome sight,' said Mary. Kit regarded her seriously. She had an elfin beauty that had beguiled him from the beginning and would do so for the rest of his life.

'Horrible,' said Kit before taking evasive action as a sausage was brandished with threatening intent.

'Poor Chris,' said Mary. 'I know you said that he had been scarred by the War, but I suppose I took this to mean mentally.'

'Sorry, I should have said,' admitted Kit. 'I haven't seen him myself since we came back. Gerry did tell me that he shunned the world now because of his injuries. He suggested there was shell shock too, but this diminished over the last year. What did Chris say?'

'He turned away from me and held his hands up to his face and said, "don't look at me". He was crying, Kit. I felt like I was some sort of monster. He dropped the knife and the plate and was about to shoot off like a jackrabbit when I stood in front of him. Poor thing.'

'I can think of worse things than having a beautiful girl grab hold of me. Anyway, it wasn't your fault that you scared him.'

'Well, it was. I gave him the most awful scare. I went over to him and told him my name. He knew who I was. He said he'd seen me arrive through his window.'

'What happened then?'

'I told him why I'd come down to the kitchen. He was still turning away from me. I think he was ashamed of his reaction. He just left without saying another word. I must say, I felt horribly guilty.'

'Don't worry my darling. What did you do then?'

'Well, he left his sandwich behind,' said Mary. Her voice was small, and she appeared to shrink into Kit.

'You didn't eat it, did you?' asked Kit. Mary was too remorseful to confirm this so Kit took her silence as an admission of guilt. 'This is the thin end of the wedge, Mary. Soon you'll be raiding collection tins in churches and stealing from beggars. Frankly, I'm appalled.'

Mary seemed a little less guilty after hearing this searing condemnation from her husband. She pointed out that Chris could always have returned when the coast was clear and made another sandwich. Kit, meanwhile, casually referred to her devious theft at breakfast by turning his body in front of his breakfast plate when Mary was near. Even Mary had to laugh by this stage. They dined alone as both Gerry and

Tamsin appeared to be locked away with Carol, no doubt to establish what they needed to do.

Kit was glad to have the dining room to themselves as he needed to think through what, if anything, should be their involvement. There were a number of options to consider; whether they should leave or not was the primary one. However, the principal argument against doing so was immediately identified by Mary.

'One thing I am confused about is why Chief Inspector Hook did not ask Carol to come and identify the body immediately. I mean, I think I would know you *sans tete*, so to speak.'

Kit smiled and raised his eyebrows momentarily, 'Yes, I thought his point around the gunshot's effect on the head seemed a tad disingenuous. Welcome to the world of Hookie.'

'And where is he this morning? I would have thought having allowed Carol some time to recover from the shock, he would want her to come in and answer some questions. I mean, he didn't seem all that curious about why Teddy might have committed suicide,' said Mary. She seemed genuinely confused about the almost negligently lackadaisical approach from a man Kit clearly respected highly.

Her husband was now sitting, gazing happily at his wife who was by the window. The storm of yesterday had abated and the sun was shining brightly, framing her head in a bright halo.

'Oh this is classic Hookie. I daresay he's somewhere nearby waiting; conducting a war of nerves.'

'Waiting for what?' asked Mary.

Kit held his hands in the air palms outwards. Rather frustratingly for Mary he, too, seemed a little bit too relaxed about the events of the previous evening. Although she was not so hypocritical to feel much by way of sympathy for a man she had never met who, apparently, had mistreated his wife, before taking his own life, nor was she happy that his death should just be accepted on a nod. Part of her recognised that a game was being played out that was new to her. Perhaps it was time to take a leaf out of Kit's book and sit back and wait to see who made the next move.

'So what do we do?' asked Mary, walking over to Kit and sitting on his knee.

Now, a question like this, in Kit's book, merited only one response. A few minutes later he answered the original exam question, impressing Mary that he could remember a question she had forgotten.

'I think we should finish our breakfast and then do what we came here to do.'

'You mean go out for a ride.'

'Yes,' replied Kit.

'But what happens if the Chief Inspector comes, and we miss him?'

'That, my dear, is the point,' replied Kit enigmatically. Despite the outward appearance of a handsome fictional hero in the English mould, Kit had learned his trade at the feet of two masters of the dark arts of deception, Eustace and Hook. When called upon to do so, he was not afraid of dipping his toes into a little intrigue himself. In fact, he rather enjoyed it.

'To the horses?' asked Mary. She was already dressed for riding, as was Kit. She received a confirmatory nod and they set off via the French windows down the hill towards the

54

enormous stables which housed close to two dozen horses, some of them belonging to the family, many just paying guests to be trained by Gerry and his team.

They met Cedric Naylor, the stables manager. Naylor had been with Gerry for as long as Kit could remember. 'I have two horses ready for you, sir,' said Naylor. 'Would you care to come this way?'

No mention was made of the previous evening's events by the veteran stable manager. Kit was sure that he knew all about what had happened. The staff would be talking about the suicide and already be forming theories about the death.

'Have you seen Mr Tudor this morning?' asked Kit.

'Yes, he and Mr Chris were down bright and early as usual. He said to have your mounts ready. We're giving you Ballygowan, I think you've ridden him before and Mrs Aston can have Fintona, she's a lovely mare we recently purchased in Ireland.'

'Wonderful,' replied Kit. 'I remember old Ballygowan. Lovely temperament and jumps a dream.'

Naylor took Kit and Mary through to the stable where one of the lads was busy tightening the buckle on Mary's horse. Then he took the lead and brought her through to meet the new arrivals. Fintona was a grey while Ballygowan was a tall chestnut horse who had been a 'chaser' for many years until the War started. Gerry was far too fond of his horse to allow him to be taken away and he'd hidden him from prying eyes little suspecting the carnage to which his other horses would experience as the War tightened its deadly grip.

Ballygowan nudged Kit which brought a laugh from Naylor. 'I think he recognises you, sir.'

'He recognises a source of food,' said Kit, putting his hand up to the horse's mouth so that it could take the carrots.

Despite his prosthetic lower leg, Kit had no problem mounting Ballygowan. Mary was, if anything, an even more confident rider than Kit. They were led out of the stables towards the paddock.

'You know your way around sir, I remember,' said Naylor. 'There's no restrictions on where you go but be careful of cars. There seems to be more of them every year.'

Kit and Mary trotted past the cottages for the staff and the large barn containing the food for the horses. Soon they were cantering out onto the gallops which led onto lush green fields. The sun was shining, but it was bitterly cold. Neither Kit nor Mary cared. For the next few hours they trotted, cantered and galloped across ten- and twenty-acre fields surrounded by low hedges which allowed them to jump safely. They headed towards a hill some three miles away from the stables which Kit informed Mary would allow them a wonderful view of the land around Newmarket racecourse.

As they emerged from a wood Kit pointed to the hill. 'That's the one I was talking about.'

'There looks to be someone up there already,' said Mary.

Although the hill was not very steep, they chose to walk up rather than tire their mounts out. The man at the top was with his own horse. He, too, appeared to have the same idea and was gazing out at the rolling landscape, eating a sandwich.

'I think that's Chris,' said Kit as they drew closer. 'He's wearing a mask.'

Ballygowan whinnied as if to confirm Kit's assessment. The man at the top of the hill turned sharply and saw that people were approaching. He leapt to his feet immediately and mounted the black colt. They were off before Kit could shout to him.

'Pity,' said Mary. 'I'd like to have apologised for last night.'

'You mean stolen another one of his sandwiches,' laughed Kit.

'Good point. I'm beginning to feel a little peckish.'

'Let's see the view then we'll head home,' agreed Kit.

They reached the top of the hill and gazed down towards the racecourse in the distance. Kit smiled as he took in the view.

'I love this place, Mary. I went so many times to the races. Lord only knows how much money I lost. Well, not much really. Father only gave me a small allowance. I'm not sure you can see, but there are actually three racecourses. The Rowley mile course and the Plate course as well as the course where the other flat racing takes place. Perhaps this summer we can come back and watch the Guineas if Northern Glory competes.'

Mary took Kit's arm and hugged him close. She said, 'I would love that, but I'm worried about what's happening to Gerry and Tamsin. Do you sense something? I know I do.'

Kit nodded. He had sensed something. There was the faint but all too distinct whiff of fear, of dark, unspoken secrets, of murder. The presence of Hook and his manner the previous evening had all but convinced Kit that there was more to the death of Teddy Harrison than had so far been revealed. It was time to return to the mansion and find out what had happened over the few hours that they had been away.

It was lunchtime when they returned. As they neared the gallops, a familiar figure appeared outside the house wearing a raincoat and a felt hat. Kit smiled as he watched the figure lope down the steps. He reached the fence of the paddock just as Kit and Mary rode up.

A pipe in his mouth, he gazed up at the couple with a swoony smile. Mary smiled back at him. His crumpled felt hat was perched on the back of his head revealing his beaming face. He genuinely seemed happy to see them both which made for a rather stark contrast to his manner the night before. Glancing towards Kit, Mary noted that her husband was smiling with pleasure too. It was quite amusing really to see them circle one another, feinting and parrying imaginary and nuanced verbal lunges.

'Enjoy your ride?' asked Hook.

'Thoroughly pleasant,' said Kit. 'I take it you still do not ride.'

Hook chuckled and replied, 'No I much prefer *terra firma*. Too dangerous, you could fall off. I'll stick to the occasional flutter, but that's all I want to do with these animals.'

Ballygowan, sensing a rather nervous spectator swung its head in Hook's direction causing the detective to step back and scowl nervously at the horse.

'Stupid animal,' said Hook, straightening his hat a little.

This made Kit grin. He asked the detective, 'For someone who professes no love for horses, why have you chosen to live in the very heart of the racing world?'

'Ask my wife,' said Hook downheartedly.

'How many cases have you worked on, related to horses, aside from the one we worked on?'

'Well over a hundred, I suppose,' said the detective. He didn't sound particularly nostalgic about this.

Kit and Mary climbed off their horses and handed the leads over to a couple of stable lads to take the horses away to the stables where they would be washed down, and fed. Kit and Mary accompanied Hook back up to the house.

'So have we missed anything?' asked Kit.

'Oh this and that,' said Hook with a chuckle. Unlike some of his smiles which had a ruthless streak embedded within them, this one had a different texture. It was one that seemed to be genuinely amused, but in the manner of unsurprised disbelief, thought Mary. There was no question, Chief Inspector Hook was an intriguing man.

They arrived at the house and stepped in through the French windows into the dining room. It was empty but places had been laid out for lunch. Mary eyed the number of settings and was gratified to see that Kit had noticed the same thing.

'Staying for lunch?' asked Kit.

'Oh I think so. Me plus our new guests,' responded Hook with an air of innocence that would have gained immediate acceptance into any order of nuns.

'Who might the guests be?' asked Mary. 'Your colleagues?'

Hook erupted into laughter at this just as the door opened. Carol entered the room followed by two men that Kit and Mary had never met before. None of them seemed very amused although given that Carol had just lost a husband, of sorts, perhaps this was not a surprise. More surprising was the sense of suppressed rage with all three. This was going to be a highly unusual interview thought Kit.

It was so typical of Hook to do it this way. Kit smiled at the detective fondly.

'I've missed you Hookie,' he murmured through the side of his mouth in Hook's direction.

The gleeful countenance of the detective became, if anything, even more amused.

One of the more unusual lunches that Kit or Mary had ever attended commenced soon after Vincent and Lisa had served the first course. In attendance were Gerry, Tamsin, Carol and the two young men that Hook had alluded to the previous evening: Roger Sexton and Jason Trent. Apparently the pair had arrived, separately, soon after Kit and Mary had departed for the stables to go riding. One would have been hard pressed to describe their expressions as rapturous. Chief Inspector Hook, true to form, had left them all to stew at the house before arriving soon after ten to see if the pot had reached boiling point and to give things a little stir. After the initial introductions by Gerry, Kit settled back to enjoy the show.

'Perhaps we should have a moment's silence for our departed friend,' said Hook with the air of a particularly virtuous vicar. This did not go down well with either Gerry or Carol, but Tamsin seemed amused, noted Mary. Crocodile tears were not her style, and she was not about to adopt the practice now.

Carol glared at Hook but said nothing. Everyone remained silent for a few moments and then Hook took a napkin, swirled it a little before placing it on his lap with a flourish.

'Now, what has cook made for us here,' asked Hook taking in the aroma of the soup.

'Cabbage soup,' said Gerry glumly.

Hook's face fell a little before he said, 'Not my favourite, but no matter. Now, where were we?'

The first to respond was Roger Sexton. He had the air of someone who was seconds away from losing his temper and duly did. He rose to his feet, 'What is your game? Are you going to tell us why we are here or not?'

Hook was a picture of faux innocence as he replied, 'Why my good man, you came here of your own accord. To see Mrs Harrison, I believe. Am I mistaken?'

Kit had to fight hard to avoid erupting in laughter. Sexton sat down on his seat with a thump. He knew he'd been made a fool of and, equally, he knew he'd brought it on himself. In those few seconds, Kit had an opportunity to appraise Sexton. He was probably his own age or maybe slightly older. His hair was sandy coloured and thinning a little. He was just under six feet tall and built like a front row rugger player. His suit was well made, and his voice suggested that he'd enjoyed the very best sort of education that England allows, if not for its brightest prospects, then certainly for those fortunate enough to afford it. As tempting as it was to assume that Sexton was not the sharpest knife in the dining room, Kit decided not to read too much into the outburst. Hookie could get to you like that.

Turning his attention to Jason Trent, Kit sensed a much shrewder individual. He was slenderer than Sexton and, to Kit's eyes, a little older, perhaps nudging forty. Unlike

Sexton, who wore a tweed suit and looked every inch a sportsman, Trent was clearly not of the country. He was wearing a business suit with a bright tie and a matching breast pocket handkerchief. Both the tie and the handkerchief were white polka dots against a scarlet background.

While Sexton fumed at the insouciance of Hook, Mary decided it was time to get to know the new arrivals better.

'Mr Sexton, are you also involved in horse racing?'

Sexton turned to Mary and some of the anger seemed to evaporate under the attention of such a young woman. His colouring was already a little red and he went a little redder. A swift glance towards Carol and then he responded, 'I own a shop. We sell and rent equipment related to horses. Horse boxes, particularly.'

'There are a lot of stables around,' suggested Mary.

'There are a lot of horses,' agreed Sexton. 'Demand is high.'

'And you Mr Trent, are you in horseracing?'

Trent smiled slowly at Mary. He dabbed the side of his mouth and sat back in his chair. This was a man to whom self-doubt was a stranger, something to be avoided like a beggar in the street. He pondered what was, on the face of it, a fairly simple question, then when he was good and ready he replied, 'In a manner of speaking. I am a money manager. I invest money for people, I connect businessmen together who wish to invest in enterprises or, in this case, partnerships who wish to become involved in racing, you know, owning a horse. A stallion is much more fun than munitions, ships, or textiles, believe me. The sport of kings. We also help finance businesses in the racing world.'

Sexton appeared to shift uncomfortably in his seat at this remark.

'I imagine there must be many people who would like to own racehorses,' said Mary.

'There are and the partnerships I bring together gives them the opportunity to have the chance of being a part owner of a Derby winner or the sire of one,' said Trent coolly. 'It's a growing business. Soon, I believe, it will be a worldwide concern. With it will be a need to have access to money. That's what I do. The banks will become more interested in loaning money into horseracing.'

Kit noticed a distinct wince from Sexton at the mention of the word 'loan'. Trent seemed to smile as he said the word. It was as if it was taunting Sexton. He studied Trent more closely and wondered if he or Sexton had fought during the War. They were both of an age to have done their bit. He also glanced towards Sexton who was glaring at Trent with undisguised loathing. There could, of course, have been any number of things to account for this, but Kit guessed what the chief reason was. He was sitting beside her, and he could not help but notice how both men glanced towards Carol as they spoke.

When he had first met Carol's husband, Teddy, he had formed an instant dislike of the man. They had met at Kit's club in London, Sheldon's. It was there that Kit was able to hear about his activities when he came to London. It was clear that marriage to Carol in no way limited his pursuit of other women. His affairs were discussed openly by him among his 'gang'. The lunch had planted a seed in Kit's mind that, perhaps, Teddy had not been the only one to stray.

As he was considering all this, he became conscious that Hook's eyes were on him. They exchanged glances. The detective's smile was dangerously benign. It was almost as if he was inviting Kit to ask questions. In fact, there was no 'almost' about it. This is why they were all together at the table.

After the soup, Carol excused herself. It was as if she sensed that the group wanted to discuss the events of the previous night. Tamsin accompanied her out of the dining room, but Mary stayed, a little to the dismay of Hook. He'd learn, thought Kit.

The main course was a ploughman's pie served with vegetables. With the lunch now served and Carol away from the rest of the group, Kit decided it was time to begin his and Mary's involvement.

'I gather you gentlemen were unfortunate enough to discover poor Teddy,' said Kit, before eating a mouthful of the ploughman's pie. It was delicious. He nodded to Gerry in approval. 'What brought you there?'

Sexton's face reddened in anger, and he glared at Trent,

'I have no idea,' he said through compressed lips.

'Nor I,' admitted Trent. 'I received a call from Teddy around four in the afternoon. He asked me to come over to discuss some horses he was looking to invest in.'

'You spoke to him?' interjected Hook. Kit glanced towards his friend. So they were to team up. Kit would introduce the topic while the detective dug a little deeper into the answer.

'No, my man Julian did. I was out at the time. He asked Julian that I come to meet him at his cottage at six on the dot. He said that he knew some people who wanted to meet me. Said they wanted to be involved in a partnership.'

'Did Teddy often introduce you to potential members of partnerships?' asked Kit. He saw Hook nod his head in approval.

'Yes. He was well rewarded for this of course,' replied Trent.

'And you Mr Sexton?' asked Kit, once more eating a mouthful of the ploughman's to disguise any hint that he was interrogating the horse box business owner.

'I don't see what business it is of yours, if I may say,' said Sexton. Then realising how rude that may have sounded in company, relented. 'There was a message for me to come over at six. On the dot.'

'You spoke with him?' asked Hook.

'No,' said Sexton. He looked extraordinarily uncomfortable. The problem with bluff individuals is that they lack any ability to dissemble or disguise their feelings. Sexton was one such individual.

Hook nodded; his eyes fixed on Kit.

'You often did business together?' asked Kit.

'No,' came the curt reply. Kit decided it was time to move off this territory and onto something new.

'I imagine, Gerry, you will have had some interest in Northern Glory.'

'I'll say,' replied Gerry and then proceeded not to say anything.

'Really? asked Mary, aware that Kit needed blood extracted from a nearby stone.

'Several people have approached me,' announced Gerry, barely looking up from his plate. He was not a man who

66

enjoyed talking at the best of times and especially when there was food in front of him. In this regard, he resembled no less than at least ninety percent of other males on the planet who have barely evolved from being hunters.

'I say old bean,' said Trent, adopting a chummier tone, 'don't do anything without letting me know. I'm sure I can find you the very best deal.'

'Not selling,' said Gerry, while finishing off a piece of carrot thereby proving that men really can multi-task. 'This is my one chance of owning and training a Derby winner. Damned if I'm passing that up.' Gerry looked up as he said this. There was a hard glint in his eye.

'What if it doesn't win?'

The question from Hook was like a stone shattering paned glass in monastery. Gerry looked up sharply from his empty plate.

'What do you mean?' snapped Gerry.

'I mean,' said Hook placidly, 'That if Northern Glory fails to win the Derby, will its value at stud not fall dramatically? That being so, I would have thought that now would be the best time.'

'To do what?' asked Gerry obtusely.

'To clear the chips from the table,' suggested Hook.

'And when did you become an expert in bloodstock?' asked Gerry. He clearly was unhappy at the hint of anything negative in the dream that he was living.

Hook held his palms up facing outwards. 'I'm sorry to rain on your victory parade. I was just curious. Tell me, were you in with Teddy yesterday?'

67

Kit was surprised at this, but then remembered that Mary had seen the car return along the driveway just before they had their pre-dinner drinks.

'What makes you ask that?'

Hook shrugged. Then he said, 'It's for my report to the coroner. We must fill in Teddy's movements up until the suicide. Just a formality, really.'

To Kit's ears, and knowing his friend, it was anything but.

'I was with Kit and Mary all afternoon from when they arrived at two until they retired to ready themselves for drinks and dinner at just after five.'

'And after that?' asked Hook.

'Nothing. I stayed at the house until we met up again and then you arrived with that horrible news.'

'I see,' said Hook. He nodded slowly and glanced towards Kit and Mary.

Kit grinned at the detective. He said, 'Do you want to know Mary and my whereabouts yesterday?'

Hook just smiled at this and shook his head. Yet something was seriously awry. Gerry had been out in the car. Or perhaps it was Tamsin. Or Carol. Someone from the house had been out between five and six. Kit felt Mary take hold of his hand and give it a squeeze.

The lunch drew to a close with conversation moving away from the murder. The more Sexton's countenance stayed unhealthily beetroot, the more Trent appeared to relax and enjoy proceedings. Hook, meanwhile, rather like Trent, appeared in a more flippant mood. This was when he was at his most alert, in Kit's experience. He loved to play people off against one another and see what it threw up. It made Kit wonder what he had gained from the lunch.

Of course, the level of insight one draws from any situation is relative to what you knew beforehand. For Kit and Mary, the lunch had been illuminating. It was clear that Carol had two suitors who may or may not have known about the other's existence. It was also clear, despite Hook's protestations otherwise, that he did not entirely buy the idea of a suicide.

What did he know?

Kit was desperate for the lunch to finish now. When Sexton and Trent both declined coffee, Kit was delighted. Sexton left immediately to return to his shop in Newmarket while Trent announced his intention to return to his rooms in London. He kept rooms in both London and Newmarket, at the Rutland Arms, as they were his two principal locations for doing business. Hook waved him away with a friendly smile.

Gerry excused himself to see to Northern Glory and the other horses under his eye in his role as trainer. All were due to have their afternoon gallop. Kit and Mary both declined his offer to join them. Soon it was just Kit, Mary and Hook in the dining room.

'I don't suppose we can see where Mr Harrison met his end?' asked Mary, a picture of innocent, disinterested curiosity.

Perhaps a little ungallantly, Hook roared with laughter at this. In fact, it took him fully a few minutes to recover his composure at Mary's request.

8

Half an hour later, Kit and Mary were travelling in a police car heading towards the market town of Newmarket. It was Mary's first visit to the town. She was immensely curious to see a town which was near to the school Kit had attended from the age of fifteen until eighteen. Kit had promised they would call in, but that was for later. They had a case to help solve, whether Hook wanted them involved or not.

'You can make your own way home,' said Hook. His mood was, once more, grouchy bordering on petulant.

'You would have us hitch a lift home?' asked Kit, his attention on the countryside passing by his window.

'I imagine Mary will have no problem finding a willing driver. You'll be walking,' he said sourly.

'Even with my leg?' asked Kit, a false tone of victim infiltrating his voice. 'And me a war hero. Put his life on the...'

'All right, all right,' snapped Hook. 'You've made your point. Laboriously, if I may say.'

Mary was sitting in the passenger seat alongside Hook, while Kit was in the back of the police car. She was giggling away at the exchange between two men who clearly adored one another and, as can only happen where men are concerned, it found expression in the mutual hurling of abuse. When in the presence of such elevating examples of mature sensibility it is incumbent upon the more intellectually gifted class to rise above the immediate company and lead by example. Mary chose to join in.

'Kit tells me he solved all the cases you worked on together.'

'What?' chorused Kit and Hook. For just a moment they were united in common cause against the monstrous regiment of women, at least until the penny dropped a quarter second later that she was giving them a taste of their own medicine.

'She's dangerous, Kit. Have you considered divorce?' asked Hook in a voice tender with genuine concern.

'I was considering taking the decent way out with my old revolver.'

'On yourself, or Mary?'

'Interesting thought, tell me more, Hookie,' said Kit.

Mary wasn't listening anymore. She was enthralled by the sight of the race course stands in the distance. They were made from red brick and had been built relatively recently. It had been a long time since she had been to a horse race, probably before the War. They were driving through the outskirts of Newmarket.

'The poor little village,' said Hook, smiling at Mary. He was echoing Charles I view when he had first visited the area.

'The resort of Kings,' replied Kit.

'You have asked such of me that was never asked of a King,' responded Hook.

Mary racked her memory for where she had heard this quote before. Then it hit her.

'Charles I?'

'Yes, the English Civil War effectively began here when Charles would not back down,' confirmed Hook. His tone was a little sorrowful. Then a degree of flippancy returned. 'My roundhead brothers took on you nobles and, if I may say, gave you quite a thrashing.'

'I'm delighted you working folk won,' said Kit. 'You must come to my mansion sometime.'

Hook scowled saying, 'You'll be first against the wall when the glorious revolution occurs.' They turned off the Main Street near the Memorial Hall and drove away from the centre until they reached a townhouse. A policeman stood outside but there appeared to be no one taking much interest in him. 'Needless to say, Teddy and Carol Harrison lived in this cottage.'

Hook pulled into an alleyway that ran alongside the house which led to a yard at the back. They stepped out of the car. Hook pointed to the back door, 'Our two friends neglected to mention that Harrison asked them to come to the back door and let themselves in.'

'Rather odd,' said Kit.

Hook turned to Kit and gave him one of those strange grins. His eyes were shining as they usually did when he knew someone was in for a shock.

'I trust Mary that you will be all right,' asked Hook. A slight frown appeared on his face.

'I imagine Mr Harrison is in the mortuary,' pointed out Mary. 'Besides which, I had my fair share of shocking sights in France, not the least of which was my future husband.'

Hook nodded to the policeman who had wandered around from the front.

72

'We're just going to inspect the scene of the...,' Hook paused dramatically before adding, 'the shooting.' Once more, noted Kit, he had refrained from saying outright that it was suicide.

They followed him towards the back door which led to the kitchen. Hook stood to one side to let Mary and Kit come through. The kitchen was empty, but the blood stains pulsed around the stone walls and even remained on the high ceiling. Mary blanched at the sight then steeled herself from the foundations laid three years and one war ago. In front of her was an oak kitchen table, a blood-stained chair where Teddy had been shot. In front of the chair, pointed directly at the occupant of the seat, lodged in a wooden shoe rack, was a shotgun. But there was something else, too, that shocked Kit and Mary.

'Oh,' said Mary as the implication of what she had seen became clear to her.

'Indeed,' said Hook.

Hook removed his felt hat as he entered. A moment of respect for an unloved man. Kit felt oddly moved by the gesture and the deep fondness he had always felt for the detective welled up within him. Their eyes met. For a moment nothing was said because nothing needed to be. At that moment, Kit knew for certain that Hook was convinced a murder had taken place here.

It had never been Hook's style to ask for help when invective could be deployed instead. It was why Kit liked him so much. No confirmation was sought because none would be given. Rather, it was time to go to work. Time to find out what had really happened. There was only one place to start. Where they were now.

At the scene of the crime.

Kit began to prowl around the kitchen. His eyes were taking in everything. What was there that should or should not be there? Hook watched on in amusement as Kit's eyes darted around the kitchen.

Finally, his eyes fell on Mary who was kneeling by the door holding what they had both seen when they'd entered. In her hands was a fishing line that led from the door handle via a system of pulleys and weights to the trigger of the shotgun which remained where Teddy Harrison, or someone, had put it.

'So, Sexton and Trent were indirectly responsible for the death of Harrison?' said Kit, looking towards the detective.

'Rather ingenious don't you think?' replied Hook.

'Diabolical,' suggested Kit. 'Why would Teddy traumatise someone like that?'

'Why indeed,' said Hook, who was busy trying to light his pipe. His face had a cherubic quality: innocent, amused and guileless.

As the detective appeared in no mood to expand on his enigmatic response, Kit continued, 'So, Sexton and Trent appear at the appointed hour. Doubtless they were surprised to see one another. They know one another clearly. There's no love lost there as each suspects that the other is trying to win the affection of Carol. It's six o'clock and they are here to meet the husband of the woman they may love. They have been told to come to the back door and let themselves in. As they do so, their opening of the door sets off this devilish mechanism which pulls the trigger on the shotgun resulting in something I can't and won't describe. How am I doing?'

'Oh as astute as ever,' said Hook gleefully. 'You still have a knack, I can see.'

'Thank you, Hookie. Praise from you is praise disguised as an insult.'

'Oh, come now,' protested Hook although he did not seem too put out by the accusation.

'What am I missing, Hookie? Come on. You look like the cat that's nicked the cream.'

'May I have a try?' asked Mary who had watched the swordplay between the old adversaries.

Hook made a gesture to indicate that the floor was all hers. He was rather curious it must be said. This was the young woman who had captured the heart of his friend, enemy and everything in between, Kit Aston. The reason was not hard to see and already there had been positive signs that her good qualities were more than skin deep.

Mary stepped forward and stood, reluctantly, by the seat.

'Mr Harrison is sitting in the seat. He really has little to think about except the rather obvious gun that is pointed at his head. I imagine he is thinking about this a lot. He can hear the two men coming to the door. Perhaps they knock. Perhaps they come straight in. Either way it does not matter because the result is going to be the same. Now, if I were going to do this and I can assure my dear husband that I have neither the desire nor, frankly, the courage to do so, I would have found those minutes leading up to my demise rather intolerable, no matter what my mood was.'

Hook nodded in approval to Kit, before saying, 'And?'

'Well, if it were me, I think that I might have taken something to sleep through the ordeal, so to speak,' said Mary.

A smile split Hook's face and he clapped his hands.

'Bravo, my dear. Wonderful. She's good Kit. No question,' acclaimed Hook. The tone was an extraordinary combination of genuine praise leavened with just a hint of mockery. Not easy to carry off, but Hook had made this into an art form. It wasn't so much that you didn't know where you stood with the detective, it was quite the opposite. You knew where you stood exactly.

In the firing line.

Kit was now beside Mary and staring at the position of the seat at the head of the table and the placement of the gun. He said, 'The one risk in drugging yourself, of course, is that your head falls on the table and then you wake up some hours afterwards to find the shot missed. It rather defeats the object of this unholy exercise.'

Hook was grinning and nodding at the same time, clearly enjoying the floor show he was witnessing.

Kit turned to Hook with a frown. Then he said, 'He was drugged wasn't he?'

'Yes. There was a handkerchief on the table with chloroform and a syringe with traces of morphine. He certainly wasn't taking any chances. What does it all mean?'

'You found the drug in his blood?'

'Enough to knock out an elephant.'

Kit and Mary looked at one another and then they returned their attention to the placement of the gun. Mary crouched down behind the barrel, closed one eye as if she were aiming at Hook who was now standing behind the chair were Teddy Harrison's head departed from his body.

'Tempting isn't it darling,' said Kit, noting how Hook was in the firing line.

Hook scowled and quickly hopped out of the way.

'But why would he want to kill himself?' asked Mary.

'Why indeed?' repeated Hook, now safely out of Mary's firing line.

'Because Carol had left him?' asked Kit. His voice was soaked in scepticism.

Mary straightened herself and pointed out, 'Well, my dear, I'd like to think that if I were to leave you, life would be so unbearable you couldn't possibly consider carrying on.'

Hook chuckled at this. He said, 'It's a fair point Kit, dear boy. What do you have to say to that?' He was now thoroughly enjoying himself in the macabre location.

Kit narrowed his eyes and said, 'Don't feed him lines, darling. 'You don't know what he's like. Has Carol been to the police station?'

'Oh yes, while you were out hacking around the country. It was a short trip.'

'Gruesome,' said Mary.

'Not really. She wasn't up to seeing his body and she claimed it had been so long since they had been intimate that the rest was pointless. She identified his clothes, though.'

Kit was not surprised that this had proved too much for Carol. It would be a lot to ask of anyone. His mind moved on to why he'd killed himself. 'There was no suicide note so we don't know exactly why he committed suicide. How was business? Were there any money troubles?'

Kit and Mary turned to Hook who nodded, 'Yes, there were troubles I gather. He had borrowed a lot of money to finance the purchase of some racehorses after the War ended. Business has not boomed in quite the way he'd hoped.'

'He borrowed money? I wonder if that's where Trent becomes involved. Perhaps this is how he and Carol met.'

Hook puffed contentedly on his pipe. He had noticed Trent's comment about Teddy investing in horses.

'Why wouldn't Carol lend him money? She must be loaded,' asked Mary.

'Not necessarily,' answered Kit. 'The family has a lot tied up in the land, their horses and their business. Or perhaps she didn't believe him to be a sound investment. Or perhaps she no longer trusted him.'

'Why do you say that?' asked Hook, looking sharply in Kit's direction.

'I met Teddy a few times at Sheldon's in London. He was not a man to let a little thing like marriage get in the way of him enjoying the company of women.'

'Nice for some,' said Hook. 'Two can play at that game, of course.'

Hook emptied his pipe out the back door and then smiled at Kit and Mary.

'Well, I must run now. Can you make your own way back to Tudor Stables? I can't spend all my time with the minor nobility, you know. I have cases to solve.'

'Busy?' asked Kit, genuinely curious.

'Oh you know. The usual. A couple of burglaries. Domestic violence, coincidentally. A possible missing person. A policeman's lot is not a happy one.' Then he added, 'My superiors are not keen on my wasting time on obvious suicides.'

'All the more reason why you should welcome the presence of the minor nobility, acting in an amateur detective capacity to provide the support you so badly need at this difficult time.'

'You're all heart,' said Hook, dolefully, thrusting his felt hat on his head and exiting the kitchen.

Kit and Mary watched him head to the car and, moments later, he was gone. Mary was quite surprised by the suddenness of his departure. She turned to Kit and frowned.

'I thought he didn't want us involved yet he leaves us here to our own devices at the scene of a possible crime.'

Kit grinned, 'So like Hookie. That speech at the end was his reluctant admission that he does want us involved.'

'It would be easier if he just came out with it and asked us.'

'Where's the fun in that?' asked Kit putting his arms around Mary's waist. The embrace, sadly, was not carried to the next stage as a noise at the door told them they were not alone. It was the policeman who had been standing guard outside.

'The Chief Inspector just asked me to ask you when you wanted to return. I have a car.'

Kit looked at Mary and then turned to the young policeman.

'Could we have twenty minutes to look around?'

9

'Anywhere you would like to begin?' asked Mary as they surveyed the kitchen.

'Not really sure to be honest. Maybe we should go to the bedroom first. Hookie mentioned Carol had identified the clothes so let's start there.'

They left the kitchen which took them into a hallway with a floor tiled in the manner of a chess board minus the pieces. Kit moved on ahead of Mary. She smiled and said, 'Rook to G6.'

Kit turned around as he reached the stairs, 'You are my Queen, so does that make me Lancelot?'

'Always, darling,' said Mary, pretending to be serious.

They climbed the stairs which led them onto a landing with what looked like four bedrooms and a bathroom. There were paintings on the walls. All twentieth century work and British. There was one piece by Roger Fry and a Vanessa Bell painting that was not to Kit's taste, but Mary rather liked it and a Laura Knight that they both admired. 'They seem to be acquiring a lot of work from the Bloomsbury set,' she observed.

'I imagine Carol would have known a few of them. Some of her former beaus were in London.'

The first three bedrooms revealed the beds made and the curtains drawn. One of them was very large, but it did not look as if it had been slept in for weeks. The last bedroom was small, but the bed looked as if it had been made up hastily. This seemed strange to the couple.

'I wonder why he would sleep here rather than in the main bedroom?' asked Mary.

'Perhaps he was waiting for Carol to return. He couldn't bear to be reminded of her absence,' said Kit. His voice was dripping in scepticism.

'Or she'd banned him from the marital bed,' replied Mary. 'Perhaps this is what she meant when she said they were no longer intimate.'

Kit opened the wardrobe and found men's clothes on hangers. Mary, meanwhile, went through the drawers. They, too, contained assorted men's socks and underwear as well as jumpers or pullovers.

'It looks as if the arrangement was quite permanent,' said Mary looking up at Kit.

They left the small bedroom and went to the largest of the rooms which they took to be the master bedroom. There were no clothes belonging to Teddy in this room. It was as if Carol had excised his presence already from her life. Mary said as much.

'Yes,' agreed Kit. 'I wonder how long they had been living together, apart?'

'If he loved her then it might explain his dejected mood,' pointed out Mary. 'Or guilt at having hurt her so. A sort of final straw for Carol and he knew this himself.'

'Doesn't seem like Teddy. I don't think he loved anyone or anything except maybe his next conquest. He really was a bounder, darling.'

They went through the motions of checking the other bedrooms but saw nothing out of place there. There were three rooms downstairs, all relatively spacious, traditionally decorated with equestrian scenes reminiscent of what were on the walls of the Tudor's.

'Look at this,' said Mary. She was pointing to a couple of small paintings in the drawing room.

Kit went over to look. The two paintings were hideous portraits of a couple of horses from the nineteenth century. A five-year-old with a crayon and fortified by a tot or two of gin would have made a better fist of them than this so-called artist. This was not what was interesting Mary. There was a discolouration on the wallpaper, around the outer rim of the frames, that suggested larger paintings had once been housed in the places of the two that currently occupied the position.

A quick check on the other paintings confirmed none of them had been moved from this position in quite some time.

'I wonder what was hanging here previously?' mused Kit out loud. There was no answer to be had at that moment, so they filed away the question for later. Returning to the kitchen they met the police constable who offered to bring them back to the house.

It was just before four in the afternoon when a police car pulled into the estate. They joined Gerry for a spot of tea in the drawing room before taking him up on his suggestion to come down and watch Northern Glory being put through his paces once more on the gallops.

As they walked down to the stables to watch him being saddled up, Kit asked, 'I know this is all in the future, Gerry, but if things go well and he wins a few big races, would you go to stud at the end of the season or continue as a four-year-old?'

'It would be a nice choice to have,' laughed Gerry. His face softened as he said this. Too often it had been Kit and Mary's feeling that he was tense; he seemed to be carrying a great burden. This burden went beyond mere worry for his sister or, indeed, a reclusive brother. Gerry did not seem the sort to admit to never mind share, any personal torment.

In the distance they could see Northern Glory galloping at full speed. He seemed to be flying such was his speed in comparison to the other colts. Struggling to keep up was his chum, Leonardo's Pride. Where one seemed to eat up the ground without obvious effort, the other's head was moving from side to side, straining to avoid being left behind.

'He's a beauty,' said Mary as the two horses slowed down.

'Knows it too,' laughed Gerry.

'Poor Leonardo,' said Kit as they reached the fence separating the gallop from the yard in front of the stables. Leonardo was bathed in sweat and was panting loudly.

'He doesn't like Glory to get the upper hand, but it takes it out of him,' replied Gerry, fishing in his pocket for carrots to reward the stalwart companion of the Derby hopeful.

'How will you manage him when he does go to stud?' asked Kit. 'Your operation is set up for training horses rather than breeding.'

Gerry looked at Kit and smiled wryly.

'We've been thinking about this too. With a horse like Glory, we could open up a whole new business for ourselves. Stud farms depend on having top-class stallions. Partnerships will pay big money for the very best. We'll see.' Gerry pointed to an empty field behind the stables. 'We could expand the yard over there. Add some stables for the breeding mares and their foals. Behind that we could have the nurseries. As I said, it's a nice problem to have. Tamsin wants to keep him, and I agree. Carol wasn't so sure, but she's never been interested in the business side of things.'

Kit nodded, 'Yes, I can see how well that could go. Is the story true about how he came to be?'

Gerry smiled wistfully, 'Luck, Kit. I buy yearlings normally, if by two-years-old they have potential, I sell them on. We had a mare here, Julia's Gift, that had never really been given a chance on the flat. She was quick and could stay a bit too. Chris has been at me for a year or two now to try our hand at breeding. He was the one who suggested we match her up. Joe Barnett who lives on the other side of Newmarket had a horse I'd always liked, Boner's Delight. Quick but a bit temperamental. Never won a race or even placed, but every time I saw him he'd had to make up so much ground on the leaders that the race was as good as over. Thing is, he usually did catch them up. I made an offer, and he nearly ripped my arm off. Anyway, we weren't intending matching him up with Julia's Gift, but he escaped one night and took matters into his own hooves so to speak.'

'That was the horse I saw this morning,' exclaimed Mary. 'She's Northern Glory's mother?'

Gerry could not hide his delight.

84

'She is. I thought that would please you. Lovely animal. Great temperament. She loves Tamsin. Feeling's mutual.'

'I feel honoured. Has Boner's Delight covered her again?' asked Kit.

'He has. Northern Wonder is going to make his debut at a juvenile race in May. We'll see how he goes before we make any decisions.'

'Ascot?' asked Mary.

'Let's not talk of such things,' replied Gerry, but the excitement in his eyes suggested he'd be thinking of little else over the next few months. He pointed in the direction of a chestnut in the far distance a stable lad was leading around the track at the far end of the gallops. 'That's him over there. He's a vain one like his brother. Two peas they are.'

They watched the slender horse for a few minutes then the worry seemed to reappear on Gerry's face. He looked at his guests and asked, 'Did Hookie take you to the cottage?' Kit nodded. 'What do you think about all this? It was suicide wasn't it?'

'Have you some doubts?' asked Kit non-commitally.

'None,' said Gerry, firmly. 'The man was a pest in life and nothing's changed now that he's dead.'

'Who are those two chaps, Sexton and Trent?' asked Kit.

Gerry made a dismissive sound and shook his head.

'Friends of Carol. I stopped asking fifteen years ago, Kit. Too beautiful for her own good.'

He might have added for the family too, for his meaning lay there plainly visible like a blood stain in the fabric of what he'd said. Kit decided not to press him any further on the nature of the friendship. Instead, they watched as Northern Wonder was led round the perimeter of the field. Soon he was heading towards them. He was almost bouncing on the grass, desperate to be set loose so that he could gallop away.

'He's the image of his brother,' observed Mary.

The horse whinnied and shook its head seemingly in disagreement. This brought gleeful laughter from the onlookers. 'As I was saying,' added Mary which brought another chuckle from Gerry.

They stayed at the gallops for another twenty minutes before returning to the house to get ready for drinks. They met Tamsin at the terrace. She looked decidedly unhappy.

'We'll have at least one extra guest for dinner.'

'Which one?' asked Gerry.

'Trent. Sexton left in a bit of a huff earlier as Carol wouldn't talk to him, but Trent asked if he could join us. A meeting he had scheduled in London has been cancelled now.'

'Is he staying over?' asked Gerry.

'Do you need me to stand guard outside Carol's room?' asked Kit.

'Outside Trent's room, more like,' suggested Tamsin dryly.

'You think Trent has his nose in front?' asked Kit, with a wicked grin.'

Tamsin thought for a moment before replying, 'Not sure from Carol, to be honest. She's been rather quiet about the runners and riders. I'd say Trent is more of a sprinter.'

'And Sexton more of a stayer?' said Kit, completing the sentence.

'Exactly. Still, if they want to win the Carol handicap then they need to be good over all grounds and be prepared to take a few jumps. Sexton looked off the pace earlier. Carol wanted nothing to do with him.'

'Steady on Tamsin,' said Gerry, trying to show some loyalty to his sister. This endeavour was somewhat undermined by the fact that he was trying to stifle a smile. 'I hope you're not going to be in this mood over dinner.'

'I hope you are,' grinned Mary.

They went their separate ways at this point to get ready for drinks then dinner. As they climbed the stairs, Kit stopped at a small painting of a child who was around ten years old.

'That's Chris,' said Kit, pointing to a boy holding a toy train. Beside him was an older boy, looking more serious.

'And this is Gerry?' asked Mary.

'Yes. They look alike but yet they're quite different.'

'How well did you know Chris?' asked Mary as they continued up the stairs to the room.

'Oh quite well, I suppose. Gerry was a few years ahead of me at school while Chris was a year behind me. He was good at sport. Perhaps not so academic. Then again, I don't think Gerry was very academic either. Horses were their lives. It was not as if they were ever going to be in any other business.'

'I suppose you didn't have to be academic either given your future inheritance, yet it never stopped you,' pointed Mary. Kit had gone to Cambridge and read mathematics and modern languages.

Kit shrugged and looked rather sheepish and then said, 'You can't hide genius I suppose.'

10

The presence of Trent at dinner at least ensured Carol's presence for the duration of the evening. All mention of Teddy's death was ignored, but the atmosphere was muted. Tamsin, sadly for Mary, was inclined to rein in her waspish wit while Gerry was a picture of a man attempting to hide the fact that he was angry at Trent's company.

If Trent was aware of this and, in Kit's estimation he could hardly be unconscious of it, then he remained outwardly oblivious. Carol was all too conscious of Gerry's manner and occasionally shot him dark looks. Mary, true to form, appeared to enjoy the tension. She sat near Tamsin and spoke a lot with her. This was a little to Kit's frustration as he was sitting near Gerry and Trent. It would have been much more fun to be at the other end of the table.

Oddly, the mood improved slightly after the ladies left the men alone for their brandy and cigars. Kit declined the cigar but was happy to help Gerry and Trent finish off a rather good Napoleon Brandy.

'How is Chris?' asked Trent, as he lit his cigar and did likewise for Gerry.

'The usual,' said Gerry, adding little to this deep insight.

'Carol was with him quite a lot today after lunch,' observed Trent.

'They spend a lot of time together,' replied Gerry. His manner was a little less curt than earlier. 'I'm not much company as you know. Carol chats away with him. You know what she's like.'

Perhaps for the first time this evening, his comment 'you know what she's like' was devoid of any meaning beyond an opinion of his sister's sociability. Trent nodded; this was what Carol was like. Gerry was not social, and Chris was a different person from the one who had gone to War. They all were, but particularly Chris and who could blame him?

Gerry had never been a gifted conversationalist; he spoke as he saw. Words, whimsy and wit were Carol's domain, and she was the Queen of all she surveyed. Only Tamsin was a match for her in this regard, but Carol also had a beauty that made men fall for her even before she made them laugh, or cry, or howl at the moon. While she loved horses, she loved people more. And she loved men in particular. It had always been this way, at least until marriage to Teddy had brought that aspect of her life to a temporary end. As much as Gerry disliked Teddy, he was a match for Carol in this regard. Perhaps that had been their undoing. There could be only one monarch in that household.

'Do you think Chris will ever…?' the question from Trent remained unfinished. How could one put words to such despair? Once more, Kit was surprised by the tone of the banker. No longer was he so supercilious as he had been at lunch. Instead, he sounded more sympathetic a character. Someone who knew how Chris must be feeling. Someone who had fought in Flanders.

Gerry shook his head sadly.

'No. He's happy enough I suppose. He has Carol and Tamsin to talk to. He doesn't want anyone to see him. Ever. He still has the nightmares.'

'I suppose we all do,' said Trent.

Silence fell on the group after this remark from Trent. It was both true and untrue for Kit. He had suffered nightmares for nearly two years following the night he'd almost died. Since meeting Mary that had changed.

'You were there, too?' asked Kit after a minute or two. He was speaking to Trent.

Trent nodded. For a few moments he could not speak and then, as if impelled by the pleas of a hundred men that he'd killed he said, 'Yes. I missed the start and then when my brother bought it I went. I found that I had a talent they could use. Who knew that shooting grouse would be perfect training for war. Oh yes, I paid them back for Simon's death all right. Every bloody one of them I killed I imagined it was him that killed my brother.'

'And now?'

The sound of the clock in the room seemed to grow louder. Its echo reverberated like the crack of rifle on a misty morning in France.

'I must have done for a hundred of them or so. I still see their faces. Every last one of them,' snarled Trent. 'I hated them. I just wanted to obliterate them. I still hate them.' Tears stung his eyes as he said this. Then he tried to smile but gave it up as a bad job, 'Sorry. I don't normally talk about this.'

Kit understood; even Mary avoided the topic. Both had seen so much albeit in different ways. Kit had been at the front. Mary in a hospital which dealt with the appalling injuries caused by the industrial level of slaughter and maiming.

Keen to change the subject, Trent fixed his eyes on Gerry and said, 'So what price for Northern Glory? I could have a group of individuals on your doorstep like that.' He snapped his finger to emphasise his point.

Gerry smiled and pointed to an antique musket hanging from the wall. It dated back to the English civil war.

'So they wouldn't be welcome,' concluded Trent, but he seemed amused all the same.

Kit was happy to observe Trent and Gerry. The frostiness of earlier had thawed considerably. This applied as much to himself as their host. There was more to Trent than he'd first thought. In fact, it was a salutary reminder that first impressions were very often a poor guide to understanding a person. Nothing was ever as it appeared. Hookie had taught him that fifteen years ago.

Nothing was ever as it appeared.

11

Mary joined Tamsin and Carol in the drawing room. She declined the offer of a drink. The two women helped themselves to a modest glass of sherry each. For a few moments there was silence. They could hear the murmur of voices in the dining room as the men chatted.

'Seems they feel able to talk now that we're gone,' observed Tamsin. She did not seem particularly put out by this. It was just a fact of life. Women found it easier to speak with women, men with men.

Carol, meanwhile, regarded Mary for a few moments. Mary smiled back at her.

'I feel as if I might be the subject of a great insight,' said Mary.

'You're very lucky,' said Carol, lighting a cigarette. ' I remember when Kit used to come here with Olly, Chubby and Spunky. We had wonderful dances. The girls were mad about Kit. Tall, fair-haired, blue-eyed. Him and Olly were very popular.'

'What was Olly like?' asked Mary.

Carol coloured a little, 'Well, he was, how shall I say, good-looking and arrogant in equal measure. I had a bit of a crush on him, but he was a year or two younger than me. I think if I had let it run on he would have had had had his way and then been on his way if you know what I mean. Did you ever meet Olly, Tamsin?'

'No, I had a few friends that did,' said Tamsin, but tactfully avoided adding anything else to this although it was all too plain what she was saying.

Carol seemed not to be listening, though. She continued on rather dreamily, 'I don't know why I gave up on Olly. He couldn't have been much worse than Teddy turned out to be. I'm such a fool where men are concerned. You'd think I would've learnt my lesson.'

'May I ask what is happening with you and your two suitors?' asked Tamsin.

Carol laughed, rather mirthlessly to Mary's ears. She was a little drunk now. There was a bitterness in her voice that translated to a rather hard look on her beautifully refined face. She said, 'I suppose they think that soon I will be needing someone to take care of me.'

Carol paused for a moment to let the tears fall and then she added as an afterthought, 'And they'd be right. I'm thirty-three now. I'm a widow a few years earlier than I thought I would be. I have no children. Even if I wanted to, there's not much prospect of me being a mother. Good old Carol. Life and soul of the party Carol. I can see what Jason and Roger want. The question is not will they get it, I think we all know the answer to that, but whether they will want to stick around afterwards. I think I know the answer to that, too.'

Tamsin leaned over to Carol and gently removed the sherry glass from her hand. She put her arm around her shoulders. Nothing was said. Sometimes it is better that way.

While men are already pondering the solution to any problem, practical or emotional, Tamsin and Mary intuitively understood that this situation would not be resolved by pity or action, never mind words.

'I think I shall become an old maid, a mad spinster aunt for the boys. Even Chris doesn't seem to want to talk much with me. I just talk at him. He might even be listening. Who knows? He never takes that mask off now, even with me.'

'Yes, he has been keeping himself to himself the last few days,' agreed Tamsin.

'That may be my fault,' admitted Mary. She then told them about her encounter in the early hours of the morning with Chris.

Carol and Tamsin were both surprised and amused.

'He never mentioned it to me,' said Tamsin. 'Mind you, I only saw him briefly this morning. He went out for his ride. Poor Chris. He's so self-conscious about his face and voice.'

'His voice?' asked Mary. Her exposure to the voice had been limited to a scream and a "don't look".

'It's a little muffled,' said Carol. 'His injuries were horrific. I can barely describe them, but his lips were welded a little together so it's difficult for him to speak clearly. I suppose you wouldn't notice it so much if you hadn't known him before.'

'How awful,' said Mary. Images of some of the horrific injuries she had encountered when she was nursing rose in front of her.

'You were awfully brave,' said Tamsin to Mary as if reading her mind. 'What on earth possessed you to run away like that to France?' She was referring to the time when Mary had famously left home and volunteered under an assumed name to join the Voluntary Aid Detachment of civilian nurses who provided nursing care for the army during the War.

'I suppose it does seem rather ridiculous now, but I'm glad that I went. I wouldn't have met Kit otherwise,' replied Mary.

Of course, such a statement was always going to be interrogated and the next twenty minutes saw Mary take centre stage to describe how she met Kit. This was delivered in a level of detail that would have been painful for the average chap to listen to, but barely covered the essentials for her two companions.

It was on this romantic note that the ladies decided to end their evening. Tamsin helped Carol to bed while Mary popped her head in through the door of the dining room to tell Kit that she was retiring. She sensed that the atmosphere in the room had become less tense, but that was just a feeling. Perhaps Trent had revealed a less arrogant side to himself when the ladies had left. Or perhaps the brandy had helped Gerry thaw a little.

Around three in the morning Mary awoke. She knew that this would happen. Kit was beside her in the bed sleeping silently. Rolling away from him, she wheeled her feet from the bed and onto the floor. She slipped her feet into her bedroom slippers and rose from the bed. She put on her dressing gown and quietly left the bedroom to go downstairs to the kitchen.

The house was dark and every creak of her footsteps on the stairs ricocheted like a machine gun fire. She grimaced with each step, but finally made it to the bottom of the stairs without setting off alarms and wreaking havoc with the dogs.

The kitchen was her destination. This time it was dark and deserted. She poured herself some milk, sat at the table in the darkness and waited. Twenty minutes later she heard a noise. Someone or something was walking along the corridor. Now Mary Aston was no one's timid little girl, jumping at the merest hint of a malevolent shadow or psychotic mouse but, just at that moment, she was seriously questioning the wisdom of her actions in an internal language that would have raised a few impressed eyebrows at a rodeo convention in Mesa, Arizona. Her rational mind discounted the possibility of a poltergeist, but this memorandum had not quite reached her heart which was thrashing away like a thirty-handicapper on the practice ground.

A masked figure appeared in the doorway.

Mary stifled a desire to scream.

'Hello,' she said nervously.

The man stopped and looked around him. It was still dark, but he could see Mary in her white silk dressing gown sitting at the kitchen table.

'I wanted to say sorry for last night. I didn't mean to give you a fright.'

The breathing behind the mask was heavy and, as yet, the man seemed unwilling to say anything. They stared at one another for a few moments which probably were no more than a couple of seconds but at that time of night it felt like hours.

'Look,' said Mary, finding her courage and a stronger voice than she had hitherto managed, 'I won't bother you anymore, but if you feel like having a chat sometime or joining Kit and I on a ride tomorrow morning then we would love to give you some company.'

Mary stood up and glided past the man in the dark mask. It was only as she was halfway down the corridor that he said, 'I'm sorry Mary.' His voice sounded as if it was speaking through layers of cloth, yet there was a hole in the mask for his mouth.

Mary turned to him. She was like a spectre to him standing in the blue light of the window.

'I mean it. We'll be riding tomorrow. Perhaps we can see you on that hill with the wonderful view.' Then Mary turned and walked down the corridor. The tension she was feeling slowly evaporated and she began to breathe more easily again.

When she returned to the bedroom she quietly crept over to her side of the bed, removed her dressing gown and lay down. A whispered voice said to her, 'Did you see Chris?'

Mary smiled at her husband and kissed him gently on the cheek.

'Sorry for waking you, darling. Yes, I saw him. I apologised for last night. I told him we'd be riding again around the same area if he would like to join us.'

She rolled over to Kit and folded herself in his arms. Within seconds she was fast asleep.

Much to everybody's surprise, not the least her own, Carol joined Kit, Mary and Tamsin for a ride. Despite her flapper tendencies and predilection for the night, she was an expert rider, no less able than either Tamsin or Mary. Trent declined to join them for a ride citing the fact that he had work to do. Kit was disappointed by this as he had hoped to get to know the banker better and, unexpectedly, wanted to.

It was a cold, damp morning and the temptation to stay in bed was overwhelming had they all not agreed on the previous evening to take the horses out. To climb down now would have caused a loss of face that would have provided the basis of gentle abuse for the rest of the weekend. Gerry, wisely, decided to stay and manage the stable. They had a few owners coming that morning to see how their investment in two-year-old horseflesh was progressing.

After breakfast, Mary read the national newspapers while Kit thumbed through the local *Newmarket Journal* that had just arrived. This was the local weekly newspaper. It was one year shy of its fiftieth anniversary, as it reminded its readers. Often. The Journal was a bedrock of grassroots journalism with hard-hitting stories on pets, school sports days and, when the stars aligned, a notable death, missing persons, or, better still, a suspicious death. The front page led with Teddy's suicide.

They set off soon after ten, cantering through the paddock into the open countryside. Tamsin suggested riding in the direction of Newmarket race track as Mary had never been there.

After an hour's riding they caught sight of Chris in the distance riding, as ever, alone. There was little point in calling to him as he was too far away. Instead, they stopped at the brow of a hill and waved. If he saw them, he gave no sign.

'He definitely saw us,' said Carol.

'Are you sure?' asked Tamsin.

Kit agreed with Carol. He had seen them, but deliberately kept his back turned to them and rode in the direction of a wooded area. This was dismissal in any language.

'He's definitely been a bit distant of late,' observed Tamsin once more. She was troubled by this as far as Mary could see. She turned to Mary and smiled, 'I'm sorry Mary. It must appear rude. It really isn't.'

Mary decided not to mention her second nocturnal excursion that morning. It would seem like she was hounding the poor man; in some senses, she probably was. Yet his reluctance to meet them was disappointing. He was among friends. Chris and Kit had known one another since school. Kit had suffered horribly during the War; his scars were just as deep and would last a lifetime also. That Chris did not want to be with them was not so much rude as a little strange.

Mary glanced towards Kit who watched as Chris disappeared into the wooded area. There was concern on his face. Nothing more was said about Chris, and they headed directly towards their destination, the race course.

'Are we allowed on the track?' asked Mary.

'Of course,' said Tamsin. 'How else are we going to have a race? There are a number of tracks. There is the Rowley Mile where they hold the Guineas. Then there is the main racecourse and then there is the one we are on.'

'Which is?' asked Mary.

'The Plate course. Every August the town holds a race which is three miles round the outside of the main course. It's an amateur race. First prize is a couple of pounds of sausages. You raced in it, didn't you Kit?''

Kit grinned at this. He said, 'Yes. A long time ago.'

'And?' asked Mary.

Kit shook his head and replied, 'A story for another time. What is the handicapping system for our race, may I ask?'

'You're a man,' replied Tamsin. 'I'm afraid there's no amount of help will ever solve that problem.'

Mary laughed disloyally which made Kit smile even more. He straightened up in the saddle, 'Well, as the sole representative of the weaker sex, I look forward to putting you three ladies in your proper place.'

'The kitchen?' asked Mary.

'Last to finish should wash up tonight and give the staff a night off,' suggested Carol. Her eyes were shining with anticipation. It seemed to Kit that this was the most invigorated she'd seemed since their arrival. The gauntlet thrown; the others accepted it on a nod.

'Where to?' asked Mary.

Tamsin surveyed where they were. At that moment they had arrived on the back straight. Half a mile across from

100

them were the stands. Then she said, 'I suppose it may not be appreciated if we race around to there, but we could certainly hack along here as there's no one around. What do you think, Carol?'

Carol pointed to a tree about four hundred yards away. The others all fixed their eyes on the tree.

'Yes, I dare say that will do,' agreed Tamsin. 'Who wants to act as starter?'

'How about the member of the weaker sex,' suggested Mary, eyes twinkling.

'Very well,' said Kit. He swung his mount around to face the distant tree. The others followed suit. He leaned forward to see that everyone was in line. 'On your marks,' said Kit. As he said this, he gave his mount a gentle nudge. In a moment, Kit was off and running. The ladies, shocked by such un-dashing behaviour from someone who would grace the pages of any romantic novel worthy of the name, howled in protest. Their remonstrations were met with stony silence and the chase was on.

Kit's manoeuvre had gained him a twenty-yard start. This was probably never going to be enough given that his horse had as much interest in sprinting as he had in needlepoint.

The trick to racing a horse, as Kit had learned many years before, was to prey on a horse's natural sense of panic while keeping it under control. Ballygowan had long ago lost that sense of panic. Despite Kit's best efforts to keep his nose in front, the ladies shot past him as if he were driving a car in reverse. The whoops and insults that came his way, were lost as the distance between his mount and the ladies' horses widened.

Mary was, if anything, a better rider than Kit with a younger, faster mount. However, even she found it difficult to keep up with Tamsin and Carol. The two ladies went past her in a blur of chestnut legs and flashing smiles. Soon she was a couple of lengths behind with Kit trailing another ten behind her. At least that was something. Bragging rights against your spouse is never to be scoffed at.

Up ahead she could see the powerful hindquarters of the horses bunching and tensing, propelling the ladies forward at great speed towards the distant finish line. Over to the right, a quarter of a mile away were the new stands. It was a thrill to be riding over such hallowed turf and Mary was enjoying every second of it. The result, except where it concerned Kit, mattered not to her.

The race finished in what Carol claimed was a photo finish, but it seemed of the two ladies, Tamsin was the one who appeared the happiest. However, Carol did not appear to resent a defeat by a head. They congratulated Mary on her effort and then they turned to jeer the arrival of Kit who had long since ceased to try and race against the ladies.

'We'll find a nice pinny for you to wear in the kitchen,' said Carol.

'How about he wear a dress to dinner?' suggested Tamsin.

Mary was almost choking with laughter at the thought of this. Kit merely grinned and pointed out that it would be a little short. Carol responded to this with a wolf whistle.

'Time to head back, I think,' said Tamsin. 'We'll walk the horses a little and then ride that last mile.'

13

The race had put everyone in fine fettle. Tamsin was too modest to make much of her victory; Carol felt delighted to have run her sister-in-law so close and Mary was perhaps even more pleased to have defeated Kit despite the nefarious measures he had resorted to during the contest. Kit had never believed that victory was possible and was gleefully unmoved by the rebukes he faced from the three ladies who spent the rest of the trip home happily ganging up on him and discussing his character, or absence of it, in the severest of tones.

The nearer to the house they came the more discernible was Carol's change in mood. After leading the scolding of Kit initially, she became quieter until for the last ten minutes her comments were almost monosyllabic. This was understandable given all that she had been through so the others avoided trying to involve her too much in the conversation.

Both Gerry and Trent were busy when they returned to the house. Kit and Mary went up to their bedroom to freshen up. When they reached the room, Mary commented on the evident anxiety that Carol felt.

'It doesn't seem like grief to me, or am I being overly suspicious? She seems worried or angry or both.'

Kit did not fully agree. He said, 'I suppose grief hits us in different ways. I imagine her feelings are complicated by the most recent memory she had of him.'

In fact, Carol's most recent memory of her dead husband was him lying face up with a halo of blood around his head, but Kit was not to know that.

'I see what you mean. Perhaps she feels guilty about how it was between them before he died,' suggested Mary.

Carol was certainly feeling guilty. She could barely look at a candlestick without a sickening feeling that started out from somewhere near her feet.

'Yes, I think that's closer to the truth. She has no reason to feel guilty, don't you think?'

The answer to this would come in the future.

'Of course. He was a brute. What makes men do this?' asked Mary. She looked at her husband, standing framed against the window. He was tall, handsome, intelligent and funny; too unflawed to make the hero of a romantic novel which convention required the male to start off being beastly before the love of a good woman made him into exactly the sort of benevolent eunuch that she would never have looked at in the first place. Of all people, Kit was potentially the last person to understand what would motivate a man to mistreat a woman.

'I don't know,' said Kit truthfully. 'I'm sorry.'

'Sorry?' asked Mary. 'You've done nothing wrong.'

'On behalf of men. We're not all like Teddy,' said Kit before adding, 'Was.'

Mary walked over to him and put her arms around his neck. She was just in time to see the police car hurtling up the driveway of the estate. They stared out of the window at the uncommon sight. It pulled up at the front entrance.

Hook hopped out of the car from the passenger side and glared at the young police constable who had been driving. Neither Kit nor Mary could hear what he said but they could certainly read his lips as he said, 'Young idiot.' He straightened his felt hat before striding purposefully towards the house. Leaving the young policeman to skip along behind in his wake.

'Do you know, I have to hand it to Hookie. He has a real nose for when lunch is likely to be served.'

Kit and Mary left it a decent amount of time, around one and a half minutes, before racing downstairs to find out what had brought the Chief Inspector along at such a clip, aside from an overly enthusiastic and heavy-footed constable.

They reached the corridor to hear the sound of raised hushed voices. This did not augur well. No one was quite shouting, but nor was there cordiality in abundance. The atmosphere was quite English in respect of the frostiness that paradoxically raised the temperature of those in the hallway.

No one's pressure gauge was more likely to pop than Gerry. He was positively bristling with rage at Hook who, having raised his voice marginally to urge calm, was enjoying the by-product of his entreaty. The policeman was well aware of the fact that since life had first emerged from the original dark pond, crawled up onto the arid rocks to towel itself dry and enjoy the view poolside, no barked request for calm had ever effected sedative outcome.

Sure enough, Gerry exploded.

105

'I will not calm down Hookie,' shouted Gerry. His rage was somewhat undermined by the use of Hook's nickname. Hook smiled broadly and tilted his hat back to reveal his expansive forehead. He leaned against the wall, hands in his pockets, a sympathetic smile creasing his face. He glanced up at the arrival of Kit and Mary on the stairs. He briefly acknowledged them with a nod before once more fixing his eyes on Gerry.

'I will not get Chris,' fumed Gerry. 'What possible reason do you have for wanting to speak to him?'

Hook's answer was confined to a shrug. This was hardly guaranteed to pour oil on troubled waters.

'What's that supposed to mean Hookie?' asked Tamsin. She was in almost tears. 'What's going on?'

Hook appeared to relent in the face of the family's opposition. He straightened himself up to his full six feet and said, 'On the afternoon that Teddy left us, someone answering Chris's description was seen at the house. The car identified that night is the one currently parked in the driveway. Are you going to tell me that Chris did not take the car out?'

The Tudor family stared back at Hook in mute rebellion.

'Very well, have it your own way,' said Hook. He turned to Vincent and said, 'Vincent, would you be so good as to get Mr Tudor for me. I will see him in the drawing room.'

With that, Hook walked in the direction of the room keeping his eyes on the family all the while. Vincent glanced nervously at Gerry. The stable owner's features which were naturally scarlet, were now considerably redder than they had been a few minutes earlier. He nodded curtly to Vincent who then did likewise to a maid. The young girl, having no

106

one to nod to, scurried off in search of Chris accompanied by the young policeman.

'I'm jolly angry at this,' snarled Gerry and, to be fair, he certainly looked it.

His eyes became flintier, and he stalked forward after Hook. On his way past the stairs he said to Kit and Mary, 'I would appreciate it if you would join us.'

Kit wasn't altogether sure that their presence would be welcomed by most policemen, but Hook was not of that category. He was predictably unpredictable.

When they entered the room, Hook had made himself comfortable on the sofa. He looked up at the group entering the room and said, 'Ah, a family affair. Jolly good. I'm not sure Chris will appreciate the crowd, but on your own head be it. Now, I haven't had a chance to have lunch. I don't suppose someone could rustle up a sandwich for me?'

'No,' snapped Gerry, but Tamsin shook her head at her husband.

'I'll tell cook,' she said, exiting almost immediately.

Gerry sat in sullen silence, so Hook decided to turn his attention to Kit and Mary. Observing their attire he enquired conversationally, 'Have you been out for a ride this morning?'

Kit smiled and replied, 'Yes, it was rather nice.'

'Jolly good,' said Hook, glancing up at the grandfather clock. Then he looked at his watch before glancing back at the clock. 'Well, one of us wrong,' he observed, giving his watch a shake.

A couple of minutes later the door opened. All eyes turned to the door. It was Carol. She had not been in the hallway earlier. Her eyes darted from Hook to Gerry and back again.

107

'What is going on?'

'I've come to see Chris,' said Hook amiably. 'I don't suppose you passed him on your way here?'

'He was out for a ride earlier. He may not be back.'

'I understand that he is,' said Hook without explaining how he knew. Carol seemed about to snap back at Hook, but at the last moment stopped herself. They waited in silence for another minute then Hook said, 'Taking their time aren't they? Young Westcott needs to be more assertive. I shall have a word with him.'

Kit studied his old friend while they were waiting. Hook seemed utterly at ease despite the frosty atmosphere. A benign smile had settled on his features like a grandfather waiting to see his grandchildren. His eyes radiated a luminous charm that not even his cynicism could dim. It was clear that he did not accept, yet, that Teddy had committed suicide. There had to be a reason for this. What did Hook know that he was not telling anyone?

The sound of voices in the hallway disturbed the quiet of the room. Gerry glared at Hook once more and turned to leave the room followed by Carol. This left Kit, Mary and Hook alone in the room. Mary clutched her two hands together. Her breathing was shallower now. As if sensing this, Kit took hold of her hand.

'Do you want us to leave Hookie?' asked Kit.

'Let's see what Chris says,' replied Hook. 'Did you see anything of interest in the cottage?'

Mary told him about the picture that had been removed. The detective's face fell as he heard Mary speak.

'I must be losing it,' said Hook. 'Well done. I should have noticed that. I suppose we should speak to the cleaner and find out what was removed.'

'I'd check a few of the auctioneers in Cambridge or London while you're at it,' said Kit. Hook nodded without replying. 'Fences, too.' This brought a smile from the policeman.

For the next few minutes they waited in a companiable silence for the Tudor family to reappear. At one point they heard what sounded like a muffled argument. It did not last long.

Finally, the door swung open. Chris walked in. He was tall, slender and dressed in a tweed suit. The appearance of country squire contrasted sharply with the large black bandana which tied around his head. There were holes for the eyes, the nose and mouth. He stopped at the door and looked over at Kit then Mary. Finally, his eyes rested on the detective.

'You wanted to see me?'

'Good afternoon, Chris. It's been quite a while,' said Hook. 'Would you mind joining us for a moment?'

Chris paused for a few seconds then walked over to the detective, taking a seat opposite him, to the right of Kit and Mary. In the driveway outside the drawing room, a car started and then drove away. All eyes turned to the window for a moment. Then Hook turned his attention back to Chris.

'I'm sorry to ask you this of you, Chris, but would you mind removing your mask?'

Part II: Back Straight

14

Jason Trent had observed the arrival of the police from his table in the library. He stood up and walked over to the window making sure to stay back behind the curtain. This provided some cover from the policeman. It was now clear to him that Hook was still assembling facts on what should have been an open and shut case. Did Hook really believe that the inquest would find anything other than suicide? Was he the one driving this or did it come from coroner?

He returned to the table and lit a cigarette. It was time to consider his position more carefully. It was time to think about Carol. There was no question that she would be an enormous asset to him. Her breeding, never mind her beauty, would set him apart from all the other hopefuls knocking on the door of the bank's boardroom. He was so close now. He could almost smell the leather of the chairs in the boardroom, smell the varnish on the oak-panelled walls.

Over the last year he had come to believe that Carol would leave Teddy. Had it not been for the blasted war she would have married him. Now that she was free, uncertainty gripped him. The manner of Teddy's death was one thing, but the continued presence of Hook was quite another. It was only a matter of time before the newspapers began to ask questions on why it was taking so long for an inquest to be held and the death confirmed as suicide. News would filter down to London. What would the bank say if they knew he was involved in the matter?

A bank survived and thrived thanks to its reputation. Clients had to be able to trust a bank. After all, they were handing over large sums of money to be invested. However, faith was a fragile thing. Every bank employee, certainly ones with ambition for higher office, had to live lives of quiet integrity. They could involve themselves in nothing that would besmirch the reputation of the bank. To marry a divorced woman was one thing. To marry a woman that had lost her husband under circumstances deemed highly suspicious by the police was another.

Trent stared out of the window at the police car. It was a visible symbol of the risks he was taking. He shook his head and lit another cigarette. No, it could not go on like this. If Teddy's death was going to turn into a full-scale police investigation then he had to stay well away. He would be caught in the crossfire.

He rose from his seat and shuffled the papers he had been working on into a neat pile then stuffed them into his leather satchel. He headed to the door of the library and opened it. The coast was clear. He saw Gerry and then Carol leave the room. He stayed back a little to avoid being seen. Gerry headed towards the kitchen while Carol went to the stairs. Trent left the library to follow Carol. He bounded up the stairs and whispered, 'Carol.'

Carol turned around. Her face was pale and drawn. She was on the brink of tears.

'The police are here,' said Carol.

112

'Yes, I saw,' said Trent, taking her in his arms.

'Why are they doing this?' asked Carol. 'Jason, I'm so scared. I don't know that I can go on like this.'

Nor could Trent. He hugged Carol and stroked her hair while counting the seconds to when he would leave. And leave he would.

'Why are they doing this?,' she continued, not waiting for an answer. This was very Carol. 'What do they know?'

Trent was barely listening. This was very male. The sound of her voice was drowned out by the silent screams of his own. He had to go. Now. What could he do? At the very least he had to allow the storm to subside. Then he would have to broach the subject of his leaving. This would go down like a broccoli lunch at a children's birthday party. Women tended to take a rather jaundiced view of men who skipped town when the weather turned sour. Worse, it would allow that red-faced buffoon Sexton back in just when he'd managed to get his nose in front. Carol was crying quietly on his shoulder. He felt like joining her.

Then inspiration struck.

'Darling, you must lie down. Rest. They won't speak to you if you say that you're unwell. It's obviously all too much for you my darling.'

Lord knows what other inanities he came out with as he held her close. It was his experience that women generally, and Carol particularly, usually fell for this nonsense. He hoped so anyway. He slowly manoeuvred Carol up the final few steps onto the landing. Then he led her towards the bedroom. Thankfully, there was no one around although he could hear some noise on the stairs that led up to the small

113

apartment used by Chris. He had to get inside to the bedroom.

With a sigh of relief, he closed the door of her room behind him. He led her over to the bed and helped her lie down. At that moment, the temptation to lie down beside her and offer her a bit of the old Trent comfort was overwhelming. How many times had he done this over the years with a succession of women, wives mostly; all misunderstood by their husbands. He stared down at her. Her long, slender body was curled up on the bed. Her beautiful face streaked by the tears she had shed. Her allure could not have been greater at that moment. Nor could his panic.

Sounds in the corridor. It was Vincent. Another voice too, more indistinct. He didn't need to be Sherlock Holmes to guess what was happening here. He sat on the bed and stroked Carol's hair. Form dictated that he do at least this while he considered his options. Well, there was only one option in his mind.

Flight.

He bent down and kissed her hair. 'Carol, my darling. I must go.'

Carol straightened a little. This wasn't going to be good. Not good at all. He thought of the boardroom again. He thought of the soft red leather seats. He thought of the membership of the Stafford Club that would surely be his were he to be invited onto the board. Most of all he thought of the deal that he had on at that moment. Could he throw it all away for one woman?

'Go?' mumbled Carol through the confusion of her tears.

He had to think quickly. He had a few seconds to say something that could justify his departure to London to lie low while the dust settled here and, at the same time, not entirely burn his bridges with Carol. Yet, he knew that this was inevitable, wasn't it? The situation was spiralling dangerously out of control.

'Darling, my presence here is only going to inflame the situation. Think about it,' said Trent in a low voice. In truth, Carol seemed beyond thought at that moment. She stared up at him with frightened, confused eyes. Lord she was beautiful, he thought. 'Don't you see? Hook will only ask questions about me. It looks bad me being here. He'll ask about us. It's all too suspicious. It's best I go to London until after the inquest.'

Carol sat up on the bed. The crying had abated, and it looked like she was trying to decide if what she was hearing was sensible or the words of a craven, cowardly, cad. Trent thought the latter but, then again, he knew what was on his own mind. Of course, the way to say these things is every bit as important as what is said. He looked deep into her eyes, willing tears to appear in his own. They didn't, but perhaps the sheer intensity of his trying might make an impression.

It did.

'Get out,' screamed Carol, rage, hatred and contempt pouring like molten lava from her eyes.

This was pretty clear and unequivocal. The breach had always been on the cards and now Carol laid it out in words that barely required one syllable never mind, two. Trent was already beyond dignity himself now and with a few swift steps, he was beyond the door too. Freedom beckoned.

He raced to his bedroom. Grabbed his bag and was out the door in seconds. He passed Carol's room and could hear her sobbing her heart out. He didn't pause for a second. He was down the stairs, past a startled Vincent and out the front door. His car was parked immediately in front. He cast a swift eye towards the police car. Thankfully, it was not blocking the driveway.

Within a minute the car was on its way. He did not see Carol standing at the window staring at his escape. He did see, however, the other car racing down the driveway so quickly that he had to swerve to avoid a collision. And, with stab of shock, he saw who was driving the car.

The last day had been a torment for Roger Sexton. It felt as if his whole life was plunging slowly, inevitably, finally into the abyss. His pursuit of Carol over the last few months had exacted a toll on his business. It was in trouble. Rather like Teddy, he was a little stretched. The situation was manageable in the short term, but he needed a long-term solution. Carol had been that solution. It was clear that she and Teddy were finished. Every horse in Newmarket, knew this. It was only a question of time.

Teddy's death had been a Godsend. There was only one blot on an otherwise sunny horizon.

Jason Trent.

Quite how and where this excrescence had come on the scene with Carol, Sexton knew not. Nor did he want to think about how far their friendship had progressed. He had come to know Trent through his own business and his desire to

116

become a horse owner. His finances could not stretch to this, of course, hence why Trent had been so helpful. But owning a horse is no guarantee of a return. He'd borrowed money from the man's bank to finance his gamble. So far it was not paying off.

This was a problem given his own relatively straightened circumstances. He owed money to Trent's bank and his dapper rival looked like a Derby colt while he was more cart horse. However, the silver lining was that he had a reputation. This, paradoxically, put Sexton in a cold sweat as well as giving him hope. Sexton, like most insecure men, had a jealous nature. The last twenty-four hours had been a torture as he thought about Trent *in situ* with Carol offering words of comfort and who knows what else? As he drove at speed through the countryside towards the Tudor Stables he had decided that it was time to have it out with Trent and Carol. She had to make her choice.

He tore around the corner of the road and into the driveway of the estate. As he came through the gates, he narrowly missed another car speeding the other way. It swerved away. A malicious smile split his face as he saw who it was. He yelped in joy and started to laugh manically. The laughter died on his lips as he neared the mansion.

There, sitting in the driveway, was a police car. He was unsure what to do. The thought of turning tail and leaving crossed his mind briefly. No one except that popinjay, Trent, would have seen him. He could do it. He slowed down so much that the car nearly conked out on him. This was a problem and no mistake. He had not bargained for Hook, for surely it was he, to return. The man was no fool.

This could ruin everything.

117

As his mind, which was not that of a thoroughbred, raced, well, trotted, through the options, he saw the front doors opening to the house. People were coming out. First out was Tamsin. She appeared angry. Or perhaps she was crying. She seemed emotional, anyway. Then Kit Aston and that rather gorgeous wife of his. Finally, Hook appeared, clutching a plate of sandwiches along with a policeman.

In between them was a man. Sexton gasped at what he saw.

15

The entrance of a masked man into any room is likely to attract attention except perhaps at Madame Fannie's place in Kensington. This was a favoured nightspot for discerning gentlemen. All eyes were on Chris as he entered the room. Initially, he was hesitant and then, slowly he remembered that this was his house and then he strode forward and plonked himself on a chair facing Hook.

The smile had left Hook's face now. If Kit did not know better, there was even a hint of surprise on his face. Or perhaps the gravity of what he was seeing had had an effect. It certainly was the case for Kit and Mary. Both hoped that Hook would make the interview a mercifully short one and not ask for Chris to remove his mask.

'I'm sorry to ask you this Chris,' said Hook. 'But I will have to ask you to remove your mask.' The stunned silence that greeted this was deafening.

It was Chris who was the first to recover.

'You've excelled yourself this time, Hookie,' said the masked man. He did not seem unduly put out by the request.

Kit rose to his feet swiftly followed by Mary.

'Chris, I'm not quite sure why Hookie would ask this,' he turned to Hook and stared at the detective meaningfully. 'I'm not sure I think it's entirely necessary, but Mary and I will give you some privacy.'

Tamsin's face was beginning to resemble Gerry's. Her response was a little less diplomatic. She, too, was on her feet.

'What's the game? How dare you ask Chris to remove his mask.'

The masked man put his hand up and said, 'It's all right Tamsin. Kit, Mary, stay if you wish. In fact, I would rather prefer it if you did.'

Kit and Mary were both standing. They glanced uneasily at one another before sitting down again. Tamsin was still glaring at the detective, flames shooting from her nostrils. Hook shifted in his seat. By Kit's estimation, this interview was not going the way he had expected. But what had he expected? Kit glanced towards Chris. He was sitting back in his chair, one leg crossed over the other. He seemed wholly at peace with himself and the world. This was in marked contrast to his rather furtive appearances over the last couple of days. Whatever game Hookie was playing, this roll of the dice was not giving him the numbers he'd anticipated.

'If you please, I have to ask. You can replace it immediately, of course,' said Hook, gesturing to Chris. There was enough sadness in his voice to ameliorate a little Kit's disappointment at the original and intrusive request. Even Tamsin sat down. Although still angry, she realised that Hook had his job to do and sometimes it required him to ask questions that might seem beyond the pale.

'Very well,' responded Chris. Slowly he put his hands behind his head and untied the black mask. He began to remove it. Both Kit and Mary steeled themselves for what they would see. Despite having seen the most horrific results

120

of the bombs and the bullets, no one could be completely inured to the injuries endured. The mask came off with a flourish.

Silence.

Hook and Chris stared at one another for a few moments and then the detective said, 'Thank you Chris. Please believe me when I say that I'm sorry that we had to put you through this.' Regret was etched deeply into every word spoken by the detective. It was a side of Hook that Kit had seen before, and it was one of the reasons that he genuinely adored the man despite his often-cantankerous manner.

'May I?' asked Chris, holding up the mask. 'It's rather a grizzly sight and I wouldn't want to put you off your lunch.' Without the mask, Chris's voice was clearer. The muffle had gone, and the sound was pleasant if rather old. It had gravel and gravitas in equal measure. His face was a patchwork quilt of scars with skin pulled over where once eyelids had been.

'Please,' replied Hook, holding out the palm of his hand. He watched as Chris expertly replaced the mask. Mary stared at his hands. One of them had clearly been badly burned while the other seemed to have escaped any sign of damage.

'I hope you're happy,' said Tamsin, a little sulkily.

'Do I look happy, madam?' asked Hook, fixing his eyes on Tamsin. Colour flooded her face. He rose from his seat at this point. 'I have one more appalling request of you Chris.'

'What's that?'

'I want you to accompany me to the station.'

'What?' exploded Tamsin. 'Have you lost your mind?' Hook did not stop looking at Chris. Tamsin was on her feet once more. 'You can't seriously expect Chris to go into the station.'

Hook looked sideways at Tamsin, 'I do.'

If Chris was surprised then no one was going to be able to see it, his voice betrayed nothing.

'You wish me to make a statement about three nights ago?'

'Yes, if you would be so kind. I'm afraid we must do it at the station.'

'Why?' demanded Tamsin.

Hook sighed, shrugged and stayed silent.

It was Kit who answered Tamsin's question. He said, 'Tamsin, would you rather Chris did this at the inquest?'

Tamsin turned to Kit. The realisation was like a scream in the night. Tears welled up in her eyes. She looked at Hook and nodded her apology. Hook shook his head sadly and waved his hand to dismiss that any apology had been requested or was necessary.

Chris rose to his feet. Kit could almost see the smile that would have been on his face had his mouth not been so horribly disfigured.

'I'll come quietly guv. It's a fair cop.'

This made Hook smile at least. Everyone was on their feet now; they headed towards the door. In the corridor, Hook asked the young constable, 'I don't suppose we know who was fleeing justice.'

Young Westcott hadn't a clue as Hook well knew that he wouldn't. It was a lesson for the young man. Hook glanced towards Tamsin with a questioning eyebrow raised. She turned to Vincent.

'It's like they're passing the ball in rugby,' said Hook sardonically.

'I believe it was Mr Trent, sir,' said Vincent. 'He seemed in rather a hurry.'

'Any particular reason why, Vincent?' asked Hook.

Vincent looked slightly uncomfortable which suggested that he knew what had happened.

'I believe he had some words with Mrs Harrison.' This confirmed everyone's suspicion that there had been an argument a few minutes earlier.

'Were those words tender or sharp?' asked Hook, standing at the doorway of the house.

'I would say the latter if the volume and content is any guide,' responded Vincent.

'It usually is,' said Hook. Just then a young maid appeared holding a plate with sandwiches on it. 'The U.S. Cavalry has arrived, I see.' Hook walked over to her, smiled and took the plate from her. 'I'll return this later.'

With that he followed Kit, Mary and Tamsin through the door accompanied by Chris. They skipped down the steps and helped Chris into the police car. As he did so, Roger Sexton pulled up.

'Well, there appears to be a revolving door to Carol,' noted Hook. He glanced sideways at Mary. 'I'd keep an eye on him if I were you,' he said, nodding towards Kit.

'You'd have another murder to investigate Chief Inspector,' replied Mary.

'I suspect I would be your accomplice,' replied Hook. He took a bite of the sandwich and was about to climb into the car when Kit approached him. He stopped and the two men faced one another.

'I'll ask again, Hookie. What's going on?'

'That's what I'm trying to find out, Kit,' came the reply. Hook turned and nodded to Roger Sexton who had blustered over then he ducked his head into the car. Sexton's eyes darted from the policeman to Tamsin then to Kit in search of an explanation. None was forthcoming. His eyes drifted up to the bedroom window of Carol. He saw her standing there: beautiful, fragile and, for the time being his, until that bounder, Trent reappeared.

Sexton decided that being ignored was a fool's game. He strode forward with purpose, past Tamsin while Vincent moved out of the way to let the coming man through. Behind him he could hear the sound of the police car receding into the distance. He bounded up the stairs towards Carol's room. He knocked vigorously.

'Come in,' came the faint reply.

Sexton burst through the door and almost ran to Carol.

'My darling, what's going on?' Of course such a question required that he take Carol in his arms and draw her close to him. Tears stained her eyes.

'It's awful, Roger. They've arrested Chris.'

Her answer did not necessarily add to Sexton's understanding of the situation although this was probably not the time to point that out. Women take a dim view of sarcasm, generally. At least she seemed in a better mood than she had been the last time he'd been with her. Perhaps it was the shock of seeing Chris arrested.

'Do they think he murdered Teddy?' asked Sexton.

Carol gazed up into Sexton's eyes. Nothing was said. He inhaled her sweet fragrance. They stayed that way for a few moments before Sexton did what any sensible man would do while holding a beautiful woman close to him.

He swore out loud and let Carol go.

'This is a bit of a pickle,' he said while reaching into his side pocket for a cigarette case and matches.

For Carol, the sight of her brother being arrested for the possible murder of a man that she had killed constituted more than a pickle. Sexton's insensitivity to the sheer scale of the unfolding catastrophe cemented a feeling that had long lurked unspoken within her: perhaps Roger isn't the brightest.

They heard noises in the corridor and Tamsin calling for them. Perhaps it was a council of war. Things were becoming complicated now. Carol smiled an apology at Sexton for being so moody. Then he took her hand in his and led her out into the corridor.

16

Kit and Mary joined the rest of the Tudor family and Roger Sexton for a dinner. No one appeared to be talking, never mind eating. The atmosphere wasn't so much subdued as an utter vacuum. Mary tried to pick at her food but was soon infected by the mood.

'I'm sure Bryn will sort this matter out in no time,' said Gerry. 'Then we'll go after them. They can't do this.'

'Kit's right,' said Tamsin. She was growing a little irritated by the mood of despondency.

'About what?' asked Gerry gruffly. He was in no mood to hear any mitigation of the actions of Hook and the police.

Kit rose from his seat and walked over to the sideboard. On it was a newspaper. He picked it up and made a quick scan of the front page and then the pages inside. Then he showed the front page. It read:

SUICIDE IN NEWMARKET

'So?' asked Gerry.

'This is about to become a very public matter, Gerry. Hookie just did you an enormous kindness if you only but knew it,' said Kit.

'I don't see how pulling Chris in and getting him to do something which will have given him untold despair counts as a kindness.'

'Did you know that Chris had taken the car away, Gerry?'

'I was with him. Of course I knew,' came the short reply. Conscious that this was bordering on rude Gerry added, 'Look, are you saying that I should have said this to Hookie?'

'Did you go to Teddy's?' pressed Kit.

Gerry was quiet for a moment. He shook his head and replied, 'No. I didn't.'

'Did Chris?'

Gerry was even redder than usual. He was also quite obviously trying to avoid the eyes of Tamsin that were burning into him like flamethrowers.

'Why on earth didn't you say something?'' snarled Tamsin. 'Hookie has every right to pull Chris in. Someone obviously saw him at the house.'

'Look you don't think Chris somehow set up this suicide do you?' shouted Gerry trying to regain some of an initiative that had been well and truly lost.

'Don't shout at me you buffoon,' whispered Tamsin. 'The reason they've taken Chris away is because you never owned up to this. Now it looks worse than it is for him.'

'Bryn will fix it,' said Gerry defensively.

'Yes he will, no thanks to you,' said Tamsin.

'I still don't see why we're treating Hookie as a hero,' said Gerry. He was sounding more and more like a fourteen-year-old boy who had been caught smoking behind the greenhouse.

Tamsin sighed and gestured towards Kit to explain it in the simplest terms to her adorable, but rather dim-witted husband. Kit nodded and handed the newspaper to Gerry. He shrugged in a "what-of-it" manner.

'This is just the start,' said Kit pointing to the headline. 'It's a local matter now. Soon this could grow into something quite a bit bigger once the national press connect Teddy to the owner of a Derby prospect.'

'But it was a suicide. Tragic I'm sure. Why are we complicating a ham sandwich?'

Kit listed the reasons. With each one, Gerry appeared to shrink into his seat.

'The manner of Teddy's death is unusual. There was no suicide note. He was visited only a few hours earlier by his brother-in-law. A brother-in-law who might conceivably have had a bone to pick with him because of the ill treatment of his sister. This visit was not admitted to by the family and only came to light, no doubt, when a witness connected him to the death of Teddy having read the morning newspaper. Hookie has understood that this suicide is about to explode and, wonderful man that he is, has managed to bring Chris in before it does so in order to take a statement. He's aiming to excise Chris from any further involvement and hopefully the need to appear at the inquest. Trust me, Gerry, if Chris appears at the inquest, it will do a lot less for him than an evening down at the nick with someone he has probably known half a lifetime.'

Gerry was almost invisible now, so much so that Tamsin began to feel a little guilty.

'Remember Gerry,' she said, 'Chris was a bit wild when he was younger. I suppose we all were before the War. He and all of us had to grow up when that all started. Hookie knows him well enough and, Lord knows, we know Hookie.

He knew Chris wasn't a bad boy. He was just, well, he was Chris...'

Gerry nodded in defeat and looked at Kit apologetically. Kit shook his head. The matter was over. Mary listened on, fascinated by what life must have been like and how they had come to know the Chief Inspector.

An hour later, a policeman dropped Chris back to the house. It was around nine in the evening. He was accompanied by the man they had met on their first day, Bryn Cain. They entered a dining room in which no one appeared to be talking never mind eating. Chris was wearing a mask. He stopped in the doorway and surveyed the room.

'Feels like a funeral, Bryn,' said Chris.

Cain followed Chris into the room. Gerry rose to his feet and went over to Cain to shake hands. There was a chilly charm to the smile on the lawyer.

'Thanks Bryn, for dealing with this matter.'

Sensing that Cain's entrance had overshadowed that of Chris, Tamsin went over to her brother-in-law and gave him a hug.

'Are you able to tell us what happened, or would you prefer to retire?' she asked.

Chris seemed to grin from behind his mask, 'I suppose there's little point in playing the hermit now. According to Hookie this is not going to go away anytime soon.'

'Did he say why?' asked Kit. He remained convinced that Hook was in possession of a piece of evidence, as yet unshared, which threw the suicide in a wholly different light.

'No, you know Hookie,' replied Chris, taking one of the empty seats at the end of the table. He motioned for Cain to join them. He sat beside Carol, much to Sexton's chagrin, noted Mary with a smile. So there were at least three people who had taken a dislike to Cain. Chris lifted a fork and stabbed a piece of pork from Gerry's plate. He brought the fork over to the hole in the mask. 'Sorry, but I am starving. They made me some sandwiches, but they were nowhere near enough.'

'What happened?'

'I arrived at the station and Bryn followed a few minutes later. Hookie was happy for him to join us, and he didn't really ask any questions until Bryn arrived which was rather sporting of him. We went through what I'd done that day. I told him, Gerry, that you and I had gone into Newmarket. I added that at the last moment you had backed out of speaking with Teddy because you were afraid of what you might do.'

'What did you do, Chris?' asked Kit.

'Gerry dropped me off and I went to the front door. I banged in it a few times and probably said a few things I shouldn't have. There was no answer. I don't blame him really. I wouldn't have answered the door to me in the mood I was in. Then I went around the back door and banged on it for a few minutes.'

'Did Hook ask you if you'd tried to open it?'

Chris fixed his eyes on Kit. It must have been quite unnerving to be stared at by a mask-wearing man, but Kit seemed unperturbed.

'He did,' replied Chris. Then he stopped for a moment. Once more, Mary had the sensation he was smiling, or at least wanted to. At those moments, Mary forgot that he was wearing a mask and began to sense the person underneath the silk and the horribly burned skin. 'You and Hookie are so alike Kit. Both bloodhounds.'

'Have you met my wife?' said Kit which made Mary smile and colour a little at the same time. She shot a sideways look to her husband who she could not have loved more at that moment.

'Lord, two of you,' said Chris. 'I can't fault your choice of bride, Kit. The invite must have been lost in the post.'

Kit laughed at this and replied, 'You were all invited. It's your own fault if you chose not to come.'

Chris was silent for a moment. Kit and Mary sensed the sadness return.

Finally, Chris said, 'It was rather tough back then. I feel a bit better now but, you know.'

Kit nodded and replied, 'I know.'

'To answer your question, yes he wanted to know the time I arrived and left and yes, he did ask about the door. He was particularly interested in that, in fact.'

'Did you try to open it?'

'Yes,' said Chris to stunned silence. 'I did and it was locked.' Kit sighed out loud and shook his head. He was unhappy. Very unhappy. Chris leaned forward towards Kit. 'That's interesting Kit. You know Hookie did exactly the same thing. Didn't say why of course. I don't suppose you could enlighten a mere mortal as to what you and Hookie's god-like genius can see that we cannot.'

Kit's voice was almost strained as he spoke. He said, 'How could an unconscious man unlock a door?'

This detonated like a belch during the Vicar's Christmas sermon. Everyone stared at Kit open-mouthed, all except

Mary and Cain. When at last Chris found his voice, 'I see what you mean. You're suggesting it wasn't suicide?'

Kit's face was grave. He looked from Chris to the other people around the table then he spoke solemnly.

'I'm suggesting it was murder, Chris.'

Next morning

'What are our plans today?' asked Mary, staring unhappily out of the bedroom window.

It was morning and not a very good one at that. Rain drizzled apologetically from the sky. It was the sort of rain that was unable to decide between becoming a shower or keeping up a steady beat that would vex everyone for the day. The prospect of going out for a ride was decidedly unenticing. This was not just a function of the inclement weather. The mood, already low before Chris returned, became positively gloomy following Kit's explanation of the state of play. The only silver lining in Kit and Mary's book was the chance to see the rather disagreeable pair of Sexton and Cain butting heads for the attention of Carol.

'My goodness,' said Mary as she recalled their thinly veiled dislike, 'I must hand it to Carol. Teddy is barely in the ground and the male stags are already trying to assert dominance. Even I can see she's a dish, but decorum seems to have been thrown out the window.'

Kit kissed her gently on the forehead.

133

'No comparison to you my dear. I think even Mr Cain would jump ship, so to speak, if the opportunity presented itself.'

'I won't be presenting myself,' said Mary, 'Although I have to say, he's not bad looking in a rough sort of way. It seemed difficult to reconcile that broken nose with his clear diction and profession. Anyway, how do we proceed. You know Mr Hook better than anyone. What will be his next move?'

'I know him well, yet I could no more predict that than the next Derby winner. He's a law unto himself. I would like to see him though. Let's see if he'll share a little bit more than he has already.'

Mary thought for a moment and then said, 'Do you mind if I leave you and Mr Hook to catch up. I thought Chris would stay longer, but once you said about the murder…'

'It did rather throw a pall over the proceedings,' agreed Kit.

'That's putting it mildly, my love. I want to get to know Chris. Just for those few minutes he seemed rather charming.'

'He is. Well, he was. Gerry was always going to be the one to take over the business not the least because he was always the more responsible. It was assumed that Chris would join as his partner. You might have gathered that Chris was a bit wild in his youth. I think his dad and mum were forever on the point of throwing him out, but he would charm them out of their anger. Then the War came and that changed things forever.'

'I think Teddy's death is going to have a similar impact,' observed Mary. 'Hiding away in a turret may no longer be an option.'

Kit was thoughtful as Mary said this. She was right. The situation would change dramatically in ways they could not predict. It was critical for the family that he and Hook worked together before it became a circus. He wondered if Hook was reaching a similar conclusion. The antagonism he presented in public, to Kit was only a public face. Unacknowledged but present was the reality that they had worked together, closely, in the past. Then, there had been no hiding Hook's reluctance because Kit was merely a precocious schoolboy and then a student at the college. Now he was an adult with the experience of war behind him. Whatever public face Hook presented to his involvement; Kit suspected that he would privately hold a more flexible view.

'I will give Hookie a call this morning. I think we need a council of war.'

'Do you think it's going to be that bad?'

Kit nodded. And he would be right. Things were soon going to get very much worse.

'May I speak with Chief Inspector Hook please. Tell him it's Lord Kit Aston,' said Kit. He hated to throw his title in, but it was sometimes necessary to cut through any resistance. Sure enough a minute later a familiar voice came on the line with an equally familiar mordant response.

'This is an honour your lordship. I hope you can see that my forelock is being well and truly touched.'

'Cut the wisecracks Hookie, you know why I said it,' said Kit. The initial tone of levity gave way to a more serious mood. 'We need to meet.'

135

This was greeted with silence at the other end of the line. Then Hook finally relented.

'I'll see you at the race course. Usual place.'

The line went dead.

Kit put the phone down and went in search of Gerry. He found him down at the paddock, viewing the horses being led out. Worry lines creased the side of his mouth. There was no question his friend was deeply concerned about what would happen next.

'I am going into Newmarket to meet Hookie.'

'Thank you Kit,' said Gerry. 'I suppose it'll be like old times for you with him.'

'Almost,' said Kit, half smiling but not really joking.

'I suppose. It's different now. When you're in it up to your eyes,' said Gerry with a frown. He turned and looked Kit in the eye. 'Kit, this could ruin us. If something is suspicious about Teddy's death then I don't know how owners will react. They may not want their horses to be trained here and it'll take Glory to come up trumps in the Derby otherwise they may not want to breed with him either. Will you help us? Will you help clear our family of any hint of suspicion?'

This was an unusually long speech by Gerry's standards. It showed Kit just how much was at stake for the family. It affected everyone now, not just Carol. Kit nodded to his friend and patted him on the arm. He said, 'I'll do what I can Gerry. There's only one thing that I ask.'

'Name it, Kit.'

'You cannot lie to either myself, or to Mary, or to Hookie. Any attempt at deception will only make matters worse. You must see that now. If Hookie hadn't found out that you and Chris went to see Teddy then Chris may not have had to go

136

and see him while the press were parked outside your house or at the police station. Everything that happened matters. We just don't know yet how it all fits together. We may never have the full picture, but we cannot have anything withheld from us.'

Gerry nodded. Then they started to walk away from the paddock towards the stables.

'I'll have one of the jockeys run you into town to see Hookie.'

A jockey was duly found, and he drove Kit to the outskirts of Newmarket where the racecourse entrance was situated.

'Drop me off here, please,' said Kit, pointing to the front entrance of the main stand. Hook was rarely prompt, so it was something of a surprise to see a police car was just pulling up as they arrived. Kit thanked the young man, a promising flat jockey called Leo and stepped out of the car.

He walked over to the car where Hook sat waiting in the back. Hook saw him and stepped out. The two men walked in silence around the side of the stand. It was eerie to see the racecourse so deserted. Kit was the first to speak. Kit said simply, 'It was murder.'

'So it would appear,' agreed Hook. Then a smile crossed his face and he glanced across at Kit. He said, 'The time?'

'The time,' answered Kit, nodding. 'How can an unconscious man unlock the door?'

'Good to see you've lost none of your mildly irritating ability to expose murder most foul,' said Hook, giving the last three words a particularly theatrical enunciation.

'You've discounted Chris?'

137

'Oh yes,' said Hook dismissively. 'The witness saw him leave within a minute or two of arriving. He stood on the street briefly and then went back to the front door. He banged it for another minute and then a car, presumably driven by Gerry, picked him up and off they went. Of course, we only have Chris's word that the back door was locked.'

'Did the witness see anyone else around the property?' asked Kit.

'That is when our luck runs out. No. Mrs Hardcastle abandoned her post at the net curtains thereby depriving of us of an eyewitness to whoever set up that ridiculous contraption that killed him.' Hook shook his head sadly and tilted his felt hat back on his head. 'All very disappointing.'

'There's one thing that is troubling me and I think it's time for you to tell me what you know.'

'Go on,' said Hook. He was smiling now like a professor watching his favourite pupil with pride slowly work out something that he had long ago divined.

'You knew it was murder right from the start. How?'

'How do you think?' asked Hook. Kit was not going to get off that easily .

The two men had reached a part of the course that was open so they stepped inside and walked over to a point where they could sit down, trackside. Kit was silent for a moment. He knew he was being tested. He sat back in his seat and began to think out loud. This always entertained Hook.

'All right, Hookie. What do we have? We know that Teddy died just after six because that is when Sexton and Trent arrived and tried to open the door. You have witnesses who can verify they arrived at this time?' Hook nodded at this so Kit continued. 'This means that the time will not have

138

been played with. So working backwards, we know that Chris and Gerry left around five-forty-five. A car arrived back at the house around six because Mary saw it but did not see who was driving. You will have confirmed from Vincent and the other staff that it was Gerry and Chris?'

Hook nodded once more.

'So we can discount them. Gerry was with Mary and me most of the afternoon, too. No, someone had to have been inside the house when Chris was there and then he, or she, escaped, just before the arrival of the two men. Sexton has a shop nearby to Teddy in Newmarket while Trent claims he came up from London on the train. Witnesses?' asked Kit.

'None. He has a train ticket, but that does not mean he could not have come earlier.'

'Or driven,' added Kit.

'Correct,' said Hook.

'So what made you suspicious aside from your naturally suspicious nature? Well, the manner of the death was so contrived it might have appeared on the pages of a particularly ingenious crime novel.'

'Ingenious? I wouldn't go quite that far,' said Hook. 'Contrived, yes.'

'So that would have raised your suspicion a little. Yet, it strikes me that you were not sure when you arrived if it was not a suicide. There's something else I am missing here.'

'Missing,' confirmed Hook with a sly grin. 'Yes, indeed.'

Kit stared out onto the track. Then he shook his head and looked glumly at Hook.

'You know how much I dislike it when you give me clues,' said Kit. This was greeted with a delighted chuckle by Hook. Then Kit slapped his forehead and groaned. The realisation had dawned on him, at long last. 'It was staring me in the face all the time. You even said it at the house.'

'To be fair, Kit old boy, I wasn't sure myself. Now I am.'

'The missing person you mentioned. It was in the newspaper too. That's who the dead body is. It's not Teddy at all. That begs an interesting question or two.'

'Where is Teddy?' said Hook.

'And who put the other young man in Teddy's place?' added Kit.

18

Early afternoon, Kit returned to the house to find Mary sitting in the library looking rather morose. It was not hard to guess why. She had hoped to see Chris again, but he had remained in his room. Instead, as it was too wet to go out for a ride, she had divided her time between chatting with Tamsin and reading from the extensive collection of books in the library.

'I don't know that Gerry has ever read a single one of them,' observed Tamsin, although she was not being unkind.

'A man of action?' prompted Mary with a smile.

'Yes. Very much so. The War took a lot out of him. He was depressed for quite some time, but since we found Glory, he's perked up a lot. He seems more like his old self,' said Tamsin.

'And Chris?'

Tamsin sighed at the mention of her brother-in-law. She shook her head and said, 'I don't know if he'll ever truly recover. What you saw last night was a lot like the old Chris. Perhaps the adrenalin. I fear he may become even more reclusive following this.

'At least he's not a suspect. The timing doesn't work unless he managed to escape the stables much earlier without anyone knowing.'

'Not much chance of that. The only way he could have done so was by car or by horse. In both cases we would have noticed.'

When Kit returned to the house he joined Mary in the library. They sat by the large window that overlooked the stables.

'I wish I'd come with you,' she said glumly. 'What did Mr Hook say?'

Kit updated her on the conversation which was always a risk when it appeared that he'd had kept something back from Mary on the missing person. Kit held his hands up, a picture of innocence.

'Honestly, it only occurred to me when I was chatting with Hookie. He has that effect on me. So do you.' Mary put a threatening hand on his thigh. 'Other effects too, that I assure you are beyond even Hookie's considerable abilities.'

'So, go on, tell me more about what he said.'

'Damien Blythe. That's the man they've been looking for over the last few days. A troubled young man I gather. He's lived on the edges of the law for some time. Apparently, he ran away from home several years ago. I dread to think what he was running from. He found casual work at the racecourse and with local stables, but rarely stayed long. He lived in a hut in the forest. Not the most social of people, I understand. He started working for the Haley Stables which are over on the other side of the hill, a week ago but after a few days he disappeared without collecting his wages. This was a surprise.

142

After a few days, the owner alerted the police. That was three days ago.'

'Is he sure that the man who died of the shotgun wound is this Damien Blythe?' asked Mary.

'He's fairly certain although one complicating factor is that his blood group matches with Teddy's. They checked Teddy's army records.'

'It looks like the murderer was a little lucky,' said Mary.

'Yes. I wonder why they took the risk though.'

'Surely they are looking for Teddy, though. Does it not point to Teddy being the murderer?' asked Mary.

'Hookie's not convinced. I can see his point. Why would Teddy do this? And why would he do it in his own home? He would have to have known he would be found out and he certainly could not be sure that the blood groups would match. It doesn't really make much sense.'

'Yes, I see what you mean,' agreed Mary. 'That means we still have to find out where Teddy is? Why has he suddenly disappeared?'

Kit went to search for the local newspaper and came back a couple of minutes later. Together they leafed through the paper until they found the story they were looking for.

Local Man Missing

Police are asking for any information related to the whereabouts of Mr Damien Blythe of no fixed abode. Mr Blythe was reported missing by his employers at Haley Stables on Friday when he failed to turn up for the second consecutive day. A spokesman for the stables, Mr Bryn Cain said that the stables would be willing to offer a small reward for any information that assists the police in locating Mr Blythe.

'Cain?' said Mary. 'He certainly gets around.'

'Did Tamsin reveal anything more about Mr Cain to you?'

'She did, as it happens,' said Mary edging closer to Kit just in case anyone was listening nearby. Eavesdropping in country houses was an occupational hazard or a perk depending on which side of the keyhole one was.

Kit smiled and leaned forward towards Mary, thought about stealing a kiss and then thought better of it as she was about to speak.

'Cain has been the family lawyer since the War ended. He was over there too before you ask. His father handled the Tudor business before him.'

'I suspect he handles a lot of the stables around here in that case,' said Kit. 'Anything else?' He asked this knowing full well that there was. Something in the brightness of Mary's eyes and the confidentiality of the whisper.

'Well,' said Mary with a grin, 'It appears that Mr Sexton and Mr Trent aren't the only jockeys in this race. Apparently, Mr Cain and Carol have raised a few eyebrows in the past. Perhaps not so recently. I think he was on the scene before Trent but Sexton pre-dates either of them. I think Mr Sexton is back out of the running again. Carol refused to see him when he came earlier.'

'Why was that?' asked Kit.

Mary held her hands up and said, 'She hasn't been down since refusing to see him. Poor chap was pretty cut up. Maybe Mr Cain has hit the front now.'

'I wonder why Teddy didn't invite him the other day,' mused Kit.

'Perhaps it was Cain who was arranging the furniture inside,' suggested Mary. 'I'm not sure I would put it past him.'

'Yes, I think I agree with you on that. But let's not play guess-the-murderer until we have some evidence. At the moment we have nothing beyond supposition,' said Kit with a grin.

'And my infallible intuition,' pointed out Mary, primly.

The conversation stopped on that point as both were lost in their thoughts. They sat quietly staring out of the window for the next few minutes reflecting on the new developments in what was now, unquestionably, a murder case.

Down near the paddock they could see the horses cantering around the field. Northern Glory and Leonardo's Pride were at the back, alongside one another. Gerry was there with his two arms on the fence.

'Are they all telling the truth now?' asked Mary.

Kit through his hands up. 'Who knows? How was Gerry today?' he asked. 'Did he seem relieved by the fact that the truth was out now?'

Mary thought for a moment. Then she shook her head.

'No, if anything he was even more distant. I think even Tamsin noticed for she shook her head at me over lunch when he was being very quiet. I don't know, but I think that he has a lot on his mind and perhaps not all of it is the death of Teddy.'

145

'I imagine he has, what with managing the stables and Northern Glory. A lot depends on him. I don't think Gerry is in straightened circumstances the way Teddy was, but a horse like Glory could change everyone's life here. I think you may be right, though. Something is definitely in the air, and I don't think it's entirely down to Teddy.'

It wasn't.

A letter arrived in the afternoon post before lunch was served. It was addressed to Mr Gerald Tudor. Inside was a typewritten letter. Its arrival could hardly have come at a worse time. It's difficult to enjoy a ploughman's lunch when you have the threat of blackmail suddenly imposed on you. The letter read:

Dear Mr Tudor

I would like you to sell Northern Glory to a consortium of my choosing. I will provide you with details in a letter very soon. If you have any doubts about what I am asking or should you wish to throw this letter in the bin, I request that you take a look at the enclosed photographs. I think you will recognise the man. It is your late brother-in-law. He was murdered by your sister.

Any attempt to involve the police will
result in the immediate forwarding of
these photographs to the press and, of
course, to the police. Neither Carol, nor
you and your family will survive scandal.
Carol will almost certainly face justice
and, possibly, the hangman.

A Friend.

To concentrate his mind a few photographs were added
to the package. They were rather small, but there was no
question about what they showed. Lying in a pool of blood
around his head was Teddy Harrison. His eyes were wide
open. So was his mouth, as if he were in shock at his own
demise.

Gerry stared at the letter before trying and failing to sit at
lunch with Mary, Tamsin and Carol. In the end he gave up
and made his excuses. He raced down to the paddock to
think. The problem, as Gerry swiftly realised, was that he was
not a thinker. Chris had been, for all his immaturity, the
smarter of the two. While Carol was smarter than both of
them, it was Tamsin who stood alone. What he would have
given to have her wise counsel now. Yet, how could he? How
could he involve her or Chris in what would amount to a
conspiracy to pervert the course of justice?

No. It would not do. It was for him, alone, to deal with.

And the nightmare he was facing did not end there.

Selling Northern Glory to a consortium would mean giving up his dream. For all his life he had dreamed of training a Derby winner. Fate had gifted him not only that chance but, by the greatest stroke of luck, he was the owner of the horse, too.

Gerry understood that he was facing the greatest dilemma of his life. The choice between giving up his sister who was a murderer, if the letter was to be believed, and Gerry did, or giving up his dream.

Tears welled up in his eyes. He turned away from the stables and walked into the paddock. He wanted to be away from people, away from any prying eyes. In fact, he just wanted to scream.

Damn Carol. Damn her to hell. Why had she married that oaf Teddy? She'd caused his family so much trouble.

At that moment he hated her. Yet, at the same time he hated himself more for being disloyal to his sister, but also to his own family: to Tamsin and the children. It was their future that would be thrown away. Keeping Northern Glory would have ensured their financial futures.

Lord only knew what knock down price would be asked for the horse. The consortium would have to be seen to pay something for the racehorse otherwise questions would be asked. But what then? Would the blackmailer demand a cut of this from him?

The answer to that question was obvious. No doubt he would receive a commission from the consortium. It would be a win at both ends of the deal. The unfairness of it all made him almost sick to the hind teeth. Yet, all the self-pity in the world could not deflect from the essential question posed.

Give up Carol or give up his dream?

19

'Darling,' said Carol.

'Darling,' said the voice on the other end of the line.

'They're saying it's murder,' continued Carol. Her voice was tremulous, close to tears. Close to breaking point. The man was unsure whether to feel afraid himself or if he should assert himself in the manner that men have through the ages with women, to the detriment of all concerned.

'There's nothing to be afraid of my love. Remember, you were at your family house when it all happened. Whatever they might think or say, you are in the clear,' said the voice.

Carol struggled to breathe. It came in spurts as she fought hard to stop breaking down into tears. Then she heard footsteps.

'I must go,' she said and hung up without waiting for a reply.

The man at the other end of the line heard the click of the phone and sighed. He turned away and went over to his desk. On it was a typewriter. He sat down and stared at the letter he had begun to type. It read:

```
Dear Gerry,
```

Remember, there will be hell to pay if you go to the police. Here is a photograph to remind you of why.

I will send you details of a place that you must go. You will find a leather satchel there. Inside the bag will be a contract and a cheque.

You will sign the contract immediately and put it back inside the leather satchel. You will take the cheque and immediately go to your bank and deposit the cheque.

The cheque will take some days to clear. Once it has, you will make an announcement to the press that you have sold Northern Glory to a consortium. You will be sent a statement to issue to the press and also to the Jockey Club. You will answer no questions on the subject of the sale other than to say that you were offered an exceptional deal. The deal means that you not only can still train Northern Glory, but you may also benefit from its future stud potential. I can arrange it that you will have one nomination for breeding purposes.

The consortium have no idea about the circumstances leading to the sale. If they become acquainted with our

151

```
arrangement then I shall have no
compunction but to send the photographs
to the police. This will mean that you
will not only have lost Northern Glory
but will also lose Carol.
```

The man read over the letter before typing the final two words: *A Friend*. Then he extracted the paper from the typewriter, checked that it made sense. He was not too worried about the grammar or punctuation; he'd let the pedants fight over that one.

He folded the letter and slipped it inside an envelope. In block capitals, with his left hand, he wrote the address of Tudor Stables. A few minutes later he was outside, braving the British weather. He made his way to the post office and posted the letter. It would reach Gerry the next morning and set up a particularly rotten day for his old friend.

Rather than head back to his house, he treated himself to a cup of tea and a scone in a Tea Room. It was nearing five o'clock when he returned to his rooms. He picked up the phone and spoke to an operator. He glanced at a number that was written on a pad on his desk and asked the operator to put him through.

A few minutes later he heard a man's voice.

'Hello, who is this?'

'It's me,' said the man. 'I can't promise anything yet, but Tudor has expressed a willingness to sell and at the price we discussed.'

'Really,' exclaimed the man delightedly. 'How on earth did you manage it?'

'I had a feeling he wanted to clear the chips off the table,' said the man. 'He'll want to remain the trainer and have access for one of his mare's to breed.'

'Of course, I quite understand, I'm sure the others won't mind.'

'Good. Well, I'll call you in a day or two when we are near the finishing post, so to speak.'

This was greeted with a loud guffaw and a 'jolly good' from the other man. The man recoiled from the sound. He would be glad when this infernal business was over. He had taken an extraordinary risk that one week ago would have seemed as insane as it was impossible.

Needs must, though.

It was all madness of course. But then again, wasn't life, death and everything in between? No one coming back from Flanders could look at life again and feel the same as they had before they had been thrown into that show. To see human beings rent apart, thrown in front of blazing metal, used as shields for those that came behind, was to understand that life, far from having value, was there to be exploited. It had taken too long for him to learn this lesson.

He picked up the phone once more and spoke to the operator. A minute later another voice came on the line. A foreign accent. French.

'Hello, Jean-Claude, it's your friend.'

'Ah hello, my friend. What news?'

'It is both good and bad. Northern Glory is up for sale. This is not going to be announced, but my source is unimpeachable. The only problem is, there is another buyer interested who has also heard that a sale is in the offing.'

'*Non*,' exclaimed Jean-Claude.

'I'm sorry. I think we both knew that this was always a possibility. I don't know who the other buyer is, but it could,' said the man, feeling his throat tighten in excitement, 'drive the price up. The advantage you have is that I have my source who can give me what that price will be.'

'Excellent,' said Jean-Claude. 'You will be well-rewarded my friend if you can do this for us.'

'Thanks, Jean-Claude,' replied the man. The conversation ended and he put the phone down. His heart was racing now. He was so close to the deal of his life. Everyone just needed to act in the way they were supposed to, and he would soon be sipping from the cup of success.

He went over to his drinks cabinet and fixed himself a gin. It was too early to toast success but, for the first time, he allowed himself to think about the future and it made him smile.

20

Chief Inspector Hook arrived just after four in the afternoon. He was brought to the library by Tamsin. His umbrella was over his shoulder holding his satchel. Raindrops dripped from his felt hat. He and Tamsin found Kit staring out of the window at the sheets of rain falling down. It seemed to make the greenness of the grass and the trees all the more vivid when set against the silvery grey sky. Mary, meanwhile, was lifting books from the shelf and studying the covers. She looked up and grinned at Tamsin and Hook as they entered.

'Who is the devotee of detective fiction, Tamsin?' asked Mary. She was holding in her hand a book by Ivor Longstaff, *The Twelve Finches*.

'Good Lord,' said Hook as he took in the cover of the book. A man, clad only in a towel, was lying on a table while another man, similarly clad, was standing over him about to give a massage that, from the look on his face, might very well be his last. 'What on earth is that?' said Hook, making no attempt to hide how appalled he was.

'Oh Agatha put me on to him,' said Tamsin. 'I'm addicted to detective books.'

'I do love *Twelve Finches*,' said Mary.

'You're welcome,' muttered Kit.

Mary and Tamsin both gave Kit quizzical looks.

Hook and Kit exchanged glances. Hook noted the half-smile on Kit's face. He shook his head and said, 'I see your sense of humour has not evolved beyond middle school.' Then he turned to Tamsin and Mary. 'I would have thought that you two, at least, would be more sensible than this.' He stared once more at the cover, in horror. Mary was grinning at the policeman's rather puritanical reaction to the literature.

'Aunt Agatha likes *Twelve Finches*, too,' said Kit looking directly at Hook, one eyebrow raised.

'I would have thought she was past all that,' said Hook drily.

Mary glanced sharply at Kit. There was something on his face that suggested he and Hook were having a different conversation. She'd noticed it before when it came to this particular writer. She handed the book to Hook who had fished a pair of half-moon spectacles from his pocket. He opened the book at a random page and began to read.

'All right, dear old Todgeman, you go round the back and watch for anyone making a getaway. I intend to go undercover,' said Inspector Bellmop. Going undercover required the noble inspector to become uncovered, paradoxically. He began to remove all of his clothes in the presence of his stalwart sergeant. To Todgeman's eyes he seemed to take an eternity doing this. Finally, he stood before Todgeman in all his glory and said, 'Hand me the towel. I'll go for a massage in the steam room and see if anything juicy comes out of it.'

'This is…' began Hook but gave up as words escaped him.

'It's a jolly good story. I was guessing who the killer might be right up until the end,' said Tamsin. There was a hint of defensiveness in her voice. Like Mary, she could not understand what was amusing Kit so much whilst, at the same time, causing the Chief Inspector to be so priggish.

'Was there a happy ending?' asked Hook, his face straighter than a high court judge facing a cane-wielding headmistress.

'Inspector Bellmop always gets his man, Hookie,' said Tamsin.

'I'll bet he does,' said Hook, starchily. Hook looked over his half-moon spectacles. His gaze shifted between Mary and Tamsin. Both ladies seemed curious as to what Hook might say next. He turned towards Kit who had turned his back to them and was staring out the window. His shoulders were shaking as he tried to suppress his laughter. This, at least, was reassuring. Then a thought seemed to strike him. 'May I borrow this?' he asked.

'Be my guest,' said Tamsin. 'I've finished it.'

'For Mrs Hook, you understand,' said Hook quickly.

'Your tastes run more to Russian literature?' asked Kit sardonically.

Hook ignored this jibe and asked Tamsin, 'I thought I saw Gerry down by the paddock.'

'Yes,' said Tamsin. 'He's been there most of the afternoon.'

'In this weather?' said Hook. He looked decidedly unhappy. 'I don't suppose you could send someone down. I need to speak with him.' He turned and looked at Kit meaningfully before adding, 'Alone.'

'Why don't you go into the drawing room Hookie. I'll organise some tea as well.'

'You are, as ever, my Queen, Tamsin,' said Hook, bowing slightly. Then he nodded to Kit and Mary before departing from the library followed by Tamsin.

Mary waited a few moments and then turned to Kit with raised eyebrows. Kit took this to mean, why is he here?

'I have a feeling that Hookie is about to break the news to Gerry that the inquest will be held either tomorrow or the next day and it will find that a man who is not Teddy has been murdered.'

'So Mr Hook has enough evidence for this conclusion to be reached?'

'Yes, I would say so,' said Kit. 'I'd love to know what he's going to say to Gerry, though. I mean, it seems like an awful lot of trouble to go to even if he does know the family well.'

'What are you suggesting?' asked Mary, intrigued. Where Chief Inspector Hook was concerned, she could see that Kit had a very good understanding of the policeman.

Kit pondered this for a moment before saying, 'Honestly, I have no idea. Remember, we still have to find Teddy. Perhaps this is what the latest line of inquiry concerns.'

Any further talk of Teddy was curtailed by the arrival of Tamsin back in the library. Her face betrayed the worry that had grown with each passing day. Mary went over to her and took her hands. This was met with a smile and a frown.

'What are they saying in there?' she asked. Her voice was a whisper.

Kit repeated what he'd just said to Mary. Tamsin said nothing to this, merely nodding in agreement. It appeared to bring her no comfort to believe that Teddy might not be dead. Instead, it raised the even more dreadful question about who the dead man was.

Kit remained silent on this point. It was not right that he should reveal the confidence shared by Hook. That would come out at the inquest. They sat in the library in mute resignation listening to the rain patter against the window. After a few minutes, Mary picked up one of the books she had taken from the shelf.

'That's a good one,' said Tamsin eyeing the front cover. The book was called *Thigh Shalt Not Kill* by Laura Norder. The cover showed three young flappers and one rather lucky young man who was ensnared in a manner that the police would do well to consider when next they interrogated someone. The tagline read: *One of them knew the Kama Sutra of killing.*

'What's the *Kama Sutra*, Kit?' asked Mary, looking at the tagline. There was a slight frown on her forehead. She hated not knowing things. She looked up at her husband who, infuriatingly, was much more widely read than she. Her reading had been confined to the classics of English and French literature. Since meeting Kit's aunt, she had developed a delightfully unseemly taste for detective literature.

Kit studied his wife for a moment. Both she and Tamsin were looking at him inquiringly. This went on for a little bit longer than he had bargained for. They really did not know, he concluded.

159

'I believe it's a book on special types of yoga,' he said finally before diving behind his newspaper.

'Sounds dull,' said Tamsin. Mary nodded in agreement. Emergency over, thought Kit.

While Kit read *The Times*, the two ladies discussed their favourite detective novels. The fascination that women had for murder never ceased to amaze Kit. It seemed to grow with age. Then he reflected on the fact that he was rather fascinated about the subject himself.

Around half past five, they heard the front door open and then shut. Kit glanced out of the window and saw Hook jogging over to the police car. So there would be no report from the great man on what they discussed. That would have to wait for tomorrow he supposed.

Gerry appeared a few moments later. He looked pale and drawn. He'd looked this way before Hook had arrived and the policeman's visit had clearly done nothing to lighten the load that he was clearly carrying.

Tamsin was on her feet immediately and over to her husband. They hugged one another tightly.

'It appears this nightmare is unending. Hookie thinks that the inquest, which is tomorrow incidentally, will find that it is an unlawful killing. Furthermore, he believes it will confirm that the dead man is not Teddy. I wish I could say that this is a relief, but Hookie says it throws up many more questions. I'm afraid it's going to become a little bit sticky now.'

'Gerry,' said Kit, setting his newspaper down. 'Is there anything I can do? You know what I've done in the past. Perhaps I can help.'

Gerry's eyes darted towards Kit and then to Mary. He shifted on his feet and then sat down near Kit.

'Look old man, I hope you won't mind, but I think that this is going to become a mess. It might be better if you cut short your break here and come back when the dust has settled. I think this would be for the best.'

'Gerry,' exclaimed Tamsin. She seemed surprised, but Mary noted that Kit was not. 'Gerry, what are you saying?'

Kit stepped in to bail out his old friend.

'I think what Gerry is saying, and I can see his point, is that my presence might be misconstrued by the press. They are aware of my involvement in some cases over the last few years. I imagine that's what Mr Cain will be saying to you anyway, Gerry if he hasn't done so already.'

Gerry would probably have made the worst poker player in the world. His ruddy face coloured even more, and he reluctantly nodded.

'Why don't you tell Bryn to go to blazes,' spluttered Tamsin. She was clearly outraged at the discourtesy.

'No Tamsin,' said Kit gently. 'It makes sense. Really, it does.'

'Well, I don't mean to be rude Kit,' replied Tamsin, 'but I don't see it myself. This is exactly when we need you to be here. I'm surprised Bryn doesn't see this.'

'Tamsin,' exclaimed Gerry. 'That's not fair. Bryn has our best interests always in mind.'

'I think he's right,' said Kit, which surprised Mary, but she did not query it.

Tamsin was clearly conflicted by this. She tangled her hands together. 'He's said some things recently with which I don't agree. I don't agree with this either.'

Both Kit and Mary's eyes shot towards their friend.

'What do you mean?' asked Kit.

161

At this point Gerry would have welcomed a short stay in a four-by-four cell in the company of a slop bucket rather than face the inquisitorial gaze of his better half. He could barely look at his friends as he muttered.

'He's keen that I sell Glory.'

Kit and Mary were both aghast at this. Mary spoke first, 'But you said you would never do that.'

Kit added, 'He knows what this means to you. I hope he and, our friend, Trent aren't trying their luck.'

'Nonsense, Kit,' said Gerry stoutly. 'Why would Cain suggest such a thing?'

'Why do you think?' said Tamsin. 'He would make a juicy fat commission on the sale from Trent.'

Gerry just wanted the conversation to end. He wanted to go his room, shut the door and howl at the moon for an eternity. This was his idea of hell. He was caught between a wife on the warpath, no husband wants this, ever, and a sister who could very well go to the gallows for killing her husband. The situation was almost impossible.

Yet the decision he had to make was inevitable and it broke his heart. Even in his worst moments in Flanders, sending horses away to their death, he had never felt more alone than he did just then.

'I'm sorry,' he said in a voice that was barely a whisper. 'I have the most awful headache. Would you mind if I went to bed early?'

Tamsin followed Gerry out of the room. There was no question that he was misleading them. He looked ill and certainly sounded it. After they had left, Mary took Kit's hand.

'I'm sorry for them. This is such a ghastly situation for all of them. I wish there were something we could do.'

'I know what you mean,' agreed Kit. 'I hate to leave them in a lurch, but I don't want to upset Gerry any more than he is already. I suppose it makes a change for us to be kicked off a case not by the police but by the very person we may have helped. Let's go upstairs and start to pack. We'll make sure that we can take a train tomorrow morning. Perhaps the 1 o'clock.'

'Good idea. Such a pity. I'd like to see Tamsin again soon.'

Kit smiled, 'Yes, I knew you would be great pals. It's a pity we didn't see more of Chris.'

The evening was as much of a washout as the day had been. Gerry was too ill to attend dinner and Tamsin sent her apologies to Kit and Mary as she stayed with her husband. Carol made a brief appearance before disappearing also, leaving Kit and Mary to pick at their food. It was proving to be a sad end to their long weekend. They decided to retire early.

Mary awoke around three in the morning from a restless sleep. She found Kit standing by the window gazing out into the night. The rain had stopped, and it was possible to see the moon peeking out from behind some clouds. Mary padded over to him and took his arm.

'Do you fancy raiding the kitchen? I'm starved.'

Kit laughed, 'Yes, good plan. I'm sure there's a lot left over from what we didn't eat earlier.'

'I dread to think. I mean it was only us for dinner. I do so feel sorry for Tamsin and Gerry. This is all becoming too much. I hope they won't feel they were being rude leaving us alone tonight.'

Kit knew that they would feel bad. He felt a little low. His mind was caught somewhere in between a desire to help them and a feeling that they would be most helped by not having him or Mary around just at that moment. It was an uncommon situation. They slipped on their dressing gowns and descended the stairs together to the main hall and then took a second set of stairs that led down to the kitchen.

As they approached the kitchen, they could see that the light was on. Kit stopped for a moment and glanced towards Mary.

'I wonder…' he said.

Mary raised her eyebrows and smiled. They stepped forward into the kitchen to find Chris sitting at the table. He was without his mask. A couple of large sandwiches sat in his plate.

'They look nice,' said Kit. 'Would you mind if we joined you?'

Chris paused for a moment and then said, 'Are you sure I wouldn't put you off your food?'

'Never,' said Kit firmly.

Chris nodded and glanced towards the cupboard, 'There was quite a lot left over from tonight. What happened?'

'Gerry was unwell,' said Mary. 'He went to bed early. Tamsin stayed with him. Carol appeared briefly but had no appetite. Both she and Gerry seem in a bad way.'

164

'Ahh,' replied Chris. 'That would explain it. Poor chap's under a lot of pressure. I suppose we all are. I'm sorry it's messed up your weekend.'

'Nonsense,' said Kit.

'I'm sorry I've been a bit anti-social. I suppose you of all people would understand, Kit. And you Mary. What you did was extraordinary, going out there and nursing at the front. I gather that's where you met.'

Mary smiled and glanced shyly up at Kit, 'Yes, in a manner of speaking. We eventually came together.'

'Fate,' said Chris and they could see that he was trying to smile. 'You are a very lucky man Kit.'

This was true, yet Kit understood that it was not exactly the whole story. Kit was a lucky man because he had met and married the woman he loved. Such an outcome was unlikely to befall Chris. As good as his heart was, it was difficult to imagine anyone being strong enough to look past the horrible scarring on his face to see the person underneath.

Mary took Chris's hand and said softly, 'What happened?'

Only Mary could have asked such a question. Only she could have made a man who was running away from what he was, speak about the worst moment of his life. About the moment his life, his future and his happiness all but ended. Kit felt he had never loved her more than at that moment.

It had all been so easy.

It was an extension of the life he had led at the stables. It was almost a life without limits, free of responsibility, free of shame, just free. The discovery of flying was the moment that Chris knew he had found the thing that would occupy him for the rest of his life. Until that point, riding had been his passion. All that changed the first time he went up in an aeroplane.

He had joined the Royal Flying Corps in late 1914 because a friend from school had suggested it. Flying seemed just the ticket for him, but not because he was afraid of the fight. It was the opposite; the challenge was something he knew would exhilarate him. And it had.

From the first moment he had stepped into the back of an aeroplane to be instructed on flying, it seemed as if he had found the reason he had been put on this planet. The instructors could see that flying was an almost mystical experience for him. He could not spend enough time in the air. Unlike the other flyers who spent their time drinking and chasing young women near their headquarters, Chris would be with the engineers and the mechanics learning everything he could about the planes and what made them work. He knew this knowledge might be the difference between life and death.

It was.

His knowledge of how a plane handled in the air gave the engineers valuable insights when he was with them on the ground. He made his planes lighter, more aerodynamic and manoeuvrable. Any edge that could be gained was sought. Chris took every aircraft to the very edge of its capability in tandem with men as passionate as he was. Most pilots went to France with as little as thirty hours flying experience. Thanks to his obsessive interest in the planes and helping the engineers, Chris had nearly double that.

He was in the grip of an obsession. They all were. It was a happy madness because they were still somewhat shielded from what was happening at the front. It's difficult to appreciate the butchery and the bloodshed when you are twenty thousand feet up in the air.

By early 1915, he was in the air over France. At the start he was an eye in the sky, observing troop movements, armaments, blind spots, weakly defended areas. Often, he would see the Hun in the air flying in the other direction. At the start, they would wave to one another. Of course there were stories that the Germans were shooting at them in the air. Then the stories were no longer stories. It was true.

Soon they went up in pairs. He would pilot, his partner, the gunner, would shoot. His first dogfight was a Pyrrhic victory. The German plane had crashed but his gunner was dead. That was the day that Chris realised he was at war.

And so Chris, just over six months after he had first stepped into a plane, entered the war in earnest. He would make them pay for killing his gunner. And he did. Dogfights were not common occurrences, but Chris slowly began to amass a decent record against the Hun. More importantly, the gunners trusted him. He took no unnecessary risks. He looked after his men.

But the Hun were always ahead of them. By late 1915, the balance of power in the air had shifted dramatically in favour of the Germans. They had developed a method for using a machine gun operated by the flyer. This gave them not only superior firepower but also quicker reaction time thanks to their smaller and more manoeuvrable aeroplanes. Chris lost a lot of friends that autumn and winter.

By then he had long since fallen out of love with flying. It was a deadly pastime. Survival was no longer in his hands; it was no longer a function of his own capability. Dogfights were not won in the skies over Flanders. Instead, victory was forged in an engineer's designs. It was a battle of superior technology and Britain was losing.

The situation was almost untenable until spring of 1916. At this point, morale was shot, and death seemed like it would be an escape from the unrelenting terror. Miraculously, the British produced a fighter plane that could match the Germans. The DH2 was a single-seater biplane with the engine behind the pilot. It carried a Lewis Machine Gun that was forward firing. The absence of an engine in front gave the pilot an uninterrupted view of his target. All of a sudden, the Germans were on the run.

Thanks to Mick Mannock, a brilliant British flyer who had advanced techniques on fighting in the sky, they were out thinking the Germans in the air. They followed his method of attacking out of the sun. Any enemy caught this way had almost no time to react. All of a sudden, Britain was beginning to rule the air as well as the waves. Chris found his love of flying returning. It was not the fighting he feared, it was the unequal battle they had faced until the new plane's arrival. Now it was the enemy who had the problem. Better aircraft and a British man's natural sporting instincts made this a very big challenge for the Germans.

It would not last long, though.

The Germans soon closed the gap in technical capability. The short period of superiority was over. Like the fighting on the ground, the war in the air was one of attrition. Slowly, inexorably, Chris saw the number of chaps he'd come over with slowly whittle away. There was barely half a dozen of the original contingent.

Many times they said to him that he could stop. He'd done his bit. Time to let the younger chaps have a crack at the Boche. He could do a better job on the ground, training the new lads.

It was tempting.

Yet, Chris knew that to leave while the War was still in the balance was not something he could do. He didn't blame those that did. Sometimes, as he lay awake at night, he cursed himself for not doing as they had done.

He knew enough about gambling to know that his chances of catching one were the same however long he had been flying. The one area where the odds became stacked against you was Balloon-busting.

'Ever been balloon-busting?' asked Chris to young Johnstone who had arrived two weeks earlier. Johnstone had just left Harrow. He had the hands of a musician, the body of a Greek God and the eye of a flyer according to those that had been up with him the previous week.

'No,' replied Johnstone. 'I gather it can be a bit hairy.'

Balloon-busting was the practice of shooting down the enemy's observation balloons. More than dogfights, this accounted for the bulk of the Royal Flying Corps casualties.

'Hairy? You can say that again. Those balloons are surrounded by anti-aircraft guns, dozens of machine guns and, oh yes, a hundred rifles all taking pot shots at you, especially once they pull the balloons down towards the ground to give their boys a better chance at shooting you.'

'Sounds fun,' said Johnstone and Chris had to admire his pluck. He hadn't batted an eyelid. What a country England was that it could produce such men as this. Men? Boys. Yet, he would be a man soon enough. War did that to you.

'That's not the worst bit,' said Chris grimly.

'I had a feeling there was more,' grinned Johnstone.

'You have to get close enough to make sure it goes up in flames.'

'How close?'

'Close enough to get your eyebrows singed,' said Chris.

They headed off soon after dawn. Did senior officers really believe that a dawn departure would catch the enemy unawares, napping in their bunks waiting for their 10am call? They never did. And this time was no different.

Chris led Johnstone and another new boy, Atkins, low over the fields, the trees, the hedgerows. So low, in fact, the occasional cow ducked for cover, and they gave a young farmer and his girlfriend a bit of a fright as they skimmed over a haystack sending the top layer of straw flying. That put a smile on their faces. It didn't last long.

They heard the enemy before they saw him. And what they saw made their hearts begin to race. All around them was a sea of mud and metal. The Germans soon began to spit out a deadly welcome. Bit by bit the Germans hauled the balloons down. Atkins banked first. Youthful bravado. Too early, thought Chris who always left it until the last minute. Perhaps not bravado. Perhaps it was just terror and a desire to get the job done and away. This Chris could understand.

As if reaching the belt of anti-aircraft guns was not bad enough, they saw the first sight of a German aeroplane. If there were more they would have to call it all off. He caught Johnstone's eye and pointed towards it. Johnstone veered off to engage the German flyer while Atkins and he continued on their path towards the balloons. Except the damn fool Atkins was now too low. Less than five hundred. He was a sitting duck…

As soon as he thought this he saw the metal rain tear the wings of the young flyer's aircraft. Then it seemed to flip over and career down to the ground. Chris looked away. His eyes were on the fast-descending balloons.

He risked a glance to his right. Johnstone was in a dogfight, but the youngster had pluck and more importantly, talent. The balloons were less than six hundred feet from the ground now. He bore down on them. The sound of the aircraft's engine wheezing under the strain was blotted out by the crump of guns and the patter of bullets. So far so good he thought grimly.

He began firing at the two balloons. The closer he got the more of a risk it became. He scored as he knew he would. But had he left it too late? He vaulted the balloon just as it went up in flames.

171

His hands and face felt as if they were on fire. Then he realised they were. He screamed. Instinct tore him away from the deadly gunfire and made him perform an Immelmann turn which saw his plane climb vertically away from the enemy and re-positioned him towards his own lines. He sensed an aircraft suddenly appear to his left.

It was Johnstone.

He was pointing frantically at Chris's engine. Yes, I can bloody see it's on fire he thought. His nerves were screaming at him as the pain almost caused him to pass out. It was a wall of heat in front of and behind. The air was burning around him. For a moment, the smoke blinded him then he saw Johnstone flying on ahead. From somewhere in the depths of his brain he realised they were going in the right direction.

How he found the capacity to keep flying while his body was shutting down, he never knew. Perhaps it would have been for the best if he had gone down in flames. His eyes could see little in the heat haze. For all he knew he was on his way to Berlin. He had to get the aircraft down. It didn't matter where.

He was screaming through a lipless mouth as he descended and seconds away from unconsciousness when he touched down somewhere in No Man's Land. He knew not where because he'd already passed out.

'Notwithstanding the evidence you see before you,' finished Chris, 'They patched me up pretty well. I was, if you'll forgive me Mary, a bloody mess.'

172

Mary smiled and nodded to Chris. No forgiveness was needed. The extraordinary story had moved her greatly. She reached out and held his hand. In the space of twenty minutes she felt she had come to know the man before her very well. It was clear from Kit that he had once had a wild side. A devil-may-care streak that had propelled him to war, towards aeroplanes in particular and a fate that was shared by so many that had joined this service. That he had survived was a minor miracle. Then again, that Kit or anyone had come through the carnage of Flanders was extraordinary.

'What about that chap you mentioned? Johnstone I think his name was. Did he make it through?' asked Kit.

'He did, oddly enough. I think what happened to me affected him. I saw a lot of me in him when he arrived, but afterwards he was a damn sight, sorry Mary, more careful. Good chap. Still writes to me. Invited me to his wedding.'

'You didn't go,' said Mary. There was just a hint of scold in her voice that made the two men smile.

'No, Mary. How could I? It's the bride's day. If I'd shown up…'

He left the rest unsaid. Mary was still holding his hand. Tears glistened in her eyes now, but she was not going to let him off so lightly.

'I think that on this one occasion if the girl is anything and your friend certainly sounds as if he is, then they would not have minded in the least. In a strange way you are probably as responsible as anyone for ensuring that he was there to be married.'

Chris suddenly inhaled deeply and looked away. A tear trickled down his face. His voice was barely a whisper when he said, 'He said that Mary. Even Martha, the girl he married, wrote to me. I just sent my apologies.'

'That was very sweet of them, Chris,' said Kit. 'I believe they meant every word.'

Chris nodded but did not reply. They were silent for a moment. The sandwiches they had made were not going to eat themselves. As if by tacit agreement they turned away from the War. For once it was a subject that had needed to be discussed but not dwelt on. They were all alive despite the risk they'd faced. In every sense it was time to move on. Mary hoped that this message would be understood by Chris without further talk. The War was over, they would have the rest of their lives to deal with what they had faced. She hoped he would see that hiding away was not the answer.

Around four in the morning, they went their separate ways to bed. He was disappointed to hear that they were leaving at Gerry's request. That they were leaving had surprised him, but he did not want to argue with Gerry. After all, he acknowledged, Hookie had, effectively, absolved him and Gerry from any wrongdoing.

On this Kit was not so sure now. A thought had occurred to him earlier in the evening that had not been discussed so far with anyone except Mary. It was one so extraordinary that he had not dared raise it with either Tamsin or Gerry.

If the body of the dead man was not Teddy's but Damien Blythe, then where was Teddy? Had he killed Blythe or was he, himself, dead? If this were the case then no one of the family would be safe from investigation. No one. The reason for this was that the time of death was independent of Gerry and Chris's visit to the cottage on the fateful night Damien Blythe died. Neither Gerry nor Chris were in the clear now.

174

It seemed all the more reason for him to stay and help Hookie. Yet, Gerry had specifically asked him to leave. Of course, he may have wanted to protect both the family and, even, Kit and Mary from the attention of the press. Yet was it possible there was another reason?

Was Gerry hiding something?

22 Tuesday

Around nine the next morning Gerry was indeed hiding something. He stared at the letter that had arrived in the post. He felt sick with anger and fear. His breathing was spasmodic such was the constriction he felt as he read what his blackmailer was asking. The nightmare of the last few days was now reaching its conclusion. He had no place to run. No one to turn to. He was alone. The decision he faced was impossible, yet it had been made. He stared at the framed photographs on his office desk. There was one with his two boys: another with all four of them.

Before the War he had not been an emotional man, aside from the occasional outburst of anger. The War had changed all that. Tears fell freely these days. And they fell now. He was glad he had taken the precaution of locking the door.

Noises outside the door.

He heard Tamsin asking Vincent where he was. Quickly he wiped his tears on the sleeve of his tweed jacket and ran over to the library door and unlocked it just as Tamsin tried to enter. He turned away immediately as she came in so that she would not see his eyes. He went over to his desk and put the letter inside a drawer.

'Why did you lock the door?'

'Oh I don't know. Must have been instinct,' replied Gerry. He turned his attention to the window. 'Are Kit and Mary up yet?' he asked casually.

Tamsin had still not quite forgiven him for the previous evening but, at the same time, she could sense the strain he was under. There was no question he had felt unwell the previous evening. He'd fallen asleep quickly and slept through until almost eight. Gerry was normally an early riser and would be up and about by six.

'No, they haven't come down yet. Gerry are you sure about this?' she asked. Her voice betrayed her anxiety while, at the same time, yielded no criticism. She trusted her husband, yet this request had come out of the blue and, to her, seemed irrational.

'It's for the best, my love,' said Gerry turning towards her. He hoped that his eyes had cleared up sufficiently to avoid arousing any suspicion about the tears he had shed earlier.

'If you say so,' said Tamsin doubtfully. This was not meant to hurt him, but it did. And worse would follow. It was like a dagger in his heart. And all because of his feckless sister.

Carol.

She had caused all of this. By marrying a man like Teddy, she had begun a slow process of trouble for this family. At that moment he hated her. Yet he did not hate her enough to send her to the gallows. Even if Carol had no sense of family, he did. He always had. He was the head of the family, and this meant doing things that truly ripped his heart apart. It had happened during the War, and it was happening again.

'Sorry,' said Gerry simply. He walked over to her and took Tamsin in his arms. 'I love you so much. You and the boys are everything to me.'

177

Tamsin held him tightly, not quite sure what had brought this sudden surge of emotion on but welcoming it anyway. Whatever was wrong and she was convinced now that Gerry had something on his mind that he was not sharing, at least he would always put his family first.

He would, but just not in the way that Tamsin would have imagined or approved of.

Kit stared at the three suitcases. Two were Mary's, one was his. He'd always travelled light. Mary did so too, but as ever, this was relative. They looked at one another. Silence hung in the air like an unspoken regret. Neither were happy about the situation yet there was nothing to be done.

Mary went over to the window. It was a frosty morning but a vast improvement on the previous day. The sun was blindingly bright. This added to the pain of leaving.

'Pity. It's such a nice day. Look, there's Glory coming out into the paddock.'

'And Leonardo,' laughed Kit, looking over her head. Rather neatly, Mary fitted directly beneath his chin.

They saw Gerry walking across the lawn and down the steps towards the stables and paddock. His stride was long and raking. It was if he was escaping from the world to a hideaway where he was invulnerable.

It was almost ten now. Time for breakfast.

'Shall we?' asked Kit.

'Yes,' breathed Mary sadly.

On the landing they ran into Carol. She was dressed in her riding gear. She saw the way Kit and Mary were dressed and frowned.

'It's a lovely day. I thought we might go out for a ride. I'm hoping we can persuade Chris too.'

Kit was surprised and said, 'You obviously didn't hear. Gerry suggested that we should cut short our stay. It might look a little bad if we are here while the inquest is on.'

'Oh,' said Carol, unsure of what to say to that. 'I thought the inquest was this afternoon. What time are you leaving?' she asked uncertainly.

'We'll have breakfast and look to catch the train after midday,' said Mary as brightly as she could manage.

'I say,' said Carol. 'That's a bit of a dog. Do you want me to say something?' She seemed genuine enough to Kit, but the matter was settled. They were leaving. Any involvement, such as it was in the case, was at an end.

They entered the dining room. Breakfast had been laid out on the sideboard so that they could serve themselves. As they were doing so, Tamsin entered. Her eyes were bloodshot.

'Oh Tamsin,' said Mary, setting down her plate. She went over to their host, and they hugged.

'What's wrong?' asked Kit.

'Where shall I start?' asked Tamsin. This at least made her smile, but it was momentary. 'I was going to ask Gerry to reconsider about you, but I could see that it would be no use. Something's wrong. I know it. He's worried and I don't know what it is. He always tells me when something is wrong. You know Gerry, he can't lie. But he's hiding something. It's so obvious.'

'He knows he could never fool you, Tamsin,' pointed out Kit.

Tamsin laughed at this. Then she looked up at Kit.

179

'He's acting strangely, though. This morning when I went to see him in the library, I could have sworn he'd locked it. Then he put a letter away in his desk and came over to talk to me.'

'What did the letter say?' asked Mary.

'I didn't look,' said Tamsin, somewhat taken aback by the question. She was met with a querulous look from Mary and a smile from Kit. There was something reassuring about being married to a woman who would not let privacy cloud her conscience when it came to uncovering exactly what was troubling her man.

'You didn't look,' said Mary slowly and deliberately. Her intention was transparent, and Kit hoped that it was clear to Tamsin that conventional notions of confidentiality could be suspended when the occasion demanded. This was one such occasion.

'Should we look?' asked Tamsin, a little shocked but also, Kit suspected, a little bit excited and hopeful too. The thought had probably crossed her mind. Now she had validation for her guilty instinct.

'Yes, let's,' said Mary firmly, but with a wide smile and wide innocent eyes.

It was a tribute to the quality of the breakfast on offer that Kit set his plate down with more than a pang of regret. This was one small trouble when married to a young woman with an insatiable appetite for detection. Kit's appetite was no less than his wife's in this regard, but still, the smell of the bacon was as powerful as the call of the Sirens faced by Odysseus.

They spilled into the library and ran over to the desk. They tried the middle drawer.

Locked.

'It's locked,' said Tamsin. Kit had worked that out for himself but wisely said nothing. Mary kept lookout while Tamsin hunted for the keys. Fruitlessly as it turned out. 'What shall we do?'

'May I?' asked Kit who, without permission, extracted a hairpin from Tamsin's hair.

'You can open it with that?' asked Tamsin askance. 'I thought this only happened in detective novels.' Apparently, it had a basis in real life too.

'A little trick I learned in Russia,' said Kit, fiddling with the lock.

'Who did you take the hairpin from?' asked Mary, eyes narrowed dangerously.

Kit's eyes shot up at this question. Only a woman could find the necessity to inquire about former flames at a time like this, he thought disloyally. Mind you, he realised, she was not wrong to wonder. A young brunette by the name of Veronika if Kit's memory served.

'Roger Ratcliffe taught me,' said Kit. This had the virtue of being half true. Thankfully, any further discussion on Kit's facility with hairpins was adjourned, permanently he hoped, by the click of the drawer lock. Kit stood back to allow Tamsin to open it.

Tamsin looked at Kit, unsure of what to do. Mary's patience was becoming Agatha-like, Kit noticed, in its sparing quantity.

'Well, go on,' said Mary, just a hint of hardness in her otherwise sweet voice.

'Very well,' said Tamsin. She opened the drawer and saw the envelope.

'Hurry,' said Mary. 'Gerry's coming.'

This sharpened everyone's thinking. Tamsin had the letter open in a moment. She read the contents and gasped.

'Oh my word,' she said.

'Quickly,' urged Mary.

Kit took the letter from Tamsin, scanned it in a moment and then stuffed it back inside the envelope. Seconds later he had it back in the drawer and was fiddling once more with the lock.

'Quickly,' hissed Mary, whose vocabulary had become dangerously limited at that moment. They could all hear Gerry's voice in the hallway. He was coming to the library.

The drawer locked clicked just as Gerry opened the door. Kit grabbed Tamsin unceremoniously and pulled her towards the bookshelf.

'Where was that book?' he asked her.

'Have you read *She Loved a Loaded Gun*?' said Tamsin, disingenuously.

Kit glanced at Tamsin to see if she was joking. She wasn't.

'Yes, that one,' said Kit doubtfully. Mary strolled over to Kit and took the hairpin from his hand. Her frown was at full Inquisition mode. Kit smiled and shrugged hopefully. Mary's eyes were now slits of suspicion. Tamsin took the hairpin back from Mary and replaced it in her hair.

'Oh, hullo, I see you're up,' said Gerry, with a pale imitation of a smile.

23

Kit, Mary and Tamsin regrouped down at the stables. They went under a pretext of making a final pilgrimage to take see Northern Glory being put through his paces. It was an impressive sight and gave them all pause for thought as they considered what Kit and Tamsin had both seen in the letter addressed to Gerry. The contents had been shared with Mary by Tamsin as they descended the steps towards the horses.

'Blackmail,' said Mary.

'Blackmail,' agreed Kit.

Tamsin was almost in tears as she stared at the horse that Gerry had reared and trained to become a Derby hopeful. Glory seemed to know it was being watched. His head was up, and he seemed to veer in the direction of the spectators.

'Show off,' said Mary.

This made Tamsin laugh, but the tears now began to flow steadily. She felt Mary's arm around her waist.

'What's happening? I don't understand it, Kit,' said Tamsin.

Kit had been silent for most of the walk down to the stables. He was lost in thought. There were a number of permutations, rather like in chess which he excelled at. He went through the various scenarios, one by one, trying them out in his mind. Without more evidence he just had speculations on the murder but, at least, a plan was forming in his mind. It would certainly find approval with Mary and Tamsin. He needed to speak to Hookie. His involvement was imperative.

Three things were now clear to Kit. Firstly, Teddy was probably dead, but this was not conclusive as the photograph might have been staged. This meant that the dead body in the house would be found by the inquest to be the missing young man, Damien Blythe. So, a murder had been committed. Secondly, Gerry was being blackmailed by someone who clearly knew that the dead body was not Teddy's. This person had to be the killer of Damien Blythe. Finally, one of the Tudor family was potentially a killer. If the blackmailer was to be believed, it was Carol. This was the only construction that Kit could put on the reason for sending Gerry a blackmail letter. The blackmailer had enough to convict one of the family and Gerry was having to contemplate the unthinkable.

So was Kit.

The idea that one of his friends was a killer was unbearable but had to be faced objectively. At least two murders had been committed. This meant that all of the alibis were redundant. As these thoughts raced around his mind he became aware that he had not yet answered the question from Tamsin.

'Gerry's being told he must sell Northern Glory. This is blackmail. It's not clear what else is being held over him beyond the photograph we saw and the accusation that Carol was responsible. For all we know, and Gerry may not realise

184

this, the photograph may have been staged; we just don't know.'

Tears fell freely down Tamsin's face as Kit was speaking. She was smart and had clearly worked out the same implications as Kit had. The only reason why they would be blackmailing Gerry is if he or Carol was connected in some way with the events a few nights ago.

'Tamsin, there's no evidence to suggest that Gerry has done anything wrong never mind Carol. At the moment we have a vile accusation and a photograph. They will need more than that if they think that they have something that will stand up in court. A body, for example. We still cannot be sure Teddy is dead.'

Kit sounded less convinced in the last point. However, there was little to be gained from alarming Tamsin and helping the blackmailer. He continued, 'Aside from his trip into Newmarket with Chris, we can all pretty much account for Gerry's whereabouts on the day that, well let's say, the man died. Or, to put it another way, unless the inquest today suggests otherwise, the dead man had to have died that day. It's impossible that any post mortem would declare otherwise because the level of rigor mortis would have been more advanced. If it had been, then Hookie would have discounted everyone's alibi before now. So we know that Gerry, or Chris, could not possibly have killed this Damien Blythe if that's who is there. As to who did, Lord only knows. It might even be Teddy for all we know.'

This seemed to reassure Tamsin a little, but Kit was still very concerned. If Teddy was dead then it was possible that he had been killed in the days before he and Mary had arrived.

185

'But what can we do?' asked Tamsin.

Kit took her hand and said, 'We are not leaving, that's for sure. Mary and I will take a room at the Rutland Arms in town and continue to investigate. The inquest today is bound to find for unlawful killing of Damien Blythe. Meanwhile, Teddy will become a suspect in his death. I will speak to Hookie about what we have seen.'

Tamsin looked at Kit fearfully.

Kit exhaled and tried to maintain a positive tone in his voice, 'Tamsin, I am certain that Gerry and Chris have done nothing wrong.'

Mary frowned and glanced up at Kit. He had made no mention of Carol. So far he had studiously avoided mentioning Carol. She wondered why. Tamsin nodded albeit a little reluctantly. She trusted Kit and felt reassured that he would not abandon them. Where the trail might lead was more disturbing.

'Incidentally, Tamsin, when Mary and I were at the house yesterday, we noticed that a painting had been removed and another put up in its place. I don't suppose you know if Teddy and Carol had any valuable paintings in the cottage. The ones I saw were not of the first rank.'

'They had a Stubbs, I remember. It was a wedding present from Gerry's dad and mum.'

Kit looked at Mary who shook her head.

'That's interesting. I'm sure I would have remembered seeing a Stubbs in the house.'

They walked back up to the house to say their goodbyes to everyone there. Chris did not make an appearance, but Gerry stayed to see them off. He looked a little sheepishly at Kit as they stood by the car.

'I'm sorry old man,' he said shaking hands. 'There's just so much going on with the inquest later.'

'I understand,' said Kit. Mary came over and gave Gerry a hug and even treated Vincent to a hug and a peck on the cheek. The venerable butler blushed furiously but seemed none the worse for his ordeal.

To Gerry's surprise, Tamsin insisted on taking them into Newmarket and they set off just after eleven. It was a short drive into Newmarket. The Rutland Arms was a large redbrick hotel at the top of the town. Kit had drunk and been drunk, there many times before with his schoolfriends Chubby, Olly and Spunky.

'How will you attend the inquest?' asked Tamsin as they stepped down from the car.

Kit answered, 'Mary will go. We shall find her an appropriately hideous wig to disguise her. I daresay I shall have to miss it.'

Mary looked at him archly and asked, 'Are you so recognisable Aston?'

Tamsin burst out laughing at this. It was a delightful sound and had happened all too rarely on this weekend. She said, 'I wonder if there are a few angry fathers or jealous husbands who might want to have a few words with him.'

'I'm not sure that's helpful Tamsin,' said Kit, trying not to look at Mary. She was giggling which in the end made Kit laugh too.

They bid farewell to Tamsin with a promise to do all they could to help clear the matter up. Both felt a tightness in their chest as they watched the car chug down the street. Mary turned immediately to Kit and asked, 'This isn't going to end happily, is it?'

187

Kit breathed in deeply before replying, 'I fear not. Now, let's check in and then go and see Hookie. The inquest starts in a couple of hours. We also need to find you a wig.'

'Not too hideous.'

'And glasses. I don't want you diverting attention from the press and all the men there. We should add a cushion or three also.'

'Beast,' was Mary's only response to this.

Half an hour later, Kit and Mary stepped into Chief Inspector Hook's office at Newmarket police station. Hook split his time between Cambridge and Newmarket as he was often called upon to investigate equine-related crime. Kit looked around the office and grinned at Hook who was scowling with undisguised displeasure.

The office was not large and consisted of a small table with a comfortable leather chair on the window side, clearly something that Hook had treated himself to as well as a couple of chairs on the other. There was a hideous painting of a hunting scene that his wife had bought him some twenty years previously. Hook hated it, which Kit knew, hence the fact it was often half hidden behind various awards that he'd collected over the years.

'It hasn't changed,' said Kit nostalgically.

'The cells haven't changed either,' said Hook irritably.

Mary glanced sharply at Kit who smiled and shrugged, 'It was only for one night.'

'Really?' said Hook.

'Each time,' added Kit, quickly.

Mary chuckled at this and said, 'We can add that to the list of many things you have yet to tell me.'

Hook rolled his eyes at this, snapping at the new arrivals, 'Enough of the romantic comedy, can we move to the detective part? Why on earth are you here? In case you were unaware, I have an inquest to attend.'

'I'm sure you'll be the star turn, Hookie,' said Kit sitting down with Mary. 'I think it would be an even better performance if you are acquainted with a few more facts than I suspect you have at your disposal currently.'

Hook leaned forward. His eyes narrowed; he was all business now.

'Go on.'

Kit glanced at Mary and sighed. It was time, for better or worse, to take the plunge.

'Gerry is being blackmailed.'

Hook's eyes widened and he sat back in his seat. Moments later a cigarette was being extracted from his silver case. He tapped it on the desk then lit it. Kit knew better than to say anything at these moments, but Mary was positively dying to hear what he thought about this development. Kit quickly summed up the contents of the letter he had seen while Hook smoked reflectively, his bright eyes taking in everything. When Kit had finished, Hook said nothing. It took a minute, but then it came in a positive rush.

'Teddy's dead,' said Hook.

'I think so, too,' agreed Kit.

'He died long before Friday night.'

Kit nodded, 'Yes, this is not the first note. It looked like the second or even third.'

'Who took the photograph?'

189

'The same person that killed Damien Blythe, I suspect. Unfortunately, I have no idea who that might be,' said Kit.

'Indeed. Who developed the photograph?'

'Had to be someone who is either very discreet, very stupid or...'

'The photographer himself. There can't be many people who have such a hobby. We can investigate who would have purchased the chemicals needed to develop such photographs. We're dealing with an amateur. I mean this is something that they should have thought of beforehand,' said Hook. He fixed his eyes on Kit. 'We need to find out where the drop off will occur and when.'

Kit put his hands up and said, 'Gerry has thrown us out.' He smiled when he saw the policeman's reaction. 'Politely, I should add. He suggested that we should curtail our trip, at least until the dust settles.'

'I see. That's unhelpful. Feels like he has something to hide,' said Hook.

Or someone, thought Kit.

'We'll have to put a man on him and see where he goes. He doesn't know you know?'

'No,' said Kit.

'You won't be able to go to the inquest. He'll be there.'

Mary extracted from her bag, and held up, a blonde wig.

'Very fetching,' commented Hook with a grimace.

Silence descended on the office for a few moments. It was a loud silence, the sort you can hear as well as feel. It was broken by Hook who pointed out what Kit had considered earlier.

Hook said, 'It puts all of them in the frame now; you do realise that, not just Carol.'

190

24

The inquest was held at the large Memorial Hall built only a few years previously in 1914. Kit and Mary walked towards the Hall which was one of the first main buildings to appear in the town. At a certain point, Kit ducked away as Mary strode forward and joined the queue looking to enter the hall to watch the proceedings.

Mary was sporting a wig, glasses and a cushion strategically placed to ensure that no one would take the risk between speaking about pregnancy or useful diets in her presence. She found a seat at the back of the room which had its numbers swelled by press and onlookers from other stables who were intrigued by what was going to take place. Teddy Harrison was known to all, and rumours had already begun to circulate as to what might crop up during the hearing.

To Mary's right, sat nine people who she took to be the jury. At the front, behind a desk, was Chief Inspector Hook and a man whom Mary took to be a lawyer. He was wearing a three-piece suit with watch chain. Hook, meanwhile, was wearing a dark rumpled suit, the top button of his shirt loose. He was calmly smoking a cigarette. His eyes scanned the room before they alighted on Mary. He nodded slowly to her, and a half-smile crossed his face.

At the front sat a number of people, including Gerry, Roger Sexton, Jason Trent and Bryn Cain. Carol sat one row back alongside Tamsin. Both were dressed in black. Everyone stood up when a door opened. In stepped the Coroner, Dr Marmaduke Pike. The Coroner was large of girth, round-faced and might have been anywhere between forty and seventy. He was a man that had experienced most things except, perhaps, hunger. On the bridge of his aquiline nose was perched a pince-nez. They partly hid a pair of eyes that even the Coroner's closest friends would have called beady. Hook rose last of all and was first to sit down. He glanced towards the coroner and smiled mirthlessly.

Dr Marmaduke Pike and Chief Inspector Hook had cordially hated one another for over twenty years. Time, far from mellowing their feelings towards the other, had only served to sharpen the sword and water the seed, so to speak. Both thought the other arrogant and while Hook would, on those rare moments of introspection, acknowledge his tendency towards being a curmudgeon, Pike was a martinet, utterly immune to the distaste he roused in people. He took himself seriously. Someone had to. Hook certainly didn't and took great pleasure in calling the coroner, 'Dukie'.

Pike surveyed the room and noted how crowded it was. A satisfied smile appeared on his face. He placed his papers down in front of him and slowly arranged them. Out of the corner of his eye he saw Hook shake his head.

'Let us make a start,' said Pike.

'Hear, hear,' murmured Hook with just enough volume to carry to his old sparring partner. The Coroner's eyes flared momentarily and then he quickly fought to compose himself.

And so began the inquest.

193

Six hours later a wigless Mary sat with Kit in the hotel restaurant ready to order dinner. The restaurant could have been called "Ye olde" such was its charm. This being England, charm was denoted by a spectacularly low ceiling which forced waiting staff and customers alike to walk in a crouch. This was a consequence of the fact that the room dated back to a time when it was accustomed to being a meeting place for undernourished, undersized serfs. The march of time had seen a rise in nutritional standards as well as the rank of the Rutland Arms' clientele.

The inquest had ended shortly before six allowing Marmaduke Pike to attend a hunt ball and the press to make it back to London before ten in the evening.

'Well, it was a bit drier than I thought it would be,' said Mary. 'The Coroner began by saying the purpose of the inquest was to ascertain identity of the deceased, the place of death, the time of death and how the deceased came by their death.'

'Usual thing. I suspect he's said it a few dozens of times,' said Kit, before drinking some white wine. 'He was Coroner back in the day when I first dipped my toes into the world of murder.'

Mary's eyes narrowed at this, but she pressed on with a summary of the afternoon.

'Mr Hook had obviously heard it a hundred times, too. He puffed his cheeks out as if it were going to be a long afternoon.'

Kit laughed at this and said, 'Yes, they have history, that pair. Still, it seemed to go rather quickly in the end.'

'Yes, I think the Coroner must have had a dinner event to go to tonight. He didn't hang around. First up was Hookie. He gave a brief run through of the events leading up to the gunshot. He mentioned about the disappearance of Damien Blythe. Then he confirmed that the police were of the view that the dead body was not Teddy Harrison but Damien Blythe. The Coroner didn't ask any questions on this. He seemed to accept it as fact. Yes, I rather have the feeling neither of them like one another.'

'They don't,' confirmed Kit, but rather infuriatingly did not expand on this point. Mary frowned but was too keen to deal with the matter in hand than Kit's past misdemeanours.

'The next person up was a Doctor Sampson. He confirmed the cause of death, by gunshot obviously. He added that the man had been drugged but was alive up until the point that the gun had been fired. I won't bore you with the finer points of rigor mortis. At this point they began to work backwards, but the Coroner asked a few questions on this. They spoke with Mr Sexton then Mr Trent next. Both explained about the calls they had received and why they had come and what had happened when they opened the door.'

'Much grizzly detail?' asked Kit.

'No, the Coroner moved them on pretty quickly through a brief description of what they saw. Mr Hook had already given more detail earlier on the mechanics of how the pulley systems had engineered the gun shot. He made it clear that this was the cause of death.'

'Anything new from our two friends?'

195

'No, not really. It was pretty dry. I think the fact that the dead man was not Teddy Harrison and neither of the two men had any earthly idea who Damien Blythe was, made it rather pointless to pursue this at the inquest. Gerry was up next. Again, it was a fairly short statement of the known facts. Chris was mentioned then, and Bryn Cain followed Gerry to make a short statement. They spoke to a number of other people then who I don't know but were known to Damien Blythe.

'Not Carol?'

'No, oddly. I think by then it was clear that it was not Teddy who had died. Mr Hook had steered them away from this, in fact, when he confirmed that Carol had not been near the house since the Wednesday night when she left.' Kit nodded without asking anything else about Carol. Mary took this as her cue to continue, 'At the end, they called Mr Hook back up to give his conclusions based on the evidence they had assembled. After this the Coroner summed it up and sent the jury away to deliberate.'

'I'll bet they didn't take long.'

Mary laughed at this.

'Yes, I can imagine the first minute was to take a vote and the next thirty to have a cup of tea and gossip.'

'So an unlawful killing it was and now Hookie will be given more resources to investigate the murder and Teddy's disappearance,' said Kit.

'And the blackmail letter,' added Mary.

'That will remain off the balance sheet for the time being, I suspect. However, it's by far his biggest lead. He won't be able to stay quiet about it for long.'

'Will he bring Gerry and Chris back in for questioning?'

196

'I imagine he will try to avoid that until he sees what develops with this blackmail attempt. The fact is both of them are under suspicion. Either Gerry is a murderer and is being blackmailed because of it or he knows who the murderer is and is trying to protect them. I don't suppose you were able to speak to Hookie?'

'No, he was surrounded by the press. I left him to it. He didn't seem to be in a good mood.'

Kit laughed at this, he added, 'I can imagine he would have been pretty short with some of the questions.'

As they were chatting, a man approached the table. Kit saw Mary's eyes widen. He turned around to find Jason Trent.

'Would you like to join us?' asked Mary.

'Would you mind?' he said. 'The place is packed. No tables left.'

He sat down and ordered a drink from a nearby waiter. Then he asked the question that was also on Kit and Mary's mind.

'Why aren't you up at Gerry's?'

Kit smiled and replied, 'Could ask you the same question old boy.'

This made Trent laugh. He said, 'You probably gather that Carol and I had a falling out the other day. My star has fallen somewhat.'

Mary looked on sympathetically. She wasn't sure that she liked Trent, but Kit's impression was that he had more to him than the poor first impression she had received gave her pause to give him the benefit of the doubt.

'How did the inquest go?' asked Kit.

'You weren't there?' said Trent in surprise.

197

'No, for the same reason that we are no longer up at Gerry's. It was felt my presence might be a distraction.'

Trent did not see why that should be but was too smart to come out and say this. Mary decided to press a little, albeit gently, on what he made of the day.

'What did they say about Teddy?'

'Bit of a shock that,' replied Trent, taking a sip of his gin and tonic. 'They don't think he was the one who died in the cottage. They think it's some young chap named Blythe. That puts Teddy in the frame for murder if you ask me.'

Kit made no comment on this. He moved in a different direction.

'Have you been down in London?'

'Yes, I only came up for the hearing and I'll be back down to London tomorrow morning. It won't do much for my banking career if I'm caught up in all of this.'

Kit and Mary eyed one another as they listened. At least they had some idea of what had caused the rupture with Carol and his sudden departure. However, it might also have allowed him to get photographs developed and have the Stubbs' painting valued or sold privately if it was the case that it had been stolen. This latter point was for Hook to follow up on with Carol.

'I suppose it won't help Gerry much either with other horse owners. They may decide to stay clear of a trainer implicated in murder,' said Kit.

'Yes,' agreed Trent. 'I can definitely see that. Of course, the fact that he has Northern Glory will help him, especially if he continues the form he showed as a two-year-old.'

'Are there many people interested in buying him?' asked Mary.

This made Trent smile.

'Oh there are. I can name half a dozen who would gladly take him off Gerry's hands. If I were Gerry, I'd have done the deal a long time ago. He won't listen to me, of course and now, well, I won't be allowed through the front door with Carol angry at me.'

'Has Sexton been at Gerry to sell Glory do you know?'

'Oh yes,' said Trent, laughing rather bitterly. 'Bryn Cain as well. I think they are all trying to muscle in on this partnership game.'

'How much would it be worth to a middle man if they were able to get Gerry to sell Glory?'

Trent's eyes narrowed and he stiffened perceptibly when Kit said this. Then, almost as if he were aware of his own physical response to the question, he relaxed and smiled.

'Thousands,' he said simply. He opened his cigarette case and offered one to Kit and Mary. Both declined. He lit a cigarette and blew a smoke ring.

'Yes, it would be worth thousands to whoever could put Gerry together with a buyer for Northern Glory.' Then he added sullenly, 'But sadly, that won't be me.'

25

Lambeth, London: November 1921

Rex Palmer, like any freeborn Englishman, enjoyed a drink or two. It was his right. His forefathers had probably fought for this right over countless generations. He worked ten hours a day at the dock and who was to say that he couldn't enjoy a convivial half or two with like-minded friends in places dedicated to providing an open door for men such as he? In fact, he supplemented his income with petty crime of the smash and grab variety rather than Raffles-like cracksmanship. Not that he would have been very familiar with EW Hornung's creation.

Palmer was a shade under six feet tall and well-made, although his penchant for ending the day with mates at the pub was seeing a noticeable widening around his girth. He was a powerful man. He liked to think of himself as a strongman. His friends thought him a strongman. They knew better than to argue that point, especially when he'd had a few.

This is what had attracted Dulcie to him. She liked men who were men. Rex was that and more. She liked to know who was boss, he claimed. This was perhaps an exaggeration, but it went down well at The Four Horseshoes when he said it. He said it often. Smiles strained to keep in his good graces when he did.

When Dulcie left him, it was, at first, a joke to him. She'll come back on her hands and knees, just you see if she doesn't, he'd say. When she didn't he pretended not to care. He'd show her that she was just another one of dozens he'd had and would have.

Yet a thought gnawed at him like a toothache. *She'd left him*. This was not part of the Rex Palmer story. He was the one that decided. Not some bird who had been sly enough to get a ring on her finger. Something was wrong and slowly he began to resent the fact that she had been the one who had gone.

In fact, he did more than resent it. At home, at night, alone, he knew that she wanted to be somewhere else. Maybe she was with someone else. Who'd have her. After him what else was there? Yet, the possibility that she had left him for someone else took root. One of the boys had suggested as much at the beginning. Palmer had set him right on that. No one mentioned it again.

Problem was, what it if was true?

Three weeks after she'd left him, Palmer began to look. At first he went to her friends. None of them had seen her. He wasn't sure he believed them, but he could hardly beat a confession out of them in the streets. It was then an idea struck Palmer. They all had husbands. He couldn't threaten the girls, but he could certainly put pressure on the men.

This was more in his line.

So he began to go to pubs where some of his wife's friends and their husbands went. He knew a few of the men anyway.

They certainly knew him. Or of him. Not one refused him. Not one. They knew the score all right.

Then he waited.

It took a few days before one of them came up with the goods. He met him at his local. He was with a couple of his boys. He took the bloke off to one side. No point in alerting his mates to the fact that he had put the word out that he wanted to find Dulcie.

The man in question was just the sort of hen-pecked dew-dropper that Palmer detested. He looked up at Palmer as if grateful to be in his presence or perhaps he was just fearful. Palmer listened to what he had to say. A house in Lambeth. There were other women there too. This sounded promising. At least she wasn't with another bloke. That would have looked bad. He pointed a large finger at the man.

'If you're lying to me it'll be the worse for you. But if it's true then there's a drink in it for you, all right?'

The man nodded gratefully and when Palmer suggested he run along, he did so. Palmer returned to his three mates.

'All right boys, time to drink up. We're going to have a bit of fun now.'

'What's happening?' asked a man named Squinty, on account of him having only one eye courtesy of Fritz.

Palmer told them as they trooped over in the direction of the house.

It would be fair to say that Dan 'Haymaker' Harris had become a frequent visitor to the house that Kit, through the generosity of Haymaker's employer, had agreed to keep an occasional eye on. As Dulcie Palmer handed him a cup of tea that same evening, it was not hard to guess why.

Haymaker, notwithstanding an appearance that could scare small children from fifty feet away, at least until they came to him, was a gentleman. He had a respect, no, make that fear, of women that had been instilled in him by his formidable mother, Dixie. Any species that could include his mother, he reckoned, was one to treat carefully.

Since being taken on the previous week as their unofficial guardsman, he had come to know the ladies in the house, and they had come to love him. It seemed an extraordinary paradox to the ladies how a man so tough looking could, in fact, be the gentlest of souls. They sensed the respect that he had for them, and he could see, in turn, that they trusted him despite how he looked and what he was.

Haymaker was under no illusion as to what he was. As a former and highly unsuccessful boxer, he had little to offer the arts, medicine or law. However, his appearance alone was worth its weight in gold when it came to ensuring that his employers, Charles 'Wag' McDonald and his brother Bert were treated with the utmost respect wherever they went.

The ladies made room on the sofa so that Dulcie could take her place beside Haymaker. She coloured slightly as she sat down and shot a glance in the direction of two of the ladies. One of them had sightless eyes, but there was a smile on her face. She could not see but she could certainly hear and feel. There was nothing wrong with her other senses and they were telling her that romance was in the air. Dulcie may have said otherwise, but there was little conviction in her disavowals that her warmth towards their guardian angel was anything other than platonic.

203

Every evening Haymaker would visit. Every evening she would sit with him and gently chide him on his life, his occupation and his interests. When he left, the ladies would gently chide her about where her interests lay.

'I'm done with all that,' she would say, and no one would believe her because none of them wanted to believe that romance was entirely dead to them. All wanted to believe that somewhere out there was someone who they could feel safe with. And feel loved.

They had moved into the new house on Saturday just gone. All were delighted that they had a place, for the time being, that was warm, comfortable and safe. Especially, that it was safe. They had met the McDonald brothers and felt that these were serious men who would not stand by and allow any threat to darken their lives. Only afterwards did they hear more about who their benefactors were. It didn't matter a jot. To them they were gentlemen, if not in shining armour, then in other ways.

Just as Haymaker was dipping his biscuit into his tea, the group in the living room heard a commotion outside. It was someone shouting. Haymaker turned to Dulcie and said, 'Is that someone calling for you?'

Dulcie, who was no one's shrinking violet, had turned pale. Tears glistened in her eyes.

'That's Rex,' she whispered.

'Who's Rex?' asked Haymaker. He didn't like the sound of what he was hearing. It was disturbing his tea and chat with the ladies. Perhaps it was time to go to work.

'Call the number we gave you,' said Haymaker rising to his feet. He added 'please' a moment later.

One of the ladies was on her feet in a moment and over to the telephone that had been installed in the corridor for just such an emergency.

'What is up Dulcie?' asked Rose Hunter, gripping the arms of her chair, voice tight with fear.

Dulcie was over by the window now. She pulled the curtain back slightly and gasped.

'There's three of them with Rex. Dan don't go out there,' warned Dulcie.

But Haymaker was not made that way. He was out in the corridor. He could hear one of the ladies talking on the phone. Upstairs a baby was crying. A mother rushed past him to see to her child.

'Don't open the door,' said Dulcie.

Haymaker had his coat off and was busy removing his tie.

'Lock the door behind me Dulcie,' he ordered.

In a nearby pub, Charles 'Wag' McDonald was with his brother Bert pondering over a telegram they had received that day from his lordship. Unusually, it was quite a lengthy epistle which must have cost a small fortune to send. He could afford it, they concluded.

'What do you think?' asked Bert. Although he was the elder brother, he deferred to Wag and his other brother Wal on matters related to business. The business in their case was illegal bookmaking, protection and a couple of public houses.

Wag puffed his cheeks and considered the question. On the one hand, they liked Kit Aston. They liked hobnobbing with nobility. He was a good guy. Like Wag, he'd done his bit in Flanders. The problem with their ongoing association was

205

that lines were becoming increasingly blurred between their activities and the requests coming from his lordship.

'He wants us to play detective,' said Wag finally. 'That's a new one.'

'What if the Sabini's find out?' asked Wal. Bert was thinking the same. I doubt Billy Kimber will think much of it either.'

Wag held his hand up and nodded. Obviously, all of this had crossed his mind. Kit wanted them to locate a painting that had probably been offered to a fence to sell on. A Stubbs no less. Of course the McDonald brothers knew who Stubbs was. In fact, the idea crossed Wag's mind that necessity might be the mother of acquisition. Of a Stubbs to be precise. As soon as the thought was in his head he dismissed it. Kit was their friend.

They would help him find the painting. Wal smiled as he read the face of his brother. He said, 'maybe a job for Romeo. Where is he anyway?'

Just as he said this the door burst open. It was Alice Diamond. Maggie Hill was beside her. Neither looked happy. They rarely did.

'Dan needs us,' announced Alice. 'There's trouble at that house.'

The three McDonald's were on their feet at the mention of Haymaker.

Rex Palmer saw a chink of light at the window. He knew it was Dulcie. He marched forward to the large red door of the redbrick Victorian villa and banged on it.

'I know you're in there Dulcie. You can't hide there forever. Open the bloody door or so help me I'll break it down.'

Just for a moment he remembered an old children's story which was like this, involving pigs, but could not recall what had happened. Just as he was about to bang on the door again, it opened, and a short man stepped out. Moments later Palmer felt himself being propelled backward by a shove in the solar plexus. It winded him slightly. To say he was annoyed was like saying Napoleon had had better days than the defeat at Waterloo.

He snarled at the man in front of him, 'Who the hell are you?'

It was only then that he managed to take in the object of his fury. The man before him was a fighter. There was no mistaking the signs of his trade on a face that had suffered a thousand blows. The next thing he noticed was that the man was a good eight inches shorter than he was, but broad. Very broad in fact. Doubt assailed him now but there were a few of his mates beside him. He was a strong man. They thought he was a strong man. What was the worst that could happen. The time for talking was over. He strode forward, cocked his right hand and smacked the man before him square on the chin.

Two thoughts occurred to him simultaneously as he did so. The first was the extreme physical pain in his right hand moments after he had connected with the granite jaw of the fighter. His hand was unquestionably broken. This was, by any objective measure, a concern. However, of greater concern was the man's reaction to the punch.

He didn't even blink.

And then he moved forward. Slowly. Palmer looked on in mute fascination as he saw a fist meandering in his direction. While Haymaker's defensive prowess was unlikely to find favour with aficionados of the sweet science, the concussive power of his fists would. Palmer, a little late in the day, moved his head. This movement probably saved the outright annihilation of his nose as well as being rendered unconscious. However, the punch did catch the edge of his nose and several teeth flew onto the street. Palmer collapsed to the ground a broken man. His friends looked down at him and then at the man who had dealt so handily with their friend. They had a decision to make. It wasn't an easy one, but it was perhaps the only one they could make in the circumstances. They had to help their pal. They slowly circled Haymaker. Even the former boxer reckoned this was a highly dangerous moment.

'Do you want some of the same?' he snarled at them.

In truth they did not, but the odds favoured them. They rushed him. A blur of fists and shouts broke the night and the roar of a car and its screech to a halt.

One of the men felt as if a crane had lifted him away from Haymaker. In fact, it was a rather tall woman with a mean look in her eye. The intent he read there was duly delivered a moment later. Her fist crashed against the side of his head, and he collapsed to the ground like a sack of coal. He was lucky.

His friend was dragged back off Haymaker and found himself confronted by an elegantly dressed man who looked like a gangland boss. He was standing with a small red-headed woman with blue eyes that glinted malevolently. The man sensibly recognised the game was up. So were his hands.

He held them up like he was at gunpoint. This left him an open target to Maggie Hill who, despite a soft spot for Haymaker, had no love for men. She stepped forward and deposited her knee so deep into the groin of the man in front of her that it might need spades to dig it out again.

The ruck had probably lasted less than twenty seconds, but three men lay on the ground, and another was haring off down the street in the direction of Hobart, Tasmania.

Charles 'Wag' McDonald knelt down and stared at Rex Palmer. He guessed this was the man who had caused the affray to begin with as he was on the ground with all the signs on his face of a disagreement with Haymaker.

'Do you know who I am?' asked Wag in a gentle voice.

Rex Palmer nodded fearfully.

'Have you been a naughty boy?'

Rex Palmer nodded fearfully.

'I'm never going to hear or see you round here again?' asked Wag, with a reasonable voice, but there was no mistaking its frightening undertone.

Rex Palmer shook his head fearfully.

The final day of the case began around nine in the morning for Kit and Mary. Their dinner guest from the previous evening was nowhere to be seen. This was either because Trent was a very late riser or, more likely, he had caught an early train down to London. This was plausible even if one discounted him as a suspect.

'So we have three definite riders in the blackmail handicap,' said Mary over breakfast.

'Yes, Sexton and Cain both appear to have potential interest in acquiring Northern Glory on behalf of partnerships,' agreed Kit.

'If Trent is to be believed,' added Mary.

Kit nodded in approval. It was one of the more unusual aspects of their relationship: a husband who wholly approved of a wife with a suspicious nature. In most marriages the opposite was a desired quality in one's partner.

'Who is your money on?' asked Kit, grinning.

'Well, if we are talking about a blackmailer then we are also talking about a potential murderer too, aren't we? I mean how else would you explain the death of Damien Blythe? If that's the case then I think all three are about equal. If we are talking solely blackmail, then I would say Mr

Trent is our frontrunner if only because he has previous form over the distance.'

'No dark horse?'

Mary pondered this for a moment before replying, 'Of the other two, I would suggest Mr Cain is the more likely. Mr Sexton strikes me a bit, oh what's the word…?'

'Thick?'

Mary giggled, 'Yes, that, too. He seems more harmless. All mouth and…'

'I'd prefer you didn't ponder about the presence or absence of men's trousers,' scolded Kit with a smile.

'I think you're pretty safe, but I must say, Cain and Trent are not bad looking, you must admit that.'

Kit was not about to do any such thing. Instead, he said, 'If you like that sort of thing. And Carol certainly appears to.'

'What do you think about Carol?' asked Mary, fixing her eyes on her husband.

'Indeed, Carol. I think that her situation has changed somewhat. If Teddy is dead, then he most likely died before Damien Blythe. There's no way to avoid considering her role in this. I mean, why blackmail Gerry if it wasn't the case? It doesn't make sense. Hookie will have worked that out by now. I think Carol will be pulled in for questioning soon about this, about the missing painting and he will be probing about the blackmail.'

'Carol wouldn't be blackmailing her own brother surely?' exclaimed Mary before lowering her voice as she was aware others might overhear. 'Why would she do such a thing?'

Kit shrugged and said, 'There are so many permutations at the moment, I'm trying to shut my mind off from them. Money would be the answer to that question. However,

Carol is not exactly in penury herself, so it only makes sense if she is doing this for someone else. Sexton is the obvious candidate if we are to believe the hints thrown out by Trent the other day on the state of his finances.'

'How do you explain the fact that Teddy rang the house and came to the door the night that Carol left?' asked Mary.

'Oh that? Well, I think that's easily explained. When I realised that the dead body was not Teddy, it occurred to me that someone could have dressed up as him and gone to Gerry's house. Remember, no one actually saw the visitor's face. Same with the phone calls. They were short and sweet enough for someone to make a passable attempt at imitating him. Rather clever misdirection if one looks at it this way. Which brings us back to our three friends, Sexton, Trent and Cain. One of them is involved in this. I'm sure of it. And I agree with you by the way. I'm not sure Sexton has the mind for it.'

Mary raised her eyebrows and nodded at this.

'Yes, it seems to me that someone is playing a very intricate, high stakes game here. Unless I'm mistaken, I think Mr Sexton takes a more two-fisted approach,' said Mary. They were silent for a minute. Mary watched Kit eat his breakfast. She had not had as much on her plate. Finally, in a manner that would have brought applause from Aunt Agatha, she said, 'Hurry up and finish breakfast, I think we should pay a visit to the Chief Inspector.'

Despite Hook's attempts to duck behind his desk when Kit and Mary arrived, he was unable to evade capture. Instead, he earned a reprimand from Mary for his childish behaviour.

As Kit was laughing at Hook while Mary said this, he too was caught in the crossfire.

'You do realise I could have you arrested,' pointed Hook defensively.

Mary ignored him and explained the reason for the visit, which was probably unnecessary, but she understood that it would nip any sixth form foolishness in the bud from Kit.

'Has Gerry received his post yet?' asked Mary, getting straight to the point without further dilly-dallying.

'Twenty minutes ago,' snapped Hook.

'No need to sulk Chief Inspector,' said Mary with a smile. She put her hand on his and this seemed to mollify him slightly. 'So we are waiting for him to make his move, then.'

'For all we know he may have already started,' observed Kit. 'How many men have you covering him?'

'Three.'

'One to follow Gerry there and back, one to keep an eye on the drop and one to keep you informed. Very good,' said Kit. 'Any news on the Stubbs painting?'

Hook folded his arms and looked thoroughly miserable.

'Carol is coming to the cottage later to be interviewed once more. We want to do a full inventory of what might have been removed.'

'Does she know about the painting?' asked Kit.

'Of course not,' snapped Hook. 'Only one of us is a dashing amateur detective, remember? Did you say you had a lead on the painting?'

Kit smiled and said, 'Not yet. Some people I trust are looking into this. I'm sure if the Stubbs is in London, they'll find it.'

Kit and Mary both sat down. They ignored Hook's sour comment to make themselves at home. While they were waiting for news of the surveillance operation, Kit picked up a picture on Hook's desk. It showed his wife and daughter.

'Gosh, Abbie certainly has grown. She's very like her mother. Your eyes,' said Kit.

The picture showed two women who could have been sisters. The younger had an expression that was quietly humorous, as if it doubted the sanity of everyone and everything around her. In this respect, she was very much her daddy's girl.

'So they say,' said Hook, his voice a little more tender.

'Have you grandchildren, Chief Inspector,' asked Mary. Hook rolled his eyes at this question which worried Mary for a second that she had made a misstep.

'Twins, if I remember,' said Kit.

'Spawn of Satan, more like,' said Hook. This provoked giggles in Mary.

'They must be seven or eight now, I suppose,' said Kit.

Hook said 'nine' just as there was a knock at the door. Constable Westcott peeked his head through the door.

'Mr Tudor, has made the drop.'

'Well? Where? Spit it out?' barked Hook, irritably.

Rain fell gently onto the wide expanse of Newmarket racecourse. Kit, Mary and Hook were positioned on the opposite side of the course from the main grandstand. Alongside them was another detective named Fredericks and a police constable named Barnett. Fredericks was around

Kit's age while the constable was probably in his forties. Kit recognised him from an earlier life. They nodded to one another. Hook made the introductions to the detective. The detective's face appeared to darken momentarily, and he shot a glance towards Hook then back to Kit and Mary. Kit ignored the frown on Fredericks' face. He was used to this reaction now. Hook, however, seemed positively delighted by Fredericks' sour attitude towards the newcomers.

'Detective Sergeant Fredericks is new from the Cambridge office,' explained Hook. 'We're expecting great things from him.'

Kit couldn't decide if Hook was joking or not, so left that alone. He extracted his old binoculars from their case.

'Good Lord,' said Hook, staring in horror at the battered pair of field glasses. 'Can you even see me with those old things?'

'They work perfectly fine,' said Kit. He put them up to his eyes and said. 'Now where should we be looking?'

The four men and Mary were standing on the other side of a high hedge which bordered a part of the course. They had to forego umbrellas, but the rain was not so heavy, just a very British spit. Half a mile in front of them was the stand. In between, was the Rowley Mile Course.

'Do you see the fence post at the two-furlong marker?' said Fredericks. Four sets of binoculars trained on the post identified by the detective sergeant. A brown leather satchel was draped from it. 'Mr Tudor put something inside it twenty minutes ago. Then he left. Gregson followed him. I presume he's gone back to the stables.'

They stood behind the hedge for another ten minutes staring through their field glasses at the mist of rain. Finally, a figure appeared near the stands. His head was hidden underneath an umbrella, but it was certainly a man. From where they were standing it looked as if he was making his way over towards the leather satchel.

A minute later, Hook was convinced this was their man. He turned to Fredericks and said, 'We'll take the car round to the stand and wait for him there. Barnett, you stay here just in case he decides not to return the same way he came in. Do not engage with him in case he is armed. Keep your distance.'

Barnett, tried to look pleased at the prospect of standing in the rain for another few minutes. Or perhaps the prospect of tailing someone who was a killer seemed less exciting when you were doing it alone. Mary put a comforting hand on his arm and smiled at him. This appeared to cheer him up.

In a few moments, they were all in the car and driving around the outer rim of the course towards the entrance that led to the main stand at Newmarket. There were a number of cars in the car park when they pulled in from the main road. Hook, for once, was happy that Fredericks had driven like a demon. Neither man wanted to let the potential killer out of their sight for very long.

They piled out of the car in a manner that would have received a nod of approval from the Keystone Cops. Mary and Kit walked at pace while Hook and Fredericks broke into a gentle jog to reach the stand.

When they reached the front of the stand, all four ducked behind a tall, white picket fence. It was clear that the man was on his way back, heading directly for them. His head was still hidden by the rim of his umbrella. Hook glanced towards Mary and frowned.

'I trust you will stay where you are young lady. We do not know if this man is armed or not.'

Mary nodded. For once, it was clear her presence might add a degree of risk to the operation. She stood well back.

The man continued his approach to the gate that led to the car park. The satchel was dangling from his shoulder like a schoolbag. There was no question, they had him with the evidence. They also had the element of surprise.

Hook glanced towards Fredericks and whispered, 'As soon as he is through the gate. Not before. I will step behind him to block off that escape route. You and Kit take the front. Don't let him use the umbrella as a weapon.'

Fredericks and Kit nodded.

Kit felt his chest become a little tighter at the prospect of the encounter. He regulated his breathing and waited. They were no longer looking now. The man's approach was marked only by the sound of his footsteps. Then he was through the gate. Hook immediately stepped behind him while Fredericks and Kit tackled him by pinning his arms.

'What the?' shouted the man. Moments later he was against the fence staring at Kit, Hook and Fredericks. Fear and disbelief was in his eyes.

The man they caught was Roger Sexton.

Part III: Final Furlong

One week earlier

The phone was ringing insistently. Roger Sexton listened to it from his bathroom. And ignored it. The ringing stopped. He finished shaving. Just as he was towelling his face dry, the ringing began once more. He swore forcefully but decided to pick the phone up lest it bother him all evening. Sexton listened to the click of the operator and then another voice came on the line. A familiar voice.

'I've killed him.'

This was probably the most unusual opening to a telephone call he'd ever had. He couldn't believe it.

'What?' he said in disbelief.

'I've killed him. I didn't mean to. I think he's dead. The blood,' said Carol.

'Carol, calm down,' he urged and immediately regretted it. Women were such emotional creatures, he thought. It's not *his* fault she'd killed him. It's not *his* fault she was fool enough to marry him. He waited for the swearing to stop. Finally, it did and in a small voice Carol said, 'I'm sorry, I don't know what to do.'

'What happened, Carol?'.

219

Carol took him through the events of the night that culminated in her striking him with a candlestick. All the while, Sexton was thinking furiously about the implications of what she was asking from him. This could affect the rest of his life, never mind hers.

Carol's sobbing grew louder, and it distracted him enough almost to the point where he was going to say 'shush, let me think'.

'Carol, listen to me,' he snapped, it was time to gain some control of the situation. Rather gratifyingly she stopped crying and listened. 'We have to play this smart.' He continued in a similar vein for a few seconds while he considered the options open to him.

'Look Carol, I'm going to come over. Do nothing except what I tell you. Now, I want you to pack a bag now. Pack a bag and wait for me to pick you up.'

'Yes,' said Carol.

He explained that he would be over soon to drive her to Gerry's. The line went dead soon after. Sexton sat down and fixed himself a drink. He had time. Knowing Carol, even when fleeing the scene of a possible crime, she would still take an age to get ready. What did women find to do?

He smoked while he drank the gin. What he was doing was madness. Then again, wasn't love madness? Yet, he knew he loved her. He always had. She had dazzled him from the first moment he saw her all those years ago. Damn and blast Teddy. Well, he was gone now if what Carol said was true. He resisted the urge to raise his glass to the fallen cad.

He drained the rest of his drink and stubbed out the cigarette. It was time to go over to Carol's. She lived at the other side of Newmarket from him which is to say less than a couple of minutes away. The road was mostly empty. Night had fallen and it was a cold one. When Sexton neared outside the cottage he saw that the light was on. He parked further up the street. Conscious that some busybodies might be observing him from behind net curtains, he took an umbrella and ducked his head underneath. He walked quickly to the alley way and went around the back.

He gave the back door a sharp rap. Moments later Carol opened it. Her face was somewhere between anger and fear. As it turned out, it was both.

'You scared the living daylights out of me,' she hissed at Sexton. He looked at her aghast for a moment. Then her face crumpled and moments later he was holding her in his arms. He glanced over her shoulder and saw the feet of Teddy.

'He's definitely?' asked Sexton.

'Definitely,' replied Carol.

'Let's go. Before we do, give me the car keys.'

'Why?'

'You'll see,' said Sexton with a grim smile. He led Carol away from the back and onto the high street. 'Teddy is going to pay you a visit tonight and he'll be calling you over the next few days, begging you to come back to him. Don't take his calls and instruct Gerry and Tamsin not to speak to him.'

Carol nodded and a glimmer of hope appeared in her eyes. More than that. It was something he had not seen before from her. It was as if she was seeing him for the first time. And she liked what she saw.

They reached the car, once more under the cover of the umbrella. Five minutes later, Sexton pulled into the Tudor's estate. He roared up the long driveway. This was showing off a little, but he was lightheaded with love and hope.

'Out you go,' said Sexton as they reached the front door.

'Aren't you coming in?' asked Carol, a little surprised and, perhaps, disappointed.

'No my darling. I have things to do back at the ranch. Trust me.'

Right at that moment, Carol did. She put her hand up to his face and kissed him. They'd kissed before, of course, but never like this. Then she was gone, and Sexton was in heaven.

He drove at full speed back into Newmarket. Once more, he took the precaution of using the umbrella to hide his face. Back at the cottage, he steeled himself for what he had to do. There was no going back from this. Fear gripped him, but only for a moment. The lingering taste of Carol's lips swept it away. Using a handkerchief, he opened the door and entered through the kitchen.

The sight of Teddy almost made him ill. He was dead all right. There was blood around his head and the eyes were staring sightlessly up at the cracked wooden beams of the ceiling.

Sexton had seen enough death in his time to be inured to it, but just at that moment he paused to pay his respects to how fragile life could be. He'd hated Teddy as much as he had ever hated anyone. He'd stolen Carol from him. He'd mistreated her and he was a bounder. Yet, seeing Teddy stripped of life, Sexton no longer felt quite so jubilant.

'Sorry old chap,' said Sexton.

Then he went over to the phone and picked it up, once more using a handkerchief. He asked for the operator to put

222

him through to Tudor Stables. He waited a few moments and then he heard the line click.

'Hello, this is the Tudor residence,' said a voice. It was that pompous ass, Vincent, realised Sexton. He would have fun with this.

'Vincent is my wife there?' he drawled into the phone in his best Teddy manner. Not bad he thought. It certainly passed muster.

'Mr Harrison, I have been instructed to tell you that Mrs Harrison is not available.'

The line went dead.

Very good, thought Sexton.

Now it was time to go to work. He lifted Teddy up, not without some difficulty and carried him to the door. Sitting by the sink was the key to Teddy's car. He grabbed it and stepped outside. No one would be able to see him, so he felt quite safe in depositing Teddy in the garage by the car. He staggered over with Teddy draped over his shoulder. The former husband of Carol hit the ground with enough of a thud to have extinguished any remaining life in the bounder.

Back inside the kitchen, he looked around for a rag to begin cleaning the floor where Teddy had bled so copiously. It took half an hour, but it was soon spotless. Thank goodness it was a stone floor and not carpet otherwise the game would have been up. He grabbed the candlestick that had delivered Teddy into the great winners' enclosure in the sky and carried it out to the car. He returned to the house and went upstairs to the bedroom. A quick search of the wardrobe uncovered a hat and a Crombie overcoat that were distinctively Teddy's.

Taking the stairs two at a time, he rushed out to the car. He wrapped Teddy's head in a towel to ensure that he did not stain the car in any way. A few minutes later he had put Teddy into the car. This was no mean feat. Teddy was beginning to stiffen. He found a spade at the back of the garage and put it in the car.

Soon he was on the road, sweating like a man with a guilty secret. His heart was thudding like a bass drum in a marching band. He had to get off the road and into the wood as quickly as possible.

Ten minutes later, he was once more wrestling with the corpse. This time his battle was to get the damn thing out of the car. He had to snap it at one point and the crack echoed around the night like a musket volley at Waterloo. A few choice words followed this, but soon he was digging like a madman. There would be time to make a better job of it in the future, but for now he managed a shallow grave for a man who deserved no eulogy.

An hour later he was back on the road, this time bound for his last stop of the evening before returning the car to Teddy's house.

He saw the dark shape of Tudor Stables ahead. There were no lights on as it was now after eleven at night. This was exactly what he had hoped for. The car pulled up to the house. He was now fully committed, he realised. His first act was to honk the horn of the car then he climbed out still wearing Teddy's coat and hat. Marching over to the front door, he began to bang on it and call for Carol. This had to be judged very finely. It wouldn't do for someone actually to open the door. He banged a little more then stood back to see if any lights were switched on.

The front of the house lit up like a Christmas tree. It had worked. He shouted a little bit more for Carol to appear before running to the car and taking off. No point in over-egging this particular cake. The car was disappearing down the driveway by the time Vincent and Gerry stumbled out on the front driveway clad in their nightshirts. Gerry let fly a volley of abuse. Vincent left it to the master to give vent to what they both felt.

Mission completed satisfactorily, Sexton drove back to Teddy and Carol's cottage with mixed feelings. The moment when Carol would be his had advanced considerably. Yet, nagging doubts remained. A number of questions circulated in his head, and none gave him anything like the comfort he had expected to feel at this juncture. Suppressing any thoughts on how exactly he felt about Carol, the one overriding question was if he had done enough to protect both her and, more importantly, himself, from any risk of being caught. He hadn't just perverted the course of justice; he was an accomplice in what may be deemed as manslaughter.

He needed a drink.

Depositing the car back to Teddy's garage, he kept hold of the coat and hat that he had found in Teddy's wardrobe. It wouldn't be the worst idea to be seen walking down the High Street. He was a similar height to Carol's husband, perhaps a bit burlier. They could easily be confused in the dark. Then an idea hit him. It was too good not to try. He went through the back door of the kitchen. One final check told him he had done a good job in tidying up the mess. He walked through to the lounge and the drinks cabinet. He found a half-drunk bottle of gin.

Perfect.

Moments later he was out the front door. He took a slug of Dutch courage and then began to stagger down the street singing *Roll Out the Barrel*. What it lacked in musicality, harmony and knowledge of the actual lyrics, was more than compensated by the volume with which he sang. It was an awful racket, and it had the desired effect. A few lights went on and windows were opened. Insults were duly exchanged, and the bottle was smashed to the ground before Sexton quietened down. Then he ducked into the shadows and stole off back towards where he had parked the car. It was too risky to drive through the town, so a roundabout route was selected to help him avoid any prying eyes that could connect his car to the activity he had engineered that night.

It was nearing midnight when he returned to his house. He was tired and far from elated. What was done was done now. The next day and perhaps the day after, he would ring the house in his role as Teddy, demanding that Carol return. Perhaps he could threaten suicide.

Suicide.

There was a germ of an idea there. It needed thinking about.

28

7 days later

'Where are you taking me?' demanded Sexton.

The fact that he was sitting in a police car between Hook and Barnett should have given him something of a clue as to his destination. Hook glanced at him sideways with a sour look which jolted Sexton somewhat. His face reddened as he'd realised himself their likely destination, but form dictated that he at least inquire.

'I should have thought that obvious Mr Sexton,' pointed out Hook.

'What am I being charged with?' demanded Sexton, growing angrier and he had been pretty angry to begin with after being manhandled by Kit Aston and Barnett before being somewhat unceremoniously deposited in the back of a police car. His increasingly loud and desperate demands for an explanation were roundly ignored.

Hook looked at him strangely and then replied in a subdued tone, 'You really don't know?'

It was pretty clear to Sexton that the game was up. He wondered what awaited him and he was not just thinking of the police station. What he'd done was beyond the pale.

Thoughts raced round his head like colts in the final furlong. He was facing the greatest crisis of his life. Nothing on the face of Hook suggested that bluster would save the day. The man was too sharp for that. Inwardly, he cursed himself for ever becoming involved with a married woman. A married woman who had a string of suitors waiting to fill the shoes of the man he had buried in the middle of a wood.

The question burning in his mind at that moment was quite simple: how much do they know?

There was another question coming up on the stand side, too. How far should he go to protect Carol? Related to that was, of course, how far would Carol go to protect him? In his heart, he knew the answer to that, and it gave him no comfort.

It was a mess. One giant mess and it was mostly of his own making.

Mostly. But not all. Fear gripped Sexton.

Kit and Mary stood by the stand as rain gently tickled their faces. They were watching the police car recede into the distance. At speed. They too had a question to contend with. It was more immediate and a little more practical.

'How do we get back into town?' asked Mary. She looked up at Kit and found no comfort in the expression on his face. It wasn't as if it was such a long walk back, but it was long enough in this weather. Kit smiled and was about to perform the 'I've-no-idea' shrug of the shoulders so beloved by women from their men when he saw something that, while not ideal, did provide him with the ghost of an idea.

228

Mary recognised the look on Kit's face. She had seen it often before. It was the prelude to a breakthrough. She loved that look. He looked so intelligent at these moments, and, for Mary, Kit's intelligence was his most attractive feature. And his sense of humour. He wasn't bad looking either. Tall, too.

'You may not like it,' said Kit.

'Does it mean we can avoid walking back into town in the rain?' asked Mary hopefully.

'Yes,' came the reply.

'Well what are we waiting for?'

The smell in the back of the horse box was overpowering to the extent that Kit and Mary would have welcomed the chance to pass out.

'You should have gone up front with the driver,' said Kit, his head out the back trying to take in the fresh air.

The thought had crossed Mary's mind, but she remembered her wedding vows – for better or for worse. This definitely qualified on the latter count. Anyway, she would have felt too guilty about travelling in relative comfort while Kit suffered in the straw and the, well, you get the idea.

'It's a pity there was no room in the police car,' said Mary.

'I doubt Hookie would have given us a lift. It would be just like him.'

'He'd have given me a lift,' said Mary with a smug grin.

Thankfully, the journey back into Newmarket was a short one as the course bordered the town. They thanked and paid the driver of the horsebox who promptly set off back to the racecourse.

'Nice chap,' said Kit.

'And a good deal richer now,' replied Mary pointedly. Then she swung around and said, 'Police station?'

'Police station,' agreed Kit and they walked up the steps of the building into the small foyer. The old police sergeant looked up and saw who it was.

'I'm sure he's expecting us, Bert,' said Kit.

'I'm sure he is,' replied Bert the police sergeant. He let them through, and they headed down a corridor. Standing outside the door was Barnett. He motioned with his head that Hook was inside. Kit nodded and they stood outside and listened to the interview.

'I'm not speaking without my lawyer,' said Sexton to Hook. To emphasise his determination on this score, he folded his arms and crossed his legs. Defences up, he was ready for anything that Hook was about to throw at him.

· 'It's becoming something of a habit. You being here, that is. Not one I would recommend I might add, and I work here. Sometimes,' said Hook, taking out his pipe. This was a sign that he was digging in for the long haul.

'I don't intend staying very long, I assure you,' said Sexton in a voice that was anything but assured. It sounded exactly like the voice of a man trying to bluster. Hook had been too long in the game not to recognise pure, unadulterated terror when he saw it. Sexton was in it up to his eyeballs and he was just the man to make him feel as if he was drowning.

'Mr Sexton, we are dealing with blackmail and murder. I can assure you,' said Hook, emphasising the 'you', 'that you are facing some serious charges.'

230

'Murder?' exclaimed Sexton and he immediately regretted it. Even he recognised, and he knew he wasn't the fastest runner in the race, being shocked at the use of the word *murder* was an admission that he knew something about the blackmail. He tried to cover his tracks. 'What do you mean murder and blackmail.'

'You know perfectly well what I mean,' snapped Hook. 'What's in the satchel?'

'You tell me.'

'Why did you go to collect it?'

'A friend asked me.'

'Who?'

'Where is Bryn Cain?' said Sexton sharply. He was now very agitated. He reached for his cigarette case before realising that it had been removed from his pockets along with all his belongings.

Hook sat back and smiled. He placed the pipe in his mouth and fixed his eyes on Sexton. His eyes were very blue and always contained a faint hint of scorn. Sexton felt himself burning up under the gently intense gaze of the Chief Inspector.

With a degree of flourish that would have earned a nod from a ham actor in a village play, Hook threw the satchel on the table between him and Sexton.

'What's in there?' asked Hook.

'You tell me. You looked at it.'

'Don't be disingenuous. You know what's in there.'

Sexton said nothing and kept his arm folded, so Hook reached inside the satchel and took out a few sheets of paper. It was full of the legalese that he had detested from the moment he'd started his course in law at Cambridge. What

231

had possessed him to follow his father into law was beyond him. He'd much rather have studied the classics and become a lecturer. However, life was never so straightforward. Most people thought they were rowers. Hook knew otherwise. The reality was you drifted towards your destination driven by currents that you could no more see than control.

Outside the room they heard some noise. There was a knock at the door and then Bert the police sergeant poked his head through the door.

'Mr Cain is here.'

Hook's face tightened into a scowl. Then he sighed and said, 'Show him in.' He rose to his feet and stretched his six feet frame. Then the door opened. It was Cain. He was dressed in a navy overcoat which fitted him perfectly. The lines were smooth, and the only sign of any imperfection was the spots of rain on his shoulders. He nodded to Hook and then glanced down at Sexton.

'So, what have we here?'

'I shall let Mr Sexton tell you,' said Hook, taking the contract from the desk and placing it back inside the satchel. 'Would either of you like a tea?'

The answer was yes. Hook took his hat from the hat stand and walked out into the corridor. It was empty save for Barnett who was still standing to attention outside the door. Hook went up to the old constable.

'Where are they?'

'In your office, sir,' said Barnett, who kept his eyes fixed on the wall in front.

Hook rolled his eyes by way of response and turned slowly towards his office door.

'Can you organise some tea for our guests?' he asked Barnett before opening the door to his office.

He walked in to find Kit slouched in his old leather chair and Mary sitting opposite him.

'Make yourself at home,' said Hook.

'Thanks. I shall,' grinned Kit. 'Have you beaten a confession out of him yet?'

'Not yet. If that doesn't work I could always send you in and you can tell him about what it's like to be a dashing hero. He'll break, mark my words. No one can listen to that nonsense for very long without cracking.'

'So Gerry has sold Northern Glory, then,' said Mary.

'Not until the contract is in the hands of the people who want him,' said Kit. 'Can I look at the contract for a second?'

Hook handed him the contract. Kit's eyes scanned the butchered language of Shakespeare. Then, as he held it he glanced up to Hook.

'Do you want to do this or shall I?' he asked.

Hook held Kit's gaze for a few moments and then he said, 'Do you mind?'

Kit shook his head and then, without any warning, he ripped the contract in two.

'Ooops,' said Kit, but nothing in the tone of his voice or expression suggested remorse.

29

Mary gasped in horror at the ripped contract. Her eyes swivelled from the contract to Kit and then to Hook.

'Kit, what have you done?' said Mary when she had regained the power of speech.

It was fairly clear what he had done, so Kit answered the question that was really implied.

'We can't have Gerry losing Northern Glory can we?' he replied which was a little too literal for Mary. She was about to point that out, once the right, ladylike, words occurred to her, when the phone rang.

Kit looked up at Hook with a question in his eyes. The detective stepped forward and said, 'The bank probably.'

Mary who had been thoroughly discombobulated now began to see a glimmer of what was happening.

'The cheque?' she asked Kit who nodded.

Hook picked up the phone and said in a deeply serious tone, 'Chief Inspector Hook.' He waited a few moments as he listened to the voice at the other end of the line. Then he said, 'Yes, I appreciate that it is highly irregular Mr York, but it is an important piece of evidence that is central to solving a murder as well as a blackmail.' He waited a few seconds longer then he said, 'I knew you would appreciate the critical nature of the request. Thank you for your help.'

Hook set the phone down. He smiled at Mary who was looking expectantly up at him. The scowl returned to his face, and he said to Kit, 'Do you mind if I have my seat back?'

Kit leapt to his feet with a guilty chuckle. He added, 'Very comfortable.'

'I know,' snapped Hook. 'Now young lady, you seem rather shocked by what has happened.'

'You could say,' agreed Mary in an extravagantly patient voice. She looked at Kit again and realised, for the first time, he was wearing gloves. She frowned at this but understood at least some of what had happened.

'The contract,' said Kit, 'was signed under duress. So, at the very least, it is not worth the paper it's written on. But best be safe anyway. Now that we have the cheque, Northern Glory is safe for the time being.' He shifted his attention to Hook. 'Is anyone checking…?'

'Yes, Fredericks is working on that,' said Hook. He looked down at the contract and read the name of the partnership who had just tried to buy Northern Glory. '*Paysan de France*. They sound suspiciously French to me. I knew we should have kept on marching after Waterloo.'

'That's the spirit,' grinned Kit. 'Germany would have thought twice about starting a war if a Union Jack had been flying on the Eiffel Tower.'

'I suspect the Eiffel Tower would have been a fifty foot column with Wellington on it, don't you?' pointed out Hook. 'We'll let Mr Sexton stew a little longer before we question him. Did you catch any of the interview?'

235

Kit nodded. He walked over to the window. There was a sense of regret in his voice when he spoke.

'I think Carol is central to this conundrum. Gerry was willing to sell Northern Glory for her. Sexton is or was her lover. Is he part of the blackmail plot? If you'd asked me two days ago, I would have put him bottom of that list of suspects. Now, it looks like he is implicated in Teddy's murder and, to boot, has decided to blackmail Gerry into selling Northern Glory to a consortium he has put together.'

'From France,' added Mary.

'From France,' said Hook. 'I agree. I didn't think he had it in him. I almost feel some admiration for him. He pulled the wool over my eyes completely. I thought he was a red-faced nincompoop. Still, it shows you never can tell.'

'Well, let's follow the line of logic through, then,' said Kit, who was still on his feet, by the window. 'He or Carol, or both, kill Teddy. He takes Carol back to her house. In the meantime, he acts out the part of Teddy for a day or two with the midnight visit and the phone calls so that Carol's alibi can be established. Then he murders this poor lad, Damien Blythe, plants his body in the cottage and fakes an apparent suicide while attempting to make it seem that it was Teddy who died. Have I missed anything?'

'No, still keeping up with you Kit, old boy,' said Hook. It must be said that Hook was almost incapable of saying anything that wasn't either ill-tempered or gave the impression that he was mocking you. Kit smiled at his old friend. It felt good to be made fun of by him. Men are a bit strange like that.

'I think there are layers upon layers of deception. Let's not look at this with our eyes open. This requires some imagination.'

Hook looked at Mary and said, 'I always hated when he said that.'

Kit ignored this and said, 'At the moment, that's the hypothesis we have to deal with here.'

'Do you have others?' asked Hook, leaning forward. His eyes were brightly intelligent as ever.

Kit paused before answering, 'They're both clearly hiding something. I think you'll put Carol and Sexton under pressure and see what comes from it. The blackmailer clearly is accusing Carol of killing Teddy. But, yes, I think there's more here than we are seeing at the moment.'

'Based on?' challenged Hook.

'Based on what we said. Do I think Sexton is the man to help Carol kill Teddy and then start blackmailing her? No. What is your plan?' asked Kit.

'I'll speak with Sexton first and then Carol and then perhaps we'll put them together and see what happens. You can take those seats and listen from the corridor if you want.'

'I wouldn't miss it for the world,' replied Kit.

Hook re-entered the interview and sat down without acknowledging either Sexton or Cain. The lawyer immediately began to speak, but Hook raised his hand sharply which stopped Cain in his tracks. Then Hook leaned forward and said, 'Your client is going to be charged with the murder of Teddy Harrison and with conspiracy to blackmail and extort the sale of a racehorse from Gerry Tudor. He has just been caught collecting the signed contract from a pre-arranged drop off at Newmarket racecourse.'

Bryn Cain visibly blanched at this. He turned to Sexton who was sitting silently sullen. His normal ruddy complexion had a distinct pallor now. He stared down at the table.

'This is an outrageous and slanderous accusation, Chief Inspector,' snarled Cain. 'What proof do you have?'

'I have sent the contract that was in the satchel that Mr Sexton collected to be fingerprinted. We have collected the cheque written by Gerry Tudor from the bank and make no mistake, we will certainly be getting in contact with Jean-Claude from *Paysan de France*, the partnership who thought they were acquiring Northern Glory, to find out exactly what their involvement is in this ghastly episode.'

Sexton was shaking his head now and seemed on the brink of a breakdown. Hook noted this and twisted the knife further.

'And to keep up the French theme of this investigation; *cherchez la femme* as our cousins across the Channel might say. Mrs Harrison has a case to answer too, Mr Cain. You will have your work cut out as both your clients stand accused of murder most foul. They will have the gallows.'

If Sexton was slowly shrinking into his chair, Cain was now no less shocked by what he was hearing. Then his face became a mask once more.

'I hope you have evidence for this Chief Inspector because if you do not it might well be your last investigation. Where is the dead body of Teddy Harrison? How was he killed? On what are you basing this vile accusation that either of my clients was responsible for this?

'We have a blackmail letter that accuses Carol Harrison of killing her husband,' snapped Hook.

'That's not evidence.'

'There are photographs of the dead body,' retorted Hook.

'Could've been staged for all you know,' said Cain sitting back in his chair. 'And the letter is clearly an attempt to smear a woman who has been mistreated and abused by her husband. Who's to say that Teddy hasn't staged this whole thing?'

Hook slowly smiled at this. He resembled nothing less than a Tiger contemplating a steak dinner. He leaned forward and said slowly, 'Whoever is dealing with the *Paysan de France* partnership is going to prison, Mr Cain. If not for murder, then for blackmail.

Sexton looked up from the table that he had been staring at for a few minutes.

'Who are *Paysan de France?*'

Twenty minutes later, Kit, Mary and Hook were sitting in the back of a police car, one of two driven by Constable Westcott, en route to the Tudor Stables. Hook sat in the back and stared out the window as they set off. He didn't seem in much of a mood to talk. They drove in silence for a few minutes until they saw the stables just ahead.

'Who are *Paysan de France?*' said Hook dismissively. 'What does he take us for?'

'What if he doesn't know?' replied Kit.

Hook glowered at Kit.

'That's hardly the point, is it? Even if he is a dupe in all of this, why doesn't he say so? You don't think I haven't considered the possibility that Sexton is some sort of,' the policeman struggled for a few moments for the right word before settling on 'Patsy.'

'Patsy?' said Mary, looking at Kit with a frown.

'An American term I believe for someone who is a…' Kit paused a moment to choose his words.

'The fall guy,' interjected Hook, thereby confirming his impressive knowledge of American underworld slang,

'Fall guy,' said Mary nodding. Although she was still no more certain of the terms used, the context at least suggested that Sexton was a convenient person to blame for something that he may not have done.

'Sucker,' added Kit, thereby earning another scowl from Hook and a gentle slap on the arm and a grin from Mary.

'I'm glad we've cleared that up,' said Mary drily.

They pulled into the estate and drove along the driveway to the front of the mansion. The two police cars parked by the front door. Kit, Mary and the policemen were hardly out of the car when Vincent appeared on the steps of the house, swiftly followed by a very worried-looking Tamsin. She spotted Kit and Mary and tears formed in her eyes.

'What's going on?' asked Tamsin.

Hook glanced towards Kit and then said, 'I think you know Tamsin. We need to speak with Carol and with Gerry.

'Tamsin, Gerry has done nothing wrong,' said Kit. 'We need to speak with them both.'

'I thought you'd left,' said Tamsin. Her hands were clutched together, and tears trickled down her cheek. Mary strode up the steps and immediately hugged her.

'Where's Gerry?' asked Mary.

'With Glory,' replied Tamsin. It was barely a whisper. Her voice hardened a little as she said, 'Carol's upstairs. Is this trouble?'

There was no way to answer this question without causing unnecessary worry, so Mary did not respond beyond a sympathetic smile. Tamsin's eyes followed the two policemen as they walked up the steps and past her into the house, swiftly followed by a perturbed Vincent.

'With Glory, you say?' asked Hook. He tapped a cigarette on his hand and lit it.

Tamsin nodded.

Hook tilted his felt hat back on his head. He turned to Kit and motioned with his head towards the paddock. He said, 'Shall we?'

Kit nodded and they set off down to the stables. They could see Gerry by the fence surrounding the paddock. He was gazing disconsolately at the horse he believed he had just sold.

'At least some good may come from this,' said Kit.

'I'm glad you think so,' replied Hook. 'I'm damned if I can see it.'

And Kit knew he was probably right.

30

Gerry barely seemed to register the arrival of Kit and Hook beside him. He stood silently looking at the horse and his chum, Leonardo's Pride, cantering together. To Kit he seemed lost as if in the final stages of a madness. His eyes stared unblinking at the horse who was the culmination of his three decades plus association with horses that had begun almost from the point at which he could walk. Finally, Hook spoke.

'Would you mind coming with us Gerry?' said Hook. There seemed little else that could be said, and Hook was not a man to say it.

Gerry nodded obediently. He turned and the three men walked in silence up the hill towards the driveway. He stopped for a second when he saw the two police cars. His breathing became irregular. He fought to control his emotions. Then he saw Carol appear with the two policemen. He wanted to run. To get away from the house, from his friend, from the police. He wanted to be ten years old again before life, responsibility and the greed of others became a storm swirling around him, tossing him hither and thither. His eyes met Tamsin's. She was crying in Mary's arms. For the first time he registered that it was Kit and Mary.

Gerry turned to Kit with a slight frown. He said, 'You didn't leave.'

'No, Gerry,' said Kit gently. 'I couldn't let you do this on your own.'

Gerry shook his head. He was unsure whether to be angry or sad. Breathing was difficult now. 'It's all a mess,' he whispered, and Kit could think of nothing to say that would comfort him.

Hook helped Gerry into the same car as Carol. Then he turned to Tamsin and said, 'You can come too if you wish or stay.'

Tamsin separated herself from Mary. She was unsure what to do. Mary said, 'Go with Gerry. He needs you.'

This was all she needed. She skipped down the steps and ducked into the police car. Mary and Kit joined Hook in the other car. A minute later they set off.

Once more, the gravity of the situation made conversation difficult. Then Kit said, 'We need Trent.' He saw out of the side of his eye, Hook turn towards him. 'He was staying at the Rutland Arms last night. He said he was going to London this morning.'

Hook laughed a little mirthlessly.

'I'm not completely in my dotage yet. I was aware of the presence of Mr Trent. Don't worry. I prevailed upon him this morning that he should stay another night. I haven't finished with him yet.' He smiled and said, 'Who's your money on, Kit?'

Kit sighed, 'I think you know what I think, but we need proof. We need to find out who this partnership is or who took the painting. If we know who they've been dealing with…'

'Then we have the killer. Yes, indeed. I hope Fredericks can help us in this matter. Do you think we should have searched Gerry's house for those photographs?'

'We both know that would have been a waste of time. Gerry has shown his loyalty to Carol by trying to sell Glory. He's hardly going to be stupid enough to keep hold of the evidence that will possibly send his sister to the gallows.'

'Do you think she planned all this?'

Kit pondered this for a few moments. In fact, he had been pondering this all morning and possibly most of the previous evening. It was a tribute, or a sad comment, on Carol that she would be either a criminal mastermind or a victim of circumstance. In deciding which she was, Kit recognised that it was his head and his heart making the case for each. As ever, in these situations, Kit always sought to screen out the existing evidence because it only directed them down certain pathways. The case was buried under layers of deception. The way through this was to create new hypotheses that somehow worked with the evidence yet were not subject to it.

After a short period of silence Kit smiled and replied, 'I'm sure she planned something, just not all this.'

Hook seemed satisfied with this answer. 'Yes,' he said but did not add anything to this rather cryptic accord.

'Why don't we go to the cottage?' said Kit suddenly.

Hook looked askance at him. 'Have you lost your mind?'

'I mean it. Let's conduct the interviews there.'

Hook leaned forward and tapped Westcott on the shoulder. 'Pull over,' said Hook and tell the others to follow us to the cottage. Then go to the station and collect Mr

Sexton and Mr Cain.' Then he leaned back in the seat and said with more than a hint of a sigh, 'I hate amateur detectives.'

'Constable Westcott, can you see if any telegrams have come for me. I asked that they be sent to the police station.'

'We're your sorting office now?' said Hook archly.

The car containing Kit, Mary and Hook pulled into the alleyway behind the cottage. It was around four in the afternoon. They made their way through the back door and into the kitchen which led through an opening to the living room. A few minutes later, the car containing Gerry, Tamsin and Carol arrived. A disgruntled Gerry was audible even from the living room. They spilled into the cottage through the same door as the others.

Mary had, with some forethought, brought some chairs from the kitchen table into the lounge as she had anticipated it would be quite a crowd. Some more guests were still expected.

'If this is a joke,' began Gerry.

'It's in very poor taste,' completed Hook. 'Yes, yes, Gerry. Very good. We know you're unhappy but so be it. Just have a seat while we wait for the others.'

'What others?' demanded Gerry trying to give some semblance that he was in control of the situation.

'You'll see,' said Hook before giving that infuriating smile and following it with a shrug. Kit almost wanted to laugh, despite the situation.

Five minutes later they heard another car pull up outside. They waited and then the back door opened. Roger Sexton,

245

Jason Trent and Bryn Cain entered, followed by Detective Sergeant Fredericks. He had the satchel around his shoulder. The eyes of Fredericks met those of Hook. Kit noticed there was an imperceptible shake of the head. Hook's face seemed to darken momentarily and then it resumed its smile. Kit assumed that this meant they had made no further progress on the mysterious buyers of Northern Glory. However, he handed an envelope to Kit. Hook and Mary glanced at the envelope as Kit opened it. He quickly read the contents and then handed it to Hook, with Mary peering over his shoulder.

'Hurry up,' barked Hook in a friendly manner. 'Take a seat. Some of us have homes to return to.'

'Are you going to tell us what on earth is going on?' demanded Cain.

'All in good time,' said Hook amiably. 'Now, are we all settled?'

The answer to this question was a sullen silence. Hook grinned and strode into the middle of the living room.

'I feel like I'm back at school. Well, let's begin, shall we? I won't bore you with why we are here. I think that's perfectly obvious. However, there are some matters which have come to light that might best be resolved in a group. At least that's what we hope, anyway.'

Hook paused to take a breath and take in the impact on his audience. They were a sombre lot and no mistake. Still, it was murder they were discussing. Murder was a serious matter, indeed.

'Very well, where were we? So, when last we were together, in a matter of speaking, at the inquest, our chief topic of conversation was the death of Damien Blythe and the disappearance and possible death of Teddy Harrison.'

Gerry gazed across the room at Kit. He seemed angry. It was as if he knew what was coming. Kit wondered if he would be on the receiving end of the blame. Carol's face was a mask. It was as if all hope had been extinguished from her eyes. She looked beautiful and fragile in equal measure. Sexton and Trent sat either side of Cain. Both seemed as if they were seconds away from a fight with Cain the referee. Bryn Cain bristled with pent up anger just waiting for an opportunity to interrupt. All in all, it was an unhappy party, concluded Kit.

'Since then,' continued Hook, extracting a piece of paper from his briefcase and handing it to Gerry, 'we've had a few developments.' He looked at Gerry and asked, 'That was your statement was it not. The one where you failed to mention your visit to this house with Chris.'

'What are you saying?' shouted Gerry.

Hook ignored him and pointed to the sheet.

'Is that your signature?'

'You damn well know it is, Hookie. What's this about?' growled Gerry. He glanced towards Cain for moral and, one supposes, legal support. Cain took the hint. He was furious now.

'Yes, Chief Inspector. You have no right to be doing this,' said Cain standing up.

'Sit down Mr Cain,' said Hook resignedly. 'I do have a right to speak to these people. Are we not all friends?'

This was disingenuous and met with a snort from Gerry. Hook eyed Gerry and pointed to the witness statement. He raised his eyebrows by way of asking the question once more about the signature.

'Yes,' snarled Gerry.

Hook walked over and took the statement away from him. Then he walked over to the satchel and fished out the contract. The ripped contract. He looked at one of the pieces and said, 'This is your signature, too then?'

Gerry stared at the contract, aghast. Kit was busy scanning the faces of Sexton, Trent and Cain. He was looking for their reaction to the destroyed contract. He saw a flicker on one of their faces.

Hook looked inside the satchel once more. He smiled and nodded to Fredericks. He took out a cheque, the same one that Gerry had thought he had banked earlier. He smiled and strolled over to Kit. All eyes turned to Kit.

'What are you waiting for?' asked Hook.

Kit fixed his eyes in the general direction of the three men he was most interested in. The sound of him tearing the cheque in half echoed like a scream at a wedding service. Mary was looking at Gerry. His face had turned white.

'What's going on, Kit?' asked Carol. She was the first to recover.

Hook smiled down at Carol and then turned to Kit. With a chuckle, he said, 'Well perhaps I should leave this to my young friend to take us to the winning post.'

Kit's eyes narrowed and he said drily, 'How very kind of you.'

'Don't mention it. Oh and…' added Hook.

'Yes?' asked Kit, frowning and smiling at the same time. Mary quite liked the combination.

'Best of luck. I've every confidence in you,' finished Hook, rubbing his hands together with the glee of someone about to watch a performance he's been looking forward to for some time.

31

Like the consummate actor he could be when the occasion demanded, Kit surveyed the room. They surveyed him back. It was difficult to ignore the grinning Chief Inspector, but Kit gave it his best shot. Outside on the street, he saw one of the constables standing guard at the front door. The room was silent. The floor his. Time to uncover a murderer.

'For those of you who are mystified about the exchange you've just witnessed between Gerry and Hookie, let me enlighten you. Gerry was the victim of an attempted blackmail. The blackmailer was trying to extort his signature on a contract of sale. The sale was, of course, of Northern Glory.'

Gerry's eyes blazed with anger, sadness and perhaps remorse.

'How did you find out?'

'It was me,' said Tamsin. She was holding his hand.

Gerry frowned and withdrew his hand from hers. 'Do you know what you've done?' he whispered in shock. Tamsin was no shrinking violet, but Lord knows, she had shed more tears in twenty-four hours than she had shed in the previous thirty-six years of her life. She was desolate. Once more, she sought refuge in Mary, who was sitting beside her on the sofa.

'Gerry,' said Bryn Cain. 'Say nothing. They have nothing on you.' Cain was staring at Gerry in the eye. 'I must say, Chief Inspector, I'm beginning to lose count of the irregularities. None of this will stand up in any court, as you well know.'

'Do I?' said Hook, who now had his hands behind his head and his long legs stretched out in front of him.

'This is not just irregular. It's improper. They need legal representation,' said the lawyer.

'They have you, do they not?' pointed out Hook.

'I mean each one needs to have their own counsel. This is illegal.'

'Let me be the judge of that,' said Hook calmly. 'Or do you mean that there may be some conflicts of interest here?'

Cain ignored Hook and addressed the others in the room. 'None of you have to say anything. You have not been charged. This is one large bluff.'

He was addressing the people in the room who were not of a detective inclination, but his eyes were on Carol, who was now weeping quietly.

She looked up at Gerry. For a moment, their eyes were locked like this and then Carol spoke.

'Gerry, tell me. Are you being blackmailed?' Her brother looked away but did not answer. 'Gerry, tell me. Were you being blackmailed to sell Northern Glory to protect me?' Still no answer from her brother but Carol took this as confirmation. She buried her face in her hands.

'Oh no. What have I done?'

Kit walked over to her and handed her a handkerchief. In a gentle voice he said, 'Carol, tell us what happened that night with Teddy. The night you left him.'

251

Cain was on his feet now.

'Carol, he has no standing,' said Cain calmly. 'You do not have to say anything. Carol, as your lawyer, as your friend, I'm telling you not to say anything. They are going to try and pin a murder on you. It will mean the gallows.'

'I didn't murder him,' shouted Carol. 'I didn't murder him. He hit me. He was going to hit me again. I grabbed the candlestick. I didn't mean to kill him.'

Tears were streaming down her face. Then she doubled over. Her body shook with the violence of her sobbing. Kit knelt beside her and put his hand on her shoulder. This was never really going to have much effect as Kit knew. Then he rose slowly to his feet and turned to Roger Sexton.

'And that's where you came in Sexton, isn't it?'

'You're all mad,' said Cain. 'I can't allow this to continue. I'm going to my office to apply for…'

'Don't be fatuous,' grumbled Hook. 'Sit down.' He seemed like an angry theatregoer trying to see the stage.

Cain sat down like a scolded schoolboy. Then all eyes turned to Sexton. He looked distraught. He looked at Carol. She glared back at him.

'What did you do to that boy?' she snarled. 'All I needed was help.'

Sexton was aghast at this. He shook his head slowly, his lines on his forehead furrowed like ravines.

'I didn't kill anyone. I swear.'

Kit turned to him and said, 'And I suppose you weren't the blackmailer either. Yet you were the one picking up the satchel with the signed contract for Northern Glory.'

'I swear,' said Sexton, but words were failing him now. He could not believe what he was hearing.

'The contract was for the sale of Northern Glory to a partnership,' said Kit. 'I suppose that's more your area, Mr Trent.'

'What?' exploded Trent. 'You can't hang any of this tawdry business on me. The last thing I need to do right now is be mixed up in this nonsense. Cain, do something.'

Cain was on his feet again.

'This has gone on long enough. I won't have my clients subjected to wild accusations and slander.'

'I haven't finished,' said Kit. 'Not by a long chalk.' He turned once more to Sexton. His facial colour was once more a livid red. He seemed as if he would spontaneously combust.

'Where did you hide Teddy's body, Sexton? It was you. It could only have been you. Carol called you, didn't she? You were the one that came here and took her home. You were the one that pretended to be Teddy for two days in order to establish Carol's alibi.'

Sexton looked up at Kit and howled like a captured animal, 'I didn't kill the boy.'

'Were you being blackmailed?' asked Kit. The quietness of his voice was stark in comparison to the seething rage within Sexton. All at once the storm abated. Tears formed in his eyes. 'Were you being blackmailed? You were protecting Carol, weren't you.'

Carol jerked up when she heard this. She stared in disbelief at Sexton. Her head began to shake slowly. Once more tears filled her eyes.

'I thought you'd killed him.'

Sexton shook his head.

'I didn't. I swear I didn't. I just took Teddy to the wood. I buried him there. I didn't kill anyone,' said Sexton. His voice

253

cracked under the strain of his despair. He was either telling the truth or this was an actor who would have given Henry Irving a run for his money, thought Kit. Sexton buried his head in his hands.

'Roger, swear to me you didn't kill that boy,' said Carol. Her voice was shaking also.

It was Kit who answered for Sexton.

'He didn't kill Damien Blythe.'

'Carol,' said Kit gently. 'Tell us what happened.'

Cain stood up to say something.

'Sit down,' hissed Hook. He was no longer the theatre-goer intent on enjoying the show. That was finished now. The final curtain had come down. All that was left was to recognise the actors.

'What does this all this mean for Carol?' asked Gerry.

'Prison,' said Cain with a snarl.

'Not necessarily,' replied Hook. 'If this was self-defence, of course.'

'But who…?' continued Gerry. He addressed the question to Kit, who was still standing in the middle of the room. All eyes turned to Kit.

'The person that killed Damien Blythe is the same person who blackmailed both Gerry to sell Northern Glory and Sexton to collect the satchel with the contract. The killer thought that if everything went wrong then Sexton would be blamed, and he had the evidence. Even the name of the partnership was something that was untraceable. But at least we had the cheque. And that is something that we can trace. We will find this Jean-Claude and he will tell us everything.'

Kit spun around and faced one man. He looked him directly in the eye and said, 'How about it Trent?'

32

All eyes swung towards Trent. He reacted immediately. He stuffed his hand into Bryn Cain's pocket and extracted a Webley revolver. He pointed it at Kit.

Tamsin and Carol screamed.

'Trent, no,' shouted Gerry.

Trent stood up and backed away from Cain. Then he looked at Kit and smiled. He said, 'You were right, Aston. I'll give you that.'

Then he flipped the revolver round and handed it grip-first to Kit. With a nod, Kit took the revolver and pointed towards Bryn Cain.

Cain, at this point, was looking a little shell-shocked by the turn of events. As the net had closed around him, he had considered his options and realised they were limited. Fight and flight had crossed his mind, but he knew that it was a fool's errand. His best bet had been to steer Carol away from any damaging admission on his own involvement with the death of Teddy. It had failed disastrously. Even this paled into comparison with the utter catastrophe that had been the blackmail attempt. He knew this would come back to bite him.

He was right.

'At the centre of all of this is greed,' said Kit, still pointing the gun at Bryn Cain. 'Thank you Trent, by the way.'

'You're welcome, Aston,' said Trent walking over to the door to stand by the policeman. Sexton, who had been sitting on the other side of Cain, rose to his feet also and walked over to the door. This left Cain, sitting alone on the sofa.

'Carol called you first, didn't she? I couldn't understand why she would call Sexton. You were the obvious person to call. She had acted in self-defence. That would have been what you would say. Once you sent the blackmail note to Gerry it all became clear to me. Carol's bruise, unless it was staged, meant she had been attacked. Once I knew that Teddy was definitely dead then I wondered...'

'We wondered,' chipped in Hook. 'You haven't changed.' There was no malice in his voice. He was looking on like a proud father who feels obliged to take his boy down a peg or two from time to time lest he became too big-headed.

'Yes, we,' acknowledged Kit with a sheepish grin, 'realised that she would had to have called you first. From that it followed that you had told her to get help in removing the body and to stay quiet about what had happened. All the time your mind was racing, wasn't it? If you could get to the house and obtain evidence of Carol's involvement with the death of Teddy then you could use that to do something you've been wanting to do for a while, grab a part of the growing demand for racehorse partnerships. Yet, that wasn't enough. You stole the painting too.'

Cain shifted uncomfortably in his seat. He glanced over to the door. Three men blocked his path to the front door. Another constable and Gerry were near the kitchen. He didn't fancy his chances in that direction. Gerry looked like he was seconds away from wringing his neck. It would save the hangman a job he supposed.

Jumping out the front window was a problem. Kit was blocking his path and Hook was just behind him, too. They were perhaps less of a problem than the other policeman, Fredericks, who looked like he could handle himself. He was right by the window. Every escape route was blocked. The game was up. He needed to bide his time. Let the arrogant Lord show off to his bint and acolytes.

'You'll be dismayed to hear that we have found the painting you tried to sell,' said Kit.

'Yes. It has turned up with a well-known fence in London, Lyndon Kelly. Once my friends persuaded him of the merit of handing it over, they can be quite persuasive, then he was happy to help the investigation.' Kit paused for a few moments to consider how the McDonald brothers might have secured Kelly's assistance. Then he wiped it from his mind. Some things were best left alone.

'I'm sure that when we find this Jean-Claude then he will confirm who facilitated the sale of Northern Glory. I doubt he will have had any inkling that the sale was arrived at through blackmail. I'm sure he'll be happy to provide evidence to this effect. Had this come off you would have made thousands from the sale of Northern Glory as well as the Stubbs painting. Have you nothing to say Cain?'

He did. And he was rather forthright too. A discreet veil shall be drawn over the comments as they reflected poorly on the lawyer's vocabulary and upbringing. It was left to Hook to comment on this.

'No tea for you and you'll be straight to bed when we get home,' he chuckled.

Ten minutes later, Cain had been led away by the constables and Fredericks. This left Hook with Kit, Mary and the other witnesses to Cain's capture. They separated into groups. Trent stood with Kit, Hook and Gerry while Tamsin comforted the distraught Carol. Sexton stood apart, not quite sure if he was arrested or a free man. Mary strolled over to him in the car park behind the cottage.

'How are you feeling Mr Sexton?' she asked.

'Like a damn fool,' said Sexton. He shook his head and then apologised to Mary. 'I appear to have lost my manners as well as my senses.'

Mary put a hand on his arm. She said, 'For what it's worth, I think you are a good man. You tried to help Carol.'

'Look where it's got me,' replied Sexton bitterly. 'A jail sentence and her undying enmity.'

Mary glanced over to Carol. Tamsin was speaking with her. Then she glanced over towards Sexton before looking at Tamsin. Mary, as only women can, read this look. She smiled at Sexton, 'I don't know what will happen to you both for trying to cover up Teddy's death, but right now, Mr Sexton, she needs you. Go to her.'

'I can't,' said Sexton.

'Go,' said Mary and she unceremoniously pushed him in the direction of Carol and Tamsin. Seeing what Mary was doing, Tamsin stood back to allow Sexton and Carol some privacy. She went to Mary and raised her eyebrows. A half-smile crossed her face.

'Perhaps some good will come of this eventually.'

Trent eyes flicked over to Carol and Sexton. For a moment he felt a stab of jealousy, but only momentarily. In truth, he'd had a very close shave. Both Carol and Sexton had effectively perverted the course of justice. There would be a price to pay on this, always assuming that the jury did not take a dim view of Carol's self-defence plea at the inquest. Listening to Hook speak with Gerry, it sounded as if the police would not charge her for murder.

Either way, none of this would do his career any good. The sooner he bid Newmarket a farewell the better. It would be a pity. He'd liked Carol and it was fun but only for a while. Once it became serious then it was time for him to bid '*adieu*' and this was serious in anyone's book. Trent became aware that Kit was speaking to him. He turned to face him.

'Thanks again, Trent. It was lucky we ran into you last night. You cleared up a few things for me.'

'Like whether I was the blackmailer or not?'

Kit laughed and replied, 'Well, now that you mention it.'

'How did you know it wasn't me?'

'I always suspected Cain, but I threw out a few things at dinner last night. You seemed oblivious to what I'd said which either made you a very good actor or you were, indeed, innocent.'

'You never suspected Sexton?' asked Trent.

Kit glanced over at Sexton standing with Carol. They did not seem to be saying much to one another, however, that would come.

'I always felt it was either you or Cain. You both had the contacts and the wherewithal to manage something like this. For what it's worth, I felt Sexton had fallen harder for Carol

260

than you. I'm no judge but Mary is, and she certainly thought so.'

Trent smiled and reached into his pocket for his cigarette case. He lit one. 'You don't?' he asked Kit. Kit confirmed that he did not smoke. 'I suspect that Mary is not far wrong. You're very lucky.'

'So she tells me,' said Kit, smiling. 'How did you know it was Cain?'

'When I saw you staring at me and then flicking your eyes down to his pocket. I saw the revolver. Before then I hadn't a clue, frankly. Not really my world.'

'I'm glad you read that look. I was caught before like that. Well done.'

'Think nothing of it,' said Trent cooly.

'What now for you?' asked Kit.

'Back to London and then no doubt back here in case I am needed at the inquest or trial,' said Trent. He glanced back towards Carol and Sexton who were now smiling at one another. He shrugged and added wryly, 'but it certainly won't be by Carol.'

With that he nodded to Kit and walked over to Carol and Sexton.

Kit watched him shake hands with Sexton and clap him on the back. He was magnanimous in defeat thought Kit. Mary, from a different angle to Kit saw Trent's face. To her, he seemed relieved. Trent kissed Carol on the cheek and took his leave.

Kit turned around to Hook and Gerry. They were watching Trent depart. Hook glanced up at Kit and said, 'I see you've lost none of your old prowess.' As ever with Hook, the compliment was accompanied by a sour face; the delivery was far from overjoyed. Kit was delighted by this.

'No need to thank me, Hookie,' said Kit gleefully before twisting the knife further. 'All in a day's work.'

Hook rolled his eyes which made Gerry grin. He was a very relieved man and he wrung Kit's hand. It must be said he had a ferociously strong grip.'

'Thank you old man. Sorry about the other day.'

Kit extracted what was left of his right hand and replied, 'Think nothing of it. You were in a sticky situation.'

'Come back to the house both of you. Chris will want to hear all about it. We can celebrate.'

Kit tried to smile at this, but there was uncertainty on his face. Gerry shrugged when he saw this. Kit put his hand on Gerry's arm and said, 'I just hope that it doesn't go badly for Carol and Sexton. She was clearly influenced by Cain. He'll deny it, of course. And we can't prove it.'

'I hope the jury see it that way,' said Gerry.

Kit turned to Hook with his eyebrows raised. Hook coloured a little and replied grumpily, 'I'll see what I can do. It really would have made my life easier if she'd just come clean. Silly girl.'

'Always has been,' agreed Gerry. He said this reflectively, without malice. She had always been a silly girl. This is what happens when you are idolised by men and treated like a princess by your family. There can be no good outcome from this. Perhaps if they had all not indulged her so much. It was too late now, or was it? Gerry looked at Sexton and Carol together. He hoped they both could come out of this without paying too great a price for their romantic folly. Perhaps then Carol would grow up.

She would have to now.

For the time being, Carol and Sexton were allowed to return to their respective homes. No charges would be brought, but Hook warned that they would be. Sexton expected no less and seemed ready for what he would face. Who knew how it would affect Carol? It was not Hook's problem. He stood with Kit and Mary to watch them leave. Now there was only the three of them.

'What will you do now?' asked Hook.

'Gerry invited us back to the house. We'll stay another night, but then I think we'll return home,' replied Kit.

'Where is home these days?' asked Hook.

'Grosvenor Square. Aunt Agatha's old house,' said Kit.

'Oh,' said Hook in surprise. 'Where is Agatha these days?'

'Living in the south of France now. Do you remember Betty and Sausage?'

The grimace on Hook's face suggested that he did. Then he brightened up although there was a slight frown too. It was never perfect sunshine with the Chief Inspector.

'Permanently?' he asked.

'Yes,' said Kit. 'Although she'll return home from time to time.'

'She gave you a house in Grosvenor Square?' said Hook in the manner of a man appalled and in awe of how the other half lived.

'She gave it to me, actually,' said Mary. There was a smile on her face, yet Hook saw a tenderness in her eyes, too.

'Yes,' he said. 'Yes, I can see that.' He turned to Kit and said, 'Well, I should be going. Stay out of trouble.'

'Some chance,' grinned Kit.

'Indeed,' said Hook. He put his felt hat on, tilting it upwards so that his full face was open to what sunshine there was. He picked up his briefcase with the hook of his umbrella handle and put it over his shoulder.

'So long,' he said and began to walk away.

'Goodbye, Mr Hook,' said Mary.

'So long, Hookie,' said Kit.

They watched the long-loping, careless stride of the detective until he rounded the corner of the cottage. A sadness fell over Kit. Mary took his hand and squeezed it.

'Why do I think we'll see him again?' said Mary.

'I hope so,' said Kit. 'I hope so.'

1 months later

Hyde Park, near the Serpentine, London: December 1921

A small group of men and women walked along the side of the Serpentine. It was a frosty morning, but the sun was shining so no one minded, least of all the couple near the front who were holding hands. Just ahead was an American lady of formidable aspect and a voice that could cut through brick walls and men's egos like a spear.

Mrs Isabella Rosling was like a sobered-up Ulysses S. Grant with the enemy in sight or, in this case, a nice spot to picnic. She was leading a diverse group. The couple at the front presented an interesting contrast, both were nearer forty than thirty, both were robust of build. The man's face was pleasant if your tastes ran to battered ex-boxers. The woman appeared to be a member of that exclusive club whose tastes ran exactly to that. She gazed upon 'Haymaker' Harris with, it must be reported, the light of love burning bright in her eyes.

She wasn't the only one. If anything the light shone brighter again behind the scar-tissued eyes of Haymaker.

265

Alongside them were a couple of young mothers pushing prams and at the back, a little way behind, walked Kit, Mary and Rose Hunter. The latter was gripping Mary's arm, her sightless eyes staring straight ahead, her gait unsteady. There was a smile on the two women's faces as they listened to Mrs Rosling issuing instructions on where they should go.

'I love her when she's in this mood,' said Rose.

'She's a force of nature,' agreed Mary.

Up ahead, Mrs Rosling stopped and then ordered Haymaker, who was carrying a disproportionate amount of bags, to deposit them in the place that she was pointing. He obeyed meekly. Despite his size and pugilistic past, Haymaker was no match for the fiery American and found that obedience was the best route to a peaceful life. On a day such as this, though, his mood was just too effervescent. Had there been the sweet smell of flowers in the air, he would doubtless have commented on it to the woman beside him. That woman was Dulcie Palmer.

Love had blossomed for them soon after he had begun his duties as unofficial security for the new shelter for women who had left their marital homes. While he was no young Lochinvar, Dulcie was no blushing maid, either. Both had been battered by the storms of life, yet they remained standing, no count taken. Now they were together, and Kit could not have been happier for his friend.

He came up beside Haymaker and said, 'Let me help you, old man.'

Haymaker, whose outlook on life was positively feudal, began to dismiss his lordship from any manual labour when a look from Mrs Rosling confirmed that Kit was, indeed,

266

required to help them set up the picnic. Haymaker smirked at Kit when he saw Mrs Rosling's flinty eyes.

'I saw that Mr Harris,' said the all-seeing American.

The two men grimaced and got on with their duties, keen to avoid any further rebuke. Mary, meanwhile, kept walking past the group as they set up the picnic. Then she said, 'Ah. Good news. He's here.'

'Where?' asked Rose. She didn't have to ask who now.

'Coming this way.'

Rose smiled and nodded. Then she turned to Mary and said nervously, 'How do I look?'

Mary giggled and replied, 'Well, if I were a man…' she left it at this. They continued walking another twenty yards. Then Mary stopped. Gently, she released her arm from Rose and stood back.

'Hello,' said the man.

'Hello Chris,' said Rose. Mary smiled and nodded to Chris. Then she turned and walked back to the picnic group.

Chris Tudor took Rose's arm and led her towards a wooden park bench by the lake.

'Shall we sit down?' he asked.

'Yes,' said Rose.

They both sat down, but Rose did not make any effort to release her arm. Chris was in no mood to prompt this either. They sat in silence for a few moments and then Rose said, 'I can feel the sun on my face.' Chris looked at her face and felt his chest tighten. Mother Nature was smiling on them at that moment and, he felt, on him particularly.

'What do you see?' Rose asked.

Chris fought to control his breathing. He didn't want his voice to crack under the painful ecstasy he was feeling. He gazed at a face whose dimensions were arranged so perfectly that, for a moment, he wondered how anyone could bear to inflict any pain or to impose control, or cause fear on such perfection. All he wanted to do was to hold her, protect her and make her happy.

'What do I see?' he said. As he said this he put his hand over hers and stared beguiled at nature's treasury laid out before him; the dappled sunlight blinking off the lake, a male duck shooing another male duck away from his girlfriend, the sun shining warm on his face. Then he turned his gaze back to Rose. Words seemed redundant.

'I see such beauty that I barely do it justice.'

The End

If you enjoyed The Newmarket Murders, please leave a review. They really help.

This is a work of fiction. However, it references real-life individuals. Gore Vidal, in his introduction to Lincoln, writes that placing history in fiction or fiction in history has been unfashionable since Tolstoy and that the result can be accused of being neither. He defends the practice, pointing out that writers from Aeschylus to Shakespeare to Tolstoy have done so with not inconsiderable success and merit.

My intention, in the following section, is to explain a little more about the connection between events / individuals mentioned and the period in which the story is set.

Newmarket & Newmarket Racecourse

Newmarket is the home of racing in Britain. The Jockey Club is located there as well as the world-famous racecourse which is home to the first two English classic horseraces: the 1,000 Guineas (fillies) and 2,000 Guineas (colts). Both are run on the Rowley Mile course. The distance for each of the races is one mile.

Also mentioned in the book is The Rutland Arms which is a hotel / bar that has recently closed down but once would have housed the great and the good, coming to the races.

One artist who stayed there was one who I learned about in a very odd way. This story will mean more to British readers than Americans.

Many years ago I owned an art gallery in Belfast. The art gallery also had a coffee shop. Occasionally, a (relatively) famous person might pop in. One day I had just such a visitor. He bought a coffee and sat down to have a smoke and read the racing pages of the *Daily Mirror*. While he was doing this, myself and a friend who owned a nearby bookshop were chatting about great sporting artists. We mentioned Stubbs, Degas, Dame Laura Knight, William Powell Frith. We ran out of steam at this point and couldn't remember any more.

At this point my famous guest, who happened to be the great Irish snooker player, Alex 'Hurricane' Higgins walked past us on his way to the door. He stopped, turned around and said, 'Munnings.' Then he walked out.

Alfred Munnings was a wonderful 19th century sporting / equine artist who stayed at the Rutland Arms on his trips to Newmarket. My friend and I chorused, 'Munnings, of course.'

1922 Epsom Derby

Northern Glory is a fictional horse. The year in which he would have run the Derby, 1922, the race was won by Captain Cuttle fairly handily by four or five lengths. There is a British Pathe film of the race if you are interested. St Louis, mentioned in the book as a potential rival to Northern Glory, won the 1922 2,000 Guineas, but could only manage 4th in the Derby.

Major Cyril Entwistle (1887 – 1974)

Sir Cyril Entwistle was an MP on and off between 1918 – 1945. He served during the Great War in the Artillery, winning a Military Cross. A lawyer by training, he became an MP and introduced the private members' bill that opened the door to women obtaining legal equality in divorce cases, in particular with respect to adultery.

Charles 'Wag' McDonald (1885 – 1943)

McDonald was a leader of a south London criminal gang known as the 'Elephant Boys' who were based in the Elephant and Castle area of London. He was assisted by his brother Wal, and they formed an effective partnership with Billy Kimber (who features in the TV series 'Peaky Blinders'). McDonald led an interesting life. He fought in the Boer War before returning to England to take over the leadership of the Elephant Boys. He then volunteered for active service during the Great War. When he came back from France, he took over leadership of the gang once more before escaping to the US in 1921. He worked in Hollywood for several years, getting to know many of the stars. His life and the

270

life of gangs in the area have been captured in a few books by his descendant, Brian McDonald.

Alice Diamond (1896 – 1952)

Alice Diamond was an English career criminal, linked to organised shoplifting. Her career in crime began in 1912. By 1915 she was the leader of a gang known as the 'Forty Elephants' due to their association with the Elephant Boys led by Charles 'Wag' McDonald. Her chief lieutenant was Maggie Hill.

They were an odd couple. Diamond was tall and had a dominating personality. Hill was much smaller, intense and violent. They lived the high life when they could, accepting the cost of this would be occasional spells in jail.

She was imprisoned on several occasions. Alice Diamond never married, but was in a relationship with Wag McDonald's brother, Bert.

Jack Murray was born in Northern Ireland but has spent over half his life living just outside London, except for some periods spent in Australia, Monte Carlo, and the US.

An artist, as well as a writer, Jack's work features in collections around the world and he has exhibited in Britain, Ireland, and Monte Carlo.

The Kit Aston series featuring Mary Cavendish was the first series that Jack created. A growing number of people around the world now follow the books.

A spin off series from the Kit Aston novels was published in 2020 featuring Aunt Agatha as a young woman solving mysterious murders.

Another spin off series features Inspector Jellicoe. It is set in the late 1950's/early 1960's.

Jack finished work on a World War II trilogy in 2022. The three books look at the war from both the British and the German side. They have been published through Lume Books and are available on Amazon.

Acknowledgements

It is not possible to write a book on your own. There are contributions from so many people either directly or indirectly over many years. Listing them all would be an impossible task.

Special mention therefore should be made to my wife and family who have been patient and put up with my occasional grumpiness when working on this project.

My brother, Edward, has helped in proofing and made supportive comments that helped me tremendously. Thank you, too, Debra Cox, David Sinclair and Anna Wietrzychowska who have been a wonderful help in reducing the number of irritating errors that have affected my earlier novels. A word of thanks to Charles Gray and Brian Rice who have provided legal and accounting support.

My late father and mother both loved books. They encouraged a love of reading in me. In particular, they liked detective books, so I must tip my hat to the two greatest writers of this genre, Sir Arthur and Dame Agatha.

Following writing, comes the business of marketing. My thanks to Mark Hodgson and Sophia Kyriacou for their advice on this important area. Additionally, a shout out to the wonderful folk on 20Booksto50k.

Finally, my thanks to the teachers who taught and nurtured a love of writing.

Printed in Great Britain
by Amazon

36809956R00162